The
MILLENNIUM
ULTIMATUM

Graham Keet

First Edition 2019
Print ISBN: 978-1-77605-614-9
e-ISBN: 978-1-77605-613-2

Editor: Sheena Carnie

Layout and Typesetting by Janet Von Kleist
jvonkleist@yahoo.com

Published by Kwarts Publishers
www.kwartspublishers.co.za

Acknowledgments

To my wife Astrid who gives me the time to write even when the lawn needs mowing; my son Ryan and daughter-in-law Ayako who quietly get stuck into pruning my neglected shrubs when they visit, and my grandchildren Hiro, Hina, Mako, Shun, Taku and new arrival Ann who make me realize that there is more to life than sitting behind a laptop. Thanks also to Karine and Astrid for their input into the final draft.

Author's Note

The Millennium Ultimatum is a fictional account of events that could take place at some future time. Actual biblical characters mentioned assume a purely fictional role in the narrative.

According to biblical prophecy, the end of world as we know it will be marked by a period of extreme turmoil. There will be a seven-year period, known as the Tribulation, during which an evil leader, the Antichrist, will rise to power under the control of Satan, the devil. The last three and a half years of the Tribulation will see God's wrath poured out upon a sinful world in the form of both natural and supernatural disasters, the likes of which have never before been experienced.

The Tribulation will end with the return of Jesus Christ ("the king" in this narrative), at which time he will judge the survivors of the Tribulation (the "Sheep and Goat" judgment) and will set up a righteous government on Earth, with Jerusalem as the seat of government. He will destroy the Antichrist in a lake of fire and Satan will be locked in an abyss for a thousand years. During this thousand-year period, known as the Millennium, Satan will be unable to influence affairs on Earth and, in particular, he will not be able to lead mankind astray.

The idyllic Millennium Earth will be inhabited by two groups of people. One group will consist of the believers, with glorified immortal bodies, who returned with Christ at the end of the Tribulation. They will have authority over a second group of people – those who survived the Sheep and Goat judgment. These people will have mortal bodies similar to ours today, except that the perfect conditions on the Millennium Earth will make extreme longevity a possibility.

According to the apostle Peter, God sees a thousand years as one day. The end of the Millennium could, therefore, be seen as the end of the Millennium "day". But whereas the Millennium will be a time of peace, the prophesied release of Satan from the abyss at the end of the Millennium will once again bring the darkness of sin and turmoil upon the earth. Satan will gather an army with the aim of overthrowing Christ's righteous government, and will set about deceiving mankind once again. He will draw his forces from both his legions of demons as well as from those who will be resurrected at the end of the Millennium (the "returnees" in this book). Once again mankind will have the choice: follow Satan or follow Christ.

At the final judgment – the Great White Throne Judgment – Satan and all his followers will be cast into the Lake of Fire, while the believers will enjoy eternity in God's holy city, New Jerusalem.

The Millennium Ultimatum is set in the tumultuous final years of the Millennium. Many believe that we are now living in the "last days" and that the seven years of Tribulation are close at hand, then to be followed by the establishment of the Millennium Kingdom.

May each reader be prompted to heed the warning of Joshua and *"choose this day whom you will serve"* (Joshua 24:15 ESV).

Prologue

"We have two alternatives facing us, Kratos, we either stand up to the king and defeat him, or we flee from his coming judgment. My followers are not equipped for a showdown with the king and his warring angels, so we've decided to escape from Earth before the judgment and head for distant galaxies. Being cast into a lake of fire is definitely not part of my future. In any case, I have special plans for those traveling with me – plans that will make me rich."

"I'm sure your plans will suit you perfectly, Draco, I have no problem with that. However, before you make any hasty decisions, bear this in mind – I have legions of demons at my command. When I have defeated the king and become supreme ruler of the universe there'll be no more Lake of Fire – not for us at any rate; I'm keeping that for the king and his followers. They've grown fat and lazy during the Millennium – their so-called thousand years of peace – so they'll be easy targets. There'll be no City of Light for them; their day will surely end in darkness."

"Then we have similar aims, Kratos. Let's not oppose each other; in many respects we can work together."

"Yes, I believe we can. You persuade those mortals, the ones resurrected to face final judgment, to either flee with you or, alternatively, they can join my forces rather than join the king's army. In the meantime I'll prepare my legions for battle."

"An alliance then?"

"Yes – an unholy one."

CHAPTER 1

JERUSALEM'S OLD CITY, MILLENNIUM YEAR 999

Pete Barnaby awoke with a jolt. For a moment he lay still, trying to piece together what had happened. He remembered the impact of the bullet hitting him in the chest, but the fact that he was still alive meant the shooter must have missed his vital organs; what luck – if one could call it luck. Barnaby rubbed his eyes and tried to penetrate the darkness around him. Was it all a dream or was he still in mortal danger?

Well, I'm not dead yet and I don't feel the pain that I expected after being shot, he reasoned to himself. *But how the hell did I get into this bed? I was in the kitchen when they shot me.*

Fearful that his attackers might still be in the house, he climbed slowly out of bed and crept towards where he thought the door might be. His eyes strained to distinguish shapes in the darkness.

It's pretty dark in here; can't be any windows in this room...

Suddenly he walked into an open cupboard door, hitting his head with a loud thud. Barnaby stifled a howl of pain, and then listened intently for any movement.

Have I given away my position?

A door slammed somewhere in the house. He held his breath and waited, his heart racing as he heard quick footsteps approaching. Desperately he looked around for a place to hide;

seeing nowhere else, he crept as far back into the cupboard as he could and pulled the door closed behind him.

Depending on how many there are I'll try to jump them from behind and then get the hell out of here.

During Barnaby's years of involvement in gang violence he had been caught up in many skirmishes, but now the chips were down – these guys were armed and he wasn't.

I've got nothing to lose; they'll probably kill me on sight anyway. I'll take them on – it's them or me.

The door opened, bathing the room in light from the passage outside. A man entered and headed for the empty bed. "Where are you? Don't be afraid, I'm expecting you."

Barnaby flung open the cupboard door and dived at the man, pinning his arms in an effort to prevent him from getting a shot off. They both collapsed to the floor, with Barnaby on top of what he assumed was his captor. He was about to deliver a blow to the man's temple when he realized his opponent was unarmed and seemingly alone.

"Are you crazy?" the man shouted. "Get off me, you big oaf. I'm here to help you, not to harm you."

Slowly Barnaby released his hold on the man and rose from the floor. He had learned to trust nobody, so he kept a watchful eye for any sudden movements.

"What do you mean, you're 'expecting' me? Either you or one of your mates shot me. Why didn't you just finish me off; why put me in that bed? You might as well kill me, I told you I don't have what you're looking for."

The other man stood up and adjusted his jacket. "My friend, I'm not armed and I didn't shoot you." He extended a hand. "The name is Jed Rich, and I'm here to welcome you as a fellow re-turnee."

The man did not look aggressive, and Barnaby's years in the racketeering business, where he had encountered all types of desperados, led him to believe that Jed held no threat. Warily he took the hand. "Barnaby, Pete Barnaby. Everyone just calls me

Barnaby. Could somebody please tell me what's going on here? What do you mean by 'fellow returnee'?"

"That's exactly why I'm here," said Rich. "I've been chosen to fill you in on all the info you need to get started. They told me you would be arriving sometime this afternoon. Let's go downstairs; I'll make some coffee and we can start at the beginning. Prepare yourself for a story that will blow your mind – it did mine when I first heard it."

CHAPTER 2

The coffee was good, and so were the muffins that Jed served warm out of the oven. After gulping down his third muffin Barnaby stood up, unbuttoned his shirt and examined his chest.

"This is very strange. I know I was shot, but now I don't appear to be any the worse for wear. Maybe only the faintest mark where the bullet must have hit me... Can you tell me what's going on here?"

"When were you shot?"

"Earlier today or maybe yesterday; I'm a little confused at the moment."

"This may seem like a stupid question to you, but what's the last date that you can remember?" Jed asked. "Think carefully, this is important."

"The day I was shot was the third of June 1925. What's to-day's date?"

"It's long, long past that date, but before I explain, please finish telling me what happened to you."

Barnaby looked skeptical, but carried on with his story. "I guess you know as well as I do about the gang wars. I was caught up in a spate of gang violence in Chicago during the prohibition years. Yesterday – I think – I was cornered in a house by a rival gang who wanted me to divulge the location of our liquor stash, which I refused to do. I saw a gap and tried to make a run for it; unfortunately the kitchen door was locked. When I turned to face them some trigger-happy recruit of theirs let me have it in the chest. That's the last I can remember. It definitely seems like yesterday, or have I been asleep longer than I think?"

"You've been asleep, my friend, and for much longer than you could ever imagine. This will be hard to believe, but you've been out of action for more than a thousand years."

Barnaby stared at the man in disbelief. "You're screwing with me! What the hell's really going on here?"

"Okay, I'm going to give you the short version first; we can fill in the details bit by bit as we go along. You say the last date you remember is the third of June 1925? You actually died on that day. The world as you knew it then carried on for another 113 years, till 2038 to be exact. You remember the First World War that ended in 1918? Well there were many other wars after that.

"The situation on Earth got worse as time progressed, until about 2035 when the world was hit with worse natural disasters and man-made conflict than ever before. This was, in fact, the Great Tribulation – the final biblical apocalypse. It ended in a huge battle between followers of an infamous leader, commonly known as the Antichrist, and the countries and peoples opposing him. Some call it the Battle of Armageddon. Things got so out of hand that God himself stepped in and defeated the Antichrist. More importantly, he locked Satan, the devil, who was behind all the turmoil, up in an abyss situated in the depths of the earth. That was sometime in 2038."

Barnaby held up his hand. "Is this some type of game you're playing with me? Do you really expect me to swallow all this stuff?"

"Give me a chance," said Jed. "Once I've filled you in a bit, we'll take a walk outside and you'll see for yourself that nothing is as you remember it. But if I don't give you some background first you'll wet your pants when you step outside."

"Carry on then," said Barnaby, "I'll reserve my judgment till you're done."

Jed sat back in his chair. "Here comes the part that you'll find the most difficult to understand. As I said, you died when you were shot, but now you've been brought back to life. After that great battle I told you about where God stepped in and defeated the evil ruler, he set up a righteous government based in Jerusalem, with his son Jesus, whom we call the king, as supreme ruler. That was nearly 1,000 years ago. Since then mankind has lived in complete peace and harmony – till now."

"Assuming what you say is true, what's happened now?"

"As was prophesied in the Bible, at the end of the period of 1,000 years, which we call the Millennium, Satan gets released from the abyss and is free to do his worst on Earth. We believe this has now happened."

"But that's crazy. If what you say is true, why let him out?" Barnaby asked, aghast.

"I don't have all those answers, yet, but I'm constantly searching for information," Jed assured him. "The society I belong to is known as the White Robes, and we have good reason to believe that Satan has been released and is, as we speak, gathering followers for a showdown with the king. I'll fill you in on all the details I have as we go along. I'm pretty much in the same boat as you – I also lived long ago, before the Millennium started, and was resurrected into this present time."

"So you're also from way back? Why are we here?"

Jed had known they would eventually get around to the reason for them all being there at that particular time. He smiled: "We're here because we all messed up in our previous lives but we're getting a second chance."

Barnaby looked confused. "A second chance to do what?"

"In a nutshell, and to put it bluntly, a second chance to follow the king instead of our own selfish and often rotten lives."

"You're still screwing with me, aren't you?"

"I'm afraid not. Believe me, things are very different from when you were last on Earth. You've a lot to learn and, for better or for worse, I've been chosen to show you the way. We can start by taking a walk outside."

CHAPTER 3

Together they walked down the single flight of stairs from Jed's apartment and out onto the pavement. Barnaby stopped and looked around.

"I thought you said we were a thousand years into the future; these buildings around us look mighty old to me. Where is this place?"

"Everything looks old because that's the way it's been kept," said Jed. "You are now in the old part of Jerusalem, but this is the only city on Earth that still looks pretty much the way it did centuries ago. That's the way the king has decreed it. He loves this city, which is why he set up his government in Jerusalem."

"By 'the king' you mean..."

"King Jesus. When he returned at the end of the Great Tribulation he banished Satan to the abyss and set up his seat of government in Jerusalem. He now reigns over the entire Millennium Kingdom which covers the whole earth. Although the old traditional country names are still used, such as the United States, Great Britain, Russia and so on, they no longer have their own governments.

"Every country falls under the King of Kings and is ruled by a hierarchy of immortals who not only govern the people, but also provide loving assistance and guidance in order to meet each individual's needs. This structure consists of the Committee of Elders headed up by the prophet Daniel..."

"The guy who was in the lion's den in Babylon?" interjected Barnaby, trying to come to grips with what he was being told.

"Yeah, that guy. The Committee of Elders takes care of the day-to-day running of the kingdom, with Daniel having regular contact with the king. Then, as I mentioned earlier, there are the immortals – those with glorified bodies who returned with the king. Each immortal has a group of mortals who report to him or her, and they attend to the physical and spiritual needs of those under them. The whole system works pretty well. Don't spend too much energy trying to work everything out at once," laughed Jed, "things will fall into place as you spend more time here."

Feeling somewhat dazed, Barnaby shook his head and stepped out into the street. He was about to take another step when a huge silver shape loomed out of nowhere and stopped about five yards from him. Startled, he jumped back onto the sidewalk and watched as the silver, cigar-shaped object continued on its way.

"What the heck was that? I could have been killed!" he exclaimed.

"Not likely," chuckled Jed. "That was a public transport vehicle; what we used to call a bus or a tram, only these vehicles are automated and don't need any human intervention to get around."

"But it moves at such a speed; how come it didn't flatten me?" asked Barnaby.

"It sensed you were in the way so it stopped before it hit you. Did you notice it had no wheels? That's because it floats on an anti-gravity field that allows it to move in any direction at great speed. The inside is pressurized to protect the passengers against the fast stops and starts. We'll take a spin in one soon, but first let's get something to eat. We still have great restaurants around here, and the food has to be tasted to be believed."

"I'm beginning to give up trying to reason things out," said Barnaby, "but I'm ready to eat a horse."

CHAPTER 4

The meal was far better than Barnaby had expected. What surprised him most was the menu – instead of having a written menu there was a small device at each place setting. Jed reached out and touched the device in front of him and a holographic list of food items appeared before him, suspended in the air.

Jed explained, "You can scroll up or down the list and if you see something you like, touch that spot on the virtual image, like this." On touching his selected choice a virtual image of the dish appeared before him on the table.

"How do you like that?" he laughed. "It's a perfect image of a fillet steak with all the trimmings. You can even smell the food, but you can't eat it. If you want the real thing you tap the box twice and within a few minutes that dish will be brought out to you."

"By a real waiter or a robot?" asked Barnaby, now expecting almost anything.

"Well, if you're lucky, by a cute young chick."

"Can I touch her?" asked Barnaby with a sly smile.

"Only if you want to be instantly vaporized," said Jed. Seeing the horrified look on Barnaby's face, he added, "I'm only kidding, but you fell for it, didn't you?"

"Now you're taking advantage of my ignorance," Barnaby complained. "Anyway, once I've eaten how do I pay for the meal? I see that next to each item on the menu are figures preceded by the letters Zn. Is that the price?"

"Yes, that's quite correct. The Zn stands for zenos which is the currency of the Millennium Kingdom. Don't ask me where it originated, all I know is it's the universal currency used by everyone."

"But I don't have any zenos," Barnaby pointed out.

"Yes you do; the moment you're resurrected into the Millennium Kingdom you get allocated a million zenos. From then on your community leader, one of the immortals responsible for your area, will allocate you more currency monthly based on the record of your dealings during the month. It seems complicated but you'll get to grips with it pretty quickly, and it works well – as does everything else in the kingdom."

"Okay, so I have a balance somewhere, but how do I actually pay for my meal or anything else that I buy?"

"I'm glad you're asking all these questions; I can see you're a quick learner so I'll soon be able to cut you loose," said Jed. "Take out the gizmo I gave you earlier."

Barnaby removed a device from his pocket and studied it. It looked like a rectangular card about four inches long by two inches wide, and was made of a hard plastic material that was slightly pliable.

"Your gizmo is tuned to your personal aura, the field that each person has around them," said Jed. "It is activated by your brainwaves, and can perform a multitude of functions. You can call up anyone else on Earth by thinking of them, and if someone calls you their personal brainwaves will direct the call to you; your gizmo will make an audible sound to which you can respond either mentally or by touching the face of the gizmo. That's also how you can pay for any item you buy – you merely think of the price and the receiver of the payment, and the task is done. Don't ask me details of how it works, but believe me it works. And relax – things will come to you pretty quickly."

Barnaby shook his head, wondering if he would ever survive in this new world. "How long does it take to get used to this place?" he asked.

"Not long. I'm going to a White Robe meeting tomorrow where Erica Merton, our leader, will be speaking. Once you meet other returnees you'll get the feeling that you're home. Believe me, you won't be sorry."

CHAPTER 5

THE WORLD ARCHIVES DOCUMENT STORAGE FACILITY, WASHINGTON DC

The hooded figure moved silently along the side of the building, then rounded the corner and stopped before a small door. He glanced at his multi-function wristwatch. It was two o'clock in the morning and a freezing minus twenty degrees. After removing a small black box from his overcoat pocket he placed it against the door lock and then pressed a red button in the center of the device.

There were a few clicking sounds as the box read the parameters of the lock, and then the door quietly swung open. The man glanced at the sign above the door: *World Archives – Entry restricted*, then made his way quickly inside, closing the door behind him. Having previously studied the layout of the building he knew exactly where to go to complete his mission.

Once inside he moved purposefully to a staircase leading down to the archive section. The main archive room was kept under strict climatic conditions to ensure that the information contained therein was optimally preserved. Silently he used his black box on the system of locks governing the door mechanism and entered the enormous storeroom with its aisle upon aisle of racks containing information on everything from paper to the latest technology. *Unbelievable,* he thought to himself, *a complete history of mankind up to this time.*

Ignoring the racks around him, the figure moved through to a door that resembled a large safe in the wall. Above the door was a sign: *Entrance restricted to elders only.* He chuckled and then muttered under his breath, "Maybe I must replace that sign with one reading, 'Under new management'." The thought made him smile broadly as he placed the black box against the door. He pushed a button and waited.

Within seconds there was a clicking noise from within the door and it opened about six inches. He slipped quickly into the room and flicked a light switch on the wall next to the door; the room became instantly illuminated in bright light from concealed sources. The man knew where to find the information he required, and headed straight for a glass case standing on a pedestal in a clearing between the other racks. Remembering what he had been told, he placed the black box on the floor and shoved it towards the pedestal. He glanced at a video monitor on the wall to his left, where the words "Protective screen deactivated" appeared.

Breathing a sigh of relief he hurried to the glass case and removed a box about half the size of a shoebox. He read the inscription on the sealed lid: *The design and manufacture of pre-millennial conventional and nuclear weapon systems.*

He gave a low whistle. *What the hell … does the boss want to start a war, or something? Guess he's mean enough to do that – I'd better get back before I become his first victim!*

CHAPTER 6

HEAD OFFICE OF THE MORTAL MOVEMENTS AND OCCURRENCES DEPARTMENT (MMOD), JERUSALEM

Luke Baron swiveled his chair around and gazed out from his twentieth floor window, enjoying the view over the park with its man-made lake.

Jerusalem sure is a beautiful city; I hope it stays this way.

He sat in silence for a moment, then spun his chair back and punched a button on his desktop communication device.

"Louise, please see if Seth Baron and Mike Cousins are available for a conference right away. They should both be in Washington DC at the moment."

"Sure thing, Luke. Do you want an audio, video or hologram conference?"

"Hologram, please."

Louise quickly called up the codes for both parties and proceeded to contact them. Having recently been appointed as personal assistant to the handsome 30-year-old head of the newly-created MMOD she was eager to prove her worth at every opportunity.

The MMOD had been formed by Daniel and the Committee of Elders to keep track of the increasing number of strange happenings in the kingdom – things that had never cropped up before. The position of head of a government department was normally reserved for an immortal, but Luke was born during the Millennium from a lineage of persons who survived the Great Tribulation and was not, therefore, an immortal with a glorified body. Luke was descended from Mark and Britt Baron, a couple who had played a large role in overcoming the Antichrist at the end of the Tribulation. Longevity being one of the perks of the Millennium Kingdom, Mark and Britt still lived active lives on their ranch in Wyoming.

Luke sat back and waited, hoping that both men would be available. He was extremely proud of his relative, Seth, who had built Baron Iron and Steel into the foremost supplier of iron and steel products to companies on Earth as well as to the Mars settlements. It was also good to have Mike Cousins in on anything going down; after all, he had been connected to the Baron family since the days of the Tribulation. Luke never tired of hearing Mark and Britt Baron sharing tales about "the good old bad days", as they put it. It was during the chaos of the Tribulation that Mike Cousins, a huge African-American fireman, had been inducted into the group of workers known as the 144,000; he had come to their rescue on many an occasion.

"They're both available and coming through now," Louise announced. Luke pressed a button on his communications console and the holographic figures of Seth and Mike appeared in the two armchairs in the lounge section of his sumptuous office.

"Good to see you again, Luke," said Seth. "How's it going in your new post at the MMOD?"

"It's been crazy here, but I'm slowly getting things sorted out," Luke replied. "Daniel has made some excellent people available to me, both on a full- and part-time basis. I even have Martin Petrovic as a consultant at the moment."

"I've heard of him," said Mike, "bit of a loner, isn't he?"

"He is, but he gets things done. You've probably heard that some unprecedented things are happening in the kingdom – things we have never been confronted with before."

"Such as?" asked Seth.

"Well, for the first time ever in the Millennium Kingdom we have started to experience gang violence. Only last week I sent Martin to Rome to find out what was causing the violence that had broken out there."

"And did he find anything?" Seth sat forward in his chair.

"Yes, and he sorted it out in one day. I haven't seen his complete report yet, but what he told me on the gizmo yesterday made me realize how useful he is to have around."

"What did he do?" asked Mike.

"For a start he got the leaders of the six gangs together in a sealed room. I still haven't been able to establish exactly what he said to them, but they left the meeting and immediately disbanded their gangs. The report I received from Rome this morning was that everything was as calm as the Dead Sea. How are things with you, Seth, how's it going with Baron Iron and Steel?"

"Business is booming," said Seth, "especially with our latest customer firmly on board; business has never been better."

"Who's the new customer?" asked Luke.

"Ever heard of Gorgonius Draco?"

"That name has come up in the meetings of the Committee of Elders," said Mike, "he's a bit of a shady character, isn't he?"

"I don't know anything about him being shady," said Seth. "All I know is that he is placing huge orders for specific cuts of iron and steel – I heard something about him being involved with the building of long-haul intergalactic spacecraft. Don't know all the details, but I don't have to; he pays for everything we deliver, so I'm quite happy. What has the committee heard?"

"The Committee of Elders is a bit restless at the moment," revealed Mike. "I don't know if this fits in with what you've told us, but there was a robbery at the World Archives the other night. First time ever that has happened."

"What was stolen?" asked Seth.

"They took the digital archive of documents under the general title of *The design and manufacture of pre-millennial conventional and nuclear weapon systems*," said Mike.

Seth gave a low whistle. "Surely they don't think Draco is making weapons? It's been a thousand years since mankind 'beat his swords into ploughshares', what would anyone want with weapons, especially such destructive weapons?"

"Beats me," said Mike. He sat back in his chair and looked at his two friends, as though coming to some deep realization of the truth, then he added, "Here's something else for you to think about – have either of you heard about the crash of a passenger-carrying spacecraft near the coast of Puerto Rico? It's been kept under wraps for some time now, but things seem to be coming to a head at this time."

Mike removed a gizmo from his pocket and flicked to a certain photograph which he projected onto a virtual screen.

"Looks like the sea has parted and there's a hole in the seabed with smoke coming out of it," said Seth. "What are we looking at?"

Mike flicked to another image. "What does this look like to you?"

Seth and Luke studied the image on the screen, then Luke spoke in a barely audible whisper. "Is that a figure coming out of the hole? If it is, it's the most grotesque thing I've ever seen. It's like something out of your worst nightmare. Where did you get these pictures?"

"They were taken by the automatic security devices of the spacecraft I was telling you about. Government boffins who studied blowups of the pictures reckoned that not only one strange creature came out of the hole which was in the seabed in what's called the Bermuda Triangle. They say a whole host of these critters, or whatever they were, came out. The whole thing was kept under wraps so as not to scare the population, and here's why – take a look at this."

The next photo revealed a huge grey shape clinging to the short wing of a spacecraft, a grotesque smile on its "face" as it stared back at the terrified faces of the passengers inside. "See now why we couldn't release these pictures."

"What on earth is that thing?" gasped Seth, still not quite believing what he had seen. "Did anyone go back to the hole in the seabed to check it out?"

"Yes," said Mike nodding, "but there was nothing to see. It was as if the 'Red Sea' had closed and everything was back to normal."

"What are the chances that those airline pilots were somehow pulling a fast one?" asked Luke. "Did anyone check their reliability?"

"Well both pilots were killed when the plane went down, so I guess they weren't joking around. According to the airline management the pilot and co-pilot had many years' experience and there was no mention of anything funny on either man's record sheet." Mike shrugged his huge shoulders before continuing. "In any case, the photos they took have been pulled apart by government lab technicians, and the chance that they were faked is virtually zero."

"This sounds serious," said Luke. "If there are no objections I'd like to get my staff to look into this. I'll get those photos from Mike and send them to Karen, my chief researcher, right after this meeting."

"Although this happened some time ago, there is still no answer to exactly what happened out there. It would be good to have fresh eyes look into the matter," said Mike. "Please go ahead."

"So where does that leave us?" Seth asked. "I still don't see what this has to do with Draco."

"Perhaps nothing at all." Mike stretched his arms and placed his hands behind his head. "But I have a strange feeling that we're about to find out, and we might not like what we discover."

CHAPTER 7

MMOD RESEARCH SECTION, JERUSALEM

Karen Leigh was worried. As chief researcher at the MMOD, she checked her data to see if she had made some mistake in her calculations; she didn't want to send incorrect information to her boss, Luke Baron. After running extensive diagnostic tests, she called over to her top electro-cyber engineer, Maribeth Markham.

"Maribeth, you're an expert on all these data systems, won't you come over and have a look at what I'm seeing on my screen? Something seems odd, but I can't put my finger on what it could be. I've checked the data and run diagnostic tests, but everything checks out."

"What seems to be the problem?" Maribeth leaned over Karen's shoulder to get a better view of the graphics on her screen; at the same time she caught a glimpse of their reflections in the glass window behind Karen's work station. The contrast between Karen's short blond hair and her own long mass of red curls was quite striking. She smiled as she recalled being called "carrots" by some of the boys at school, but that was only until the captain of the athletics team invited her to the senior prom where she was voted prom queen. That ended any further teasing. She shook her head and turned her mind back to the screen.

"Well, as you know, the MMOD keeps records of every birth that occurs anywhere in the kingdom, including the Mars settlements. All our databases are linked and the integrity of the software is constantly checked."

"Okay, so what's the problem?"

"I'll show you – have a look at the large virtual screen." A six-by-ten foot virtual screen appeared in the center of the office floor and a graph appeared on the screen. "The problem is that, according to the births and deaths records, the population should be roughly 15.5 billion mortals."

"Does this tally with our annual census scans?" asked Maribeth. She looked closer at the screen in front of her.

"Last year's census gave a count of 26.8 billion mortals, and this year we counted nearly 40 billion."

Maribeth now understood Karen's concern. "But wasn't this picked up and checked last year? How come we didn't see this before?"

"This is precisely why our department was formed," clarified Karen. "There was a general belief that things were falling through the cracks, but nobody had the specific job of keeping track; now we can see that something is wrong somewhere. The world population is growing enormously, but somehow the origins of billions of people are not accounted for.

"I thought some of our cities seemed a bit more crowded than usual, but then the planet can easily accommodate billions of people now that every square inch of the surface is capable of producing some or other crop."

"Does Luke know about this population increase?" asked Maribeth.

"He knows part of it, but he's been away visiting his family for the last ten days, so he isn't aware of the latest figures. I'm having a meeting with him tomorrow where I hope to get to the bottom of many strange things that have cropped up recently. We've also invited Martin Petrovic to join us at the meeting."

"You mean the new super whiz-guy who's making a name for himself as a problem solver?" asked Maribeth. "I've seen photos of him, is he as good as people say he is?"

"Well, if you look at his track record it seems that he's one of those guys who can analyze any number of random facts and come to a rational conclusion. I'm still trying to work out whether he's a mortal or an immortal."

"I thought for sure he was an immortal, but either way, mortal or immortal, he is jolly good-looking. Where's he from? What's his background?" pressed Maribeth.

"He's a bit of a mystery; the name Petrovic suggests Serbia or Croatia, but nobody seems to know for sure," Karen replied. She hit a button on her computer to save her latest calculations on a tiny thumbnail memory stick. "You'll get a chance to meet him tomorrow; be sure to ask him those questions."

"Maybe I'll do that," said Maribeth, obviously intrigued at the thought of striking up a conversation with the new genius on the block. "Any idea how old he is?"

"Easy girl," chuckled Karen, "a guy like that probably has no time for dating."

Maribeth smiled. "No man is an island."

"I sure hope you're right on that one," said Karen with a shy smile, her mind elsewhere.

"Could it be that our chief researcher has her eye on our boss?" asked Maribeth, grabbing the opportunity to poke fun at her superior. "Well, if it means anything to you," she continued when Karen didn't respond, "I've noticed Luke casting a bit more than a casual glance in your direction. I think you're in with a good chance."

"Oh rubbish, you're imagining things," Karen replied with a dismissive wave of her hand. "Anyway, he's far too busy to get involved with anyone at the moment." She returned to her work, then smiled to herself: *You're right, Maribeth, no man is an island – not even you, Mr. Luke Baron.*

CHAPTER 8

ESTATE OF GORGONIUS DRACO, WASHINGTON DC

Gorgonius Draco looked out over the lush lawns surrounding his country estate complex. Catching a glimpse of himself in a full-length mirror, he stopped for a moment to admire what he saw reflected there. Roughly six foot four in height, he had the athletic build of a gymnast – not over muscular, but firm and well-conditioned. His most striking features were his eyes – a piercing light blue in color that seemed to change slightly in different lights. Draco straightened up as the image in the mirror met his approval. *Not bad at all,* he thought to himself. *It's no wonder that people not only respect me, but also fear me. Good; it keeps them on their toes.*

His attention was drawn to a gardener who had started to trim a large bush near the front entrance of the mansion. "Damn fool," Draco muttered as grabbed his gizmo to call his secretary.

"Judith, get my head of gardening services to call me *immediately.*"

A few moments later his secretary came back to him. "He's on lunch at the moment, sir; can I get him to call back?"

"I don't care where he is, get him right now." Draco pocketed his gizmo and stormed over to open the window. "Hey you! Stop what you're doing immediately, and wait for me," he called to the gardener below. As he stormed out of the room his gizmo rang.

"Creighton here, sir, Judith said you were looking for me?"

"Meet me in front of the main entrance; there's an idiot gardener who is busy ruining one of my bushes."

Draco stormed out of the front door and reached the terrified gardener just as Creighton arrived on the jet-propelled hover bike he used for quick coverage of the Draco estate. "Didn't I tell you that I wanted all the bushes in the front entrance area to be trimmed in the shape of ball? This ... this fellow here is clearly trimming this bush in a prehistoric Christmas tree shape. I hate that shape and all its sordid memories – I want these bushes to be round. Now what wasn't clear about that instruction?"

Creighton turned to the gardener, an elderly worker named Sidney, who looked as if he wanted the ground to open up and swallow him. "Didn't you get the daily instructions I sent on everyone's communication devices, Sidney? My instructions were very clear, were they not?"

"Sir, I did get a message but I couldn't read it."

"Why not?"

"Sir, my vision is too blurry at the moment – my 100-year medical checkup is way overdue, but due to work pressure I have not been able to visit the medics. My most humble apologies, Mr. Draco – it won't happen again."

"It had better not," said Draco, already becoming bored with the conversation. "Creighton, make sure that your entire staff knows what they're supposed to be doing – I don't want this to happen again."

"Of course, Mr. Draco, it won't happen again," said Creighton, but Draco was already striding to the front door. He marched up the stairs, taking them two at a time, and entered his office at the same moment that the floor-to-ceiling virtual screen behind his desk came to life. At first he thought it must be Seth Baron calling to confirm the large order he had placed that morning, but as the full message appeared his blood ran cold. He looked in horror at the words that appeared on the screen, emblazoned in red with simulated red drops dripping off each letter, as though written in blood.

Be warned, we know your true plans and you will pay the price!

For a moment Draco was at a loss as to who would have the audacity to threaten him, but then he remembered ... A month before he had fired two of the men working on the space exploration project. They had discovered something that he preferred to keep secret for the time being, and they tried to blackmail him in return for their silence. Nobody pulled something like that on him. He fired them instantly and threatened that if they mentioned his secret to anyone they would be ... terminated.

It would seem they did not heed his warning. Draco took out his gizmo and called a number.

"Those two I spoke to you about ... yes, those two – do as we discussed. Call me when it's done." Draco replaced his gizmo and erased the message from the screen behind his desk.

CHAPTER 9

HEADQUARTERS OF BARON IRON AND STEEL, WASHINGTON DC

Seth Baron was deep in thought as he entered the main lobby of Baron Iron and Steel Headquarters and made his way to the elevators. If what he had heard about Gorgonius Draco was true, it was possible that Baron Iron and Steel was helping to create the weapons that would soon be used against the king's government. Privately Seth did not believe that anyone could even think of succeeding with such a stupid move – it just wasn't possible. Or was it? He couldn't get the image out of his head of the grotesque figure that Mike had shown him clinging to the aircraft wing, causing it to crash. But could Draco really be behind that? After all, he had met Draco; they had even had business lunches together. Seth resolved to find out more about his best customer, but in such a manner that he did not ruin the business relationship.

"Morning, sir, have a good Thanksgiving?"

Seth immediately snapped back to the present to concentrate on Pete Simpson, the information desk attendant resplendent in his new uniform with the discreet BIS badge on the jacket. *The new Baron Iron and Steel outfit looks good*, thought Seth.

"Yes, very good thanks Pete. And you and your family, every-one well?"

"Yes, thank you sir. What do you think of our new uniforms?"

"Looks real neat, Pete. What's your wife say about them?"

"She likes the color and the fabric – says they're very service-able. She reckons a woman must have chosen them, if you don't mind me saying so, sir."

"Tell her she's quite correct," Seth chuckled. "We had a size-able team working on the project, but it was headed up by Mrs. Goodwill from human resources." Seth entered the elevator and proceeded up to his top-level office suite. As the door opened his gizmo vibrated in his pocket; he answered quickly, without first looking at the caller ID.

"Seth Baron."

"Seth, Draco here. I need to speak with you urgently."

"Sure thing, I've just walked in but I'm free to talk. What's on your mind?"

"Can't talk about it over the phone. I have a problem; I need to see you face to face – urgently."

Seth could hear the tension in Draco's voice. It was the first time his big client had given any indication that he was not in complete control of everything. Was that really the case or was he putting on a very good act? If so, for what reason?

"Sure thing Draco; your office or mine?"

"Neither, I need to speak to you in a place where there is no chance of us being bugged, overheard or lip read."

"I can assure you my office is secure, but where did you have in mind?"

"You know the Millennium Sports Stadium about a mile north of the old Smithsonian Museum?"

"Yes, I've been there before," Seth replied.

"Can you make tomorrow morning at 10:30? I own the sta-dium - it will be empty except for the maintenance staff. I'll contact you again once you arrive at the stadium. Will you be there?" Draco demanded.

Seth glanced at his electronic diary. "I have meetings tomor-row, what about the following day?"

"Okay, see you then." With a "click" he was gone.

Seth sat back and scratched his head. *What on earth is this all about?* Then, as he recalled the conversation with Mike and Luke, and the fact that some believed Draco could be involved in a revolt against the king's government, Seth wondered whether Draco was setting a trap for him. Yet again the question: *Why?*

There was only one way to find out. Seth decided to go through with the meeting, but to let Mike know what was going on – just in case.

"Do you want me to go with you?" Mike asked when Seth called him that evening.

"No, I promised Draco I would go alone, but just stay alert," Seth responded, a nagging doubt lingering in his mind. *If what some say about Draco is true, then I could be stepping straight into the devil's lair ...*

CHAPTER 10

MMOD BOARDROOM, JERUSALEM

When Karen Leigh entered the boardroom at ten minutes before nine, Luke Baron and Martin Petrovic were already seated.

"I hope I'm not late," she said looking at her watch.

"Not at all," said Luke rising from his seat. "Martin and I got in early to discuss a few matters before the meeting." Placing a hand on her shoulder, he turned to the other man in the room. "Martin, I know you've spoken to her on the gizmo, but now I'd like you to meet Karen Leigh, my chief researcher. I'm not ashamed to admit I'm entirely dependent on her amazing ability to gather and analyze data that nobody else even dreams exist. No doubt you'll see this for yourself as the meeting progresses.

"Karen, Martin will be working with us on certain matters on a consultancy basis."

Karen accepted Petrovic's outstretched hand. The handshake was firm without being overpowering in any way. *Maribeth was right about him, he is good-looking.* She made a quick mental comparison between Luke and Martin and came to the conclusion that they looked very much alike. Both men were about six foot three, athletically built and with clean-shaven faces. If it were not for the fact that Luke had the characteristic pitch black hair common to Baron men, while Martin sported neatly trimmed blond hair, they could have been related.

Soon the three other members of the team joined them. Maribeth smiled as she took a seat next to Martin who stood to his feet and introduced himself. Luke opened the meeting and gave a brief overview of the purpose of the MMOD and some of the projects they were working on. "One of the issues that concerns us most at the moment is the theft of the documents from the World Archives in Washington."

"Do you have any suspects who might want information of that sort?" asked Martin.

"Not at the moment," answered Luke, "but certain people have suggested that Gorgonius Draco might have something to do with it."

"I've met him on a few occasions," said Martin, "a very strange character all round. I really don't know what to make of him."

"In what way is he strange?" asked Maribeth.

"His mood changes all the time, and I'm talking about extreme changes. I think a shrink would label him manic-depressive."

"Well, my relative Seth Baron is doing business with Draco at the moment – and very good business I'm told," said Luke remembering his conversation with Seth and Mike Cousins.

"Do you mean iron and steel?" asked Martin. "Is Draco buying iron and steel from Seth Baron?"

"Yes, and lots of it. I discussed the matter with Seth and also brought it up with Daniel. Seth didn't seem to have a problem with Draco, especially as the man is a very good paying customer."

"And Daniel – what did he have to say about Draco?" asked Karen.

"I think Daniel was a bit concerned about the sale of such large quantities of iron and steel, especially in light of the theft of the weapons plans," replied Luke. "He said he'd he would watch the situation."

"I think it's a good idea for Daniel and the Committee to keep an eye on things," Martin said. "We must not lose sight of the fact that the Millennium has now come to an end, so things could be hotting up soon."

"Hotting up?" enquired Maribeth. "In what way?" Then she remembered the prophecy in Revelation. "Oh, you mean the final revolt. But surely you don't think Satan would want to use weapons that are so hopelessly outdated?"

"Well, we don't have any weapons at all at the moment," Luke reminded her. "Nobody's bothered about weapons for a thousand years – we had no need to. But that could be where the problem lies. As the old saying goes, '*In the land of the blind, the one-eyed man is king.*' In a similar manner, in a world where nobody has any weapons at all, a group with high-powered firearms, long range missiles and a few nuclear bombs could do a lot of persuasion."

"Let's not even go there," said Maribeth with a shiver. "Part of my studies covered pre-millennial conditions, particularly the last years of the Tribulation. They weren't pretty. If that had to happen again to our present over-protected society, we would be like lambs to the slaughter."

"But surely the king would step in and take control?" interjected Karen. "After all, he has on a number of occasions ruled very decisively on high-level matters."

"I believe he *will* use his rod of iron when needed," concurred Martin.

Luke completed the quotation: "'And he will smash them like earthen pottery.' But let's not get too concerned with things beyond our control. Always remember that the final chapter has already been written, and the ultimate victory belongs to the king."

"But when will he step in and take full control?" Maribeth asked. "It seems that the time is right now."

"It's not for us to question the king's methods or his timing," reprimanded Luke. "He has entrusted day-to-day affairs to the Committee of Elders headed up by Daniel. They in turn have the immortals responsible for sections of the population. Daniel is in constant contact with the king, so let's leave the details up to them. We receive direct feedback from Daniel; in fact, we will be meeting with him soon."

"Let's hope he can give us some answers," said Karen. "I have a strange feeling that things are getting out of hand fairly rapidly."

CHAPTER 11

It was Karen's turn to address the meeting. She rose and started with the bad news. "Unfortunately the data I am about to present will add more fuel to the fire. I think everyone has noticed the dramatic increase in the world's population in the last couple of years; our cities are becoming more crowded by the day. Maribeth and I have been keeping stats on the increase in different cities and countries, and it's really quite mind-blowing. According to stats I drew this morning of births and deaths, the population of Earth should be no more than 15 billion, but in actual fact our automatic census that scans brainwaves present in the atmosphere indicates more than 40 billion, and growing exponentially.

"We have tried to question many of these people for whom we have no birth records, but they are either not willing to discuss their origins with us, or they really don't know where they came from."

"Sounds odd to me," said Luke. "Is there any logical explanation that you've come across?"

"There might be," interjected Martin taking his gizmo device from his jacket pocket. "We all believe in the Bible, don't we?" Nods all round. "I have the Bible on my gizmo, and in Revelation 20 the apostle John describes a judgment that will take place at the end of the Millennium. It's called the Great White Throne Judgment. All the dead of all the ages will come back to life to be judged. This will..."

"This will cause the population to swell enormously," Maribeth interrupted. Do you think..."

"It's definitely a possibility," Martin replied. "The timing is perfect."

"But I thought the dead would be raised to life and be judged immediately," said Luke. "And after judgment they would be thrown into the Lake of Fire. These people that are currently swelling the ranks don't seem to be going anywhere – and certainly not into a lake of fire."

"What makes you think that they will all automatically be condemned?" asked Martin.

"Isn't that what the Bible says will happen?" asked Karen.

"No, not really. A judgment can have different results depending on the case at hand. A judgment might go in favor of the person being judged, in which case they will be acquitted. However, if the judgment goes against them, they will suffer the prescribed consequences. In any case, most of the people who have ever lived never had the chance to learn about the God of Israel, let alone his son, Jesus. So how can they be condemned if they never knew any better?"

"That's sounds fair, but on what basis will they be judged?" asked Karen.

"I think I know the answer to that one," said Luke, eager to show that the spiritual knowledge of the Baron family had not passed him by. "At the final judgment books will be opened in which will be recorded every good and bad deed and action of every single person that didn't accept Christ during their life on Earth. There will also be a second book, the Book of Life, and if the Lord decides that your life's deeds do not condemn you, then your name will be retained in the Book of Life. Anyone not found in the Book of Life at the end of the judgment period will ... will suffer the prescribed consequences."

"The Lake of Fire," said Karen with a shiver. "Perhaps that's why they're reluctant to talk about themselves. Many of them may have been felons of some sort in their previous lives and won't open up to us as they see us as being part of the king's government and therefore someone to be wary of."

"That makes sense," said Luke, "but where do we go from here? Do we see a picture forming?"

"I think we do see something taking shape," said Karen checking the notes she had been making, "but there's still a lot of work to be done."

"Let me summarize and suggest a plan of action," said Luke switching on the virtual screen behind him to reveal the points he had been jotting down on his media device. "We've discussed various issues, some of which may not fall within our jurisdiction. I don't want anything to slip through the cracks, so let's do a bit of investigation before we hand a matter over to someone else. I think there are more commonalities here than may be obvious.

"Firstly, Maribeth, regarding those photos I sent through of the crash of the airliner in the Bermuda area, could you check with the airline to see if they have any new evidence, or even photos that may have come to light in the meantime."

"Sure thing, Luke, I'll get onto it right away," said Maribeth, making hurried notes.

"Secondly, we have the robbery of the weapons plans and the possibility that Draco may have something to do with it."

"Leave that to me," offered Petrovic raising his hand. "As I said, I have had dealings with Draco before and I'm scheduled to have follow-up meetings with him next week. I can easily ask some surreptitious questions without raising suspicion that we are investigating him and his activities. I'll get back to you as soon as we've had our meetings."

"Thanks Martin," said Luke, confident that someone of Martin Petrovic's standing would be able to enquire into Draco's affairs in a way that would not arouse suspicion. "Lastly, Karen, we need to prepare a presentation for our monthly meeting with the Committee of Elders; they must be brought up to date on our findings and conclusions regarding the population explosion.

I'm sure many people are asking difficult questions at the moment."

"Wouldn't the king have kept the elders informed? After all, he knows everything," queried Maribeth cautiously, wondering if this was an impertinent question.

"That might well be the case, Maribeth," replied Luke, "but as we discussed earlier, the king has delegated the day-to-day running of the Millennium government to the Committee of Elders and the various departments – including the MMOD. We do our duty as prescribed and provide feedback on important issues to the committee; it's then up to Daniel as chairman of the committee to liaise directly with the king."

"The system has worked well for a thousand years," said Karen packing away her gizmo and various other notes, "so I guess it doesn't need changing now."

"Definitely not," said Luke exchanging grins with Martin. "One last thing before we break – I have arranged to meet with Mike Cousins over the weekend. He is working closely with the elders on several key issues and I think it's essential that we keep in touch."

"You mean that huge fella they call 'the Fireman'?" Martin looked a bit concerned. "I didn't realize that he was involved with key matters. Shouldn't knowledge of some of the things we've been discussing be limited to only a few individuals?"

"I can assure you that Mike is the one man you can trust with your life, if it ever comes to that," said Luke giving Martin a reassuring smile. "He is 200% reliable and trustworthy. Remember he was a key member of the 144,000 during the Tribulation and has been working closely with the elders since the dawn of the Millennium. Do you have concerns about him?"

"No, not at all," demurred Martin. "I've never met the man in person, but of course his reputation precedes him, and it goes without saying that anyone you trust has my trust as well."

"Well, that's settled then," said Luke. "We'll meet again next Friday for progress updates. Let's hope we can come up with some rational explanations for what's been going on around us."

Luke remained seated for a moment as the group moved out to prepare for the week ahead. *What am I getting my team into now? It seems that we have no idea at the moment who or what we're dealing with. Please God give me the wisdom to deal with these challenges; and to keep them all safe.*

CHAPTER 12

"End of a long day; mind if I walk you home?" Karen looked up from her work screen as Luke entered the room.

"That would be great, but it's out of your way. You live on the other side of town, don't you?"

"I do, yes, but it's the weekend and I'm free until Mike arrives tomorrow morning at eleven."

"Is he flying in? Oh, that's stupid of me," Karen reproached herself. "Mike is an immortal and immortals don't need physical means of transportation."

"Well, if the prophets are correct, which I'm sure they are, it won't be long before we all receive our glorified immortal bodies, then we too can teleport ourselves from one place to another. Think of how my marathon time will improve; I could be a champion," Luke said with a broad grin.

"Only if you beat me," teased Karen. She stood up and collected her handbag from her drawer. "Remember, I'm a lot lighter than you so I'll teleport much faster, so don't get your hopes up too high, Mr. Baron."

"We'll see about that," said Luke taking her arm and escorting her out of the building. "It's a really beautiful evening for a walk; I'm going to enjoy this."

As they walked Karen was very aware of Luke moving his hand from her elbow down to her fingers. He eventually took her hand and she felt a warm glow as his hand enveloped hers. "This okay for you?" he asked, glancing down at her.

"Sure," she smiled back and gave his hand a gentle squeeze. They walked in silence along the street bordering the northern wall of the Old City, still known as Sultan Suleiman Street. After a while they entered the park and walked slowly towards the Garden Tomb and Karen's apartment block.

"Look at that, they actually still hold hands here; I thought they'd skip that stage here in the kingdom." The voice was rough and mocking. Luke and Karen swung around to see three men approaching from behind some bushes. "Me and my mates are a little skint at the moment, I'm sure the lady must have a small donation for us in that handbag." The tallest of the three lunged forward and grabbed Karen's handbag, snatching it from her grasp.

"Hey, cut that out," Karen shouted indignantly. "You can't do that; give my bag back!"

Immediately Luke stepped forward and grabbed the other side of the handbag. "What are you playing at?" he hissed between clenched teeth. "Let go of the bag and get out of here."

"Whoa, what have we 'ere?" the second thug said in a British accent. "Don't try to be a hero, matey, let go of the bag and then you two clear off."

Luke felt anger rise up inside him. Although he had taken part in sport wrestling at college, real aggression was not something that expressed itself in normal everyday society anymore. Probably his closest encounter with hard self-defense was the training he received from his great aunt, Britt Baron, who had been a top martial artist prior to the Millennium. Since the banishing of Satan to the abyss nearly 1,000 years ago, however, such extreme behavior was virtually unknown.

For this reason Luke was more perplexed by the absurdity of anyone wanting to take an item that belonged to someone else than he was about the rudeness of the three men facing them now. Suddenly one of the men lunged forward and shoved Karen so hard that she went flying a few feet backwards, landing on her back on the gravel pathway.

In a blind fury Luke turned on the man, punching him on the side of the head. As the man collapsed in a heap on the ground, the other two grabbed Luke, each one taking an arm. The man on the ground slowly stood up, and while his accomplices held Luke's arms, he struck Luke hard in the solar plexus. Luke doubled over as his diaphragm contracted in spasm, forcing the air from his lungs. As he struggled to regain his breath, the thug hit him again.

Filled with rage, Karen sprang up from the ground where she had been flung and, retrieving one of her high-heeled shoes that had come off during her fall, she charged at one of the men holding Luke's arms and struck as hard as she could at his head with the sharp point of the heel.

The man screamed as the heel gashed his face. He released Luke's arm and turned on Karen. He was about to crash his fist into her face when a blur from the side upended him and he crashed to the ground with a newcomer to the fray on top of him. The fracas lasted only a few seconds as a couple of well-placed blows rendered Karen's attacker unconscious.

In the meantime, another newcomer on the scene had grabbed the second thug in a chokehold. The third assailant, seeing what had happened to his two cronies, decided that discretion was the better part of valor, and fled the scene.

"Sorry about that, guys," said the man who had upended the first thug. "Looks like my days of playing rugby were not wasted – I enjoyed that tackle. I see that your handbag has a long detachable strap; do you mind if I use it to tie up these two? You'll get it back later."

"Sure, go ahead," said Karen passing him the handbag. "It will be good to get them immobilized so they can't cause any more trouble. Then she turned to Luke who was breathing normally again. "You okay?" she asked, putting an arm around his shoulder. "I thought those hooligans were going to kill you."

"I thought so too for a moment," said Luke with a wry smile, "it was jolly brave of you to attack this one with your shoe. Well done." Then he turned to the two rescuers. "I'm sure glad you guys came on the scene when you did; things were looking bad for us. But I still don't understand why they wanted to attack and rob us – we had done nothing to them; never even seen them before."

Having tied the two thugs back to back with their arms behind them, the shorter of the two men rose up and extended his hand to Luke. "Pete Barnaby's the name – just call me Barnaby; my friend here is Jed Rich. We were in the area looking for a place for me to stay when we heard the lady here shouting and thought we should see what was going on; and a good thing we did."

"Sure was," Karen agreed, "but what prompted them to want to steal my handbag? Such behavior is unheard of."

"Not anymore," said Jed, shaking his head. "Your days of peace and tranquility are over now – for a while, at any rate."

"What do you mean?" Karen looked worried. "Are you saying there are more of this type around?"

"Plenty, I'm afraid," said Barnaby, "but let's call the local patrol to take care of these two, then Jed and I will carry on looking for a place for me to stay."

"You could be in luck," said Karen, "I know of an apartment in my block that is becoming vacant. That's my block on the corner there, Hebron Towers. The superintendent is a Mrs. Zelda Cohen – just ask for her and tell her I sent you. Hopefully the apartment will still be available."

CHAPTER 13

Early the next morning Karen left her apartment for her regular morning jog. As she approached the front door leading out to the street, a voice behind her made her stop.

"Morning Karen. Good news, you were right about there being an open apartment in the block and the superintendent let me move in immediately." Karen swung around to find Barnaby approaching, a broad smile on his face. "I don't have any furniture of my own yet, so it's a good thing the apartment comes furnished."

"That's wonderful," said Karen, "we must get together and have a good chat; I think we have lots to learn from you and Jed."

"What about this evening – let's say at six thirty? Would that be okay for you and Luke?"

"I'll check with Luke at work today, but I know that he is also very keen to find out what you know about all these strangers that are popping up, so I'm sure he will be there."

"Six thirty then; and oh, I don't have my kitchen going yet, so I'm a bit short of chocolate cake..."

Karen laughed. "That's the strongest hint I've heard in a long time – chocolate cake it will be."

* * *

Over coffee and cake that evening Luke decided that it was time to find out more about what Barnaby and Jed knew of the current happenings. "Jed, yesterday you mentioned that our days of peace and tranquility are over; exactly what did you mean by that?"

"When last did you hear of anyone being mugged like you and Karen were yesterday?" Jed asked in response. "It's something completely foreign to your whole way of life in the Millennium Kingdom, is it not?" Jed looked from Luke to Karen waiting for an answer.

"Well, as we mentioned earlier, Karen and I both work for a government department known as the Mortal Movements and Occurrences Department – MMOD for short. It's a new department created by the Committee of Elders. Obviously they had reasons for creating a department to do what we do, and our recent observations definitely validate their beliefs."

"Ah, so you've picked up that people are appearing from nowhere and that the world population is growing at an alarming rate," said Jed, receiving a nod from Barnaby.

"Tell them," said Barnaby, "they will find out pretty soon anyway."

"What will we find out?" Luke asked.

"We're aware that the population is exploding to an extent that is not justified by the record of births," said Karen. "What we haven't worked out is where the people are coming from. Our plan was to start interviewing people who don't have birth records to find out more."

"Look no further," said Barnaby with a smile, "we can be your first interviewees."

At that moment Luke's gizmo buzzed in his pocket. Seeing that the call was coming from his relative Seth Baron, Luke excused himself and left the room. He returned a few minutes later, a worried look on his face.

"That was Seth calling, Gorgonius Draco has requested a meeting with him, alone and at a rather deserted venue. Seth will meet with him, but he naturally has concerns about the unusual circumstances of the meeting. He has asked me to send him all the information we have on Draco so that he can be prepared for the meeting."

"Do you have information on Draco?" asked Jed.

"We have certain information that we have put together for the Committee of Elders," said Luke, "hopefully something will be of use to Seth. Anyway, I'm afraid we'll have to postpone our chat this evening as Karen and I will need to go back to the MMOD and get the information for Seth. This meeting he has with Draco seems pretty important."

"That's fine by us," said Jed, "give us a shout when you are ready to meet again, our time is pretty flexible."

"Thanks guys, I'll call you tomorrow," said Luke, as he and Karen made their way towards the elevator.

"Watch out for malevolent returnees," Barnaby called after them, but the elevator doors had already shut.

CHAPTER 14

MILLENNIUM SPORTS STADIUM, WASHINGTON DC

The anti-gravity boosters hissed gently as Seth Baron brought his vehicle to a slow vertical descent in the deserted parking lot of the Millennium Sports Stadium. Having parked his vehicle, Seth looked around the deserted parking lot for any sign of Draco. He still had an uneasy feeling about this meeting, especially after hearing the rumors that Draco could be Satan now released from the abyss. He was startled when his gizmo buzzed in his pocket.

"Seth here."

"Come up to row FF in the block you are now in. I will direct you from there." It was Draco's voice.

Seth entered the main stand and proceeded to climb up to row FF; when he got there he stopped and looked around. "This is crazy," he said aloud to himself. "We could have been sitting in the comfort of my office enjoying tea and cake. Why this place..."

"Because there's a very good chance we could be overheard in either of our offices." The voice came from behind him. Seth swung around to see the tall figure of Gorgonius Draco striding silently up the stairs; Seth noticed that his movements were almost cat-like – smooth and agile.

"Sorry about that, Seth, I didn't mean to give you a scare."

"What's going on?" asked Seth, the anxiety in his voice obvious as the thought crossed his mind again that this was some sort of trap he had walked into.

"I was checking up on something. I saw some movement on the grandstand on the far side of the playing field and thought it could be a sniper taking a bead on me. You may think it strange that anyone would be in possession of a rifle in this day and age, but ancient weapons are being produced on a large scale at the moment." Draco's agitation was obvious. "Have you heard of Kratos?"

"I've heard the name mentioned. Not sure who he is or what he does though," Seth replied cautiously.

"Nobody really knows where he came from. Some say Cuba, others say somewhere in South America. Anyway, he is gathering many followers with his 'teachings', if you can call them that. He also has a number of scientists and engineers working for him, and rumor has it that he is producing weapons similar to those used in pre-Millennium times, only greatly improved by his army of scientists. One of my customers says he witnessed Kratos' workers testing some pretty destructive firearms, one of them being something called an impulse rifle that can vaporize any target."

"Sounds like something our authorities should look into," said Seth. "But what makes you think someone would want to shoot you? Why are you worried?"

"Some people out there don't like what I'm doing; they think I'm involved with something both illegal and immoral. I was also forced to fire two of my workers recently so they're not happy, and there could be others who bear a grudge against me. I can't take any chances."

"They? Are you referring to the government's security detail? Exactly what are you doing that would make someone want to kill you?"

Draco pointed to a seat and Seth sat down. "You know of course that I'm ordering large amounts of iron and steel from you, but do you know what I'm doing with the iron and steel?" Draco lowered his voice as he asked the question.

"You told me at the start of our relationship that you were building some sort of spacecraft; is that still the case?"

Draco took a long breath. "As you know, during the peaceful Millennium years scientists had an opportunity to work unhindered on a variety of projects, some of which had their origins way back in the past. One such project, which my personal scientists have been working on, is the development of string theory and its by-products. That includes the harnessing of gravitons to not only enable spacecraft to break free of any gravitational field, but also to be able to use the pull of other large objects in space to attract them at speeds far in excess of the speed of light. By focusing its graviton detectors on something like a distant galaxy, a spacecraft could be drawn there at phenomenal speeds."

"You've lost me," said Seth, shaking his head. "Just give me the nitty gritty."

"I'm constructing a fleet of space vehicles capable of carrying vast numbers of people beyond the reaches of our solar system, in fact of our galaxy, to the planets we have discovered that could support life as we mortals know it. Two of these planets are in the galaxy closest to our Milky Way – the Andromeda galaxy. They orbit a star known as 103. Some of my space vehicles will be equipped to carry passengers while others will carry vast amounts of materials to build suitable dwellings, set up factories and, in general, house a population in a manner similar to what we have on Earth today." Draco looked around once again to make sure nobody was within earshot. "Of course, as my supplier, I would expect you to keep this information confidential."

"I never guessed that is what you were using the material for," said Seth. "Some believed that you were ... well ...."

"Yes, I know some of the rumors. I'm being accused of wanting to build weapons and start a revolution, and I've even heard that I'm the devil himself," Draco chuckled. "It's all nonsense, of course. The only thing I'm building is space vehicles."

Seth now understood why Draco needed the vast quantities of iron and steel that were already on order, especially the high-quality steel required for building the very tough outer skin of large space vehicles. But that still left one important question unanswered. "Why do you want to do this? What makes you think that so many people would want to travel across galaxies to settle on distant planets?"

"Because it's the end of the Millennium," said Draco as if that was reason enough to leave Earth, possibly forever.

"And so? Why would people want to leave merely because the Millennium has come to an end?" Seth asked, still not sure where Draco was coming from. "We now look forward to our conversion from mortal to immortal and the promise of an eternal life of bliss in New Jerusalem. Jesus himself has explained how wonderful the next life will be."

Draco's face clouded over and he fixed Seth with a look that caused him to go cold inside. "What if your destiny is not New Jerusalem but the Lake of Fire? Don't you see? We read that thousands upon thousands will be cast into the Lake of Fire as a result of being found wanting in the final judgment, the White Throne Judgment. Don't you think that people would pay a premium to escape from Earth before that judgment?"

"But is that possible? In any case, most of those who have come through the Millennium have lived lives that qualify them for eternal life. There are a few mortals who have done their 'own thing' and have not obeyed the king's standards, but the numbers of such people are nowhere near to what you're talking about. Where are all your space passengers going to come from?"

"They are the resurrected 'returnees', like me," said Draco almost in a whisper.

"What do you mean by 'returnees'? Returned from where?" Seth was completely confused.

"Returned from our previous lives, wherever and whenever they took place. In my case I lived during the twentieth century AD. I was a successful businessman, but not always an honest one, I'm sorry to admit. But here I am in the Millennium – still a

57

businessman and still not always as honest as I probably should be – another reason to be careful when appearing in public. So where will that leave me and the millions like me, or worse than me, when it comes to the White Throne Judgment?"

"You mean you weren't born during the Millennium, but were resurrected at the end of it...?"

"I was resurrected ten years ago to face the final judgment," Draco finished the sentence for him. "At that stage I was one of the first returnees. Now there are millions of us. Most of us have a reason to want to avoid any form of judgment."

"But nobody can flee from the final judgment – you can't flee from God," Seth said, not quite understanding where Draco was going with his line of thought.

"Maybe, maybe not," said Draco, "but there are thousands of us returnees, and many thousands of people born into the Millennium who would welcome a chance to escape a bad judgment."

"It still seems crazy to me." Seth still was not convinced that Draco was on the right path.

"Because of the things we've done, and the way we've spent our lives, many of us are not at all sure that our names will appear in the famous Book of Life on Judgment Day – and you know what that means."

"Well, according to the book of Revelation, those whose names are not found in the Book of Life are cast into the Lake of Fire."

"Exactly. Don't you think it's worth taking the outside chance to escape to a distant galaxy rather than to remain here and face the furnace? Let me assure you, we have hundreds of enquiries daily; people are prepared to pay premium prices for a chance to escape. Do you think a good businessman would pass up an opportunity like this?"

"Still doesn't make sense to me," Seth said scratching his head, "but what do you want me to do? Why this extremely secretive meeting?"

"Two things," said Draco coming to the point at last. "First, I'm asking you again, as a client of yours, to keep what I have told you to yourself – for the time being at any rate. I have contacts everywhere, so I know that certain information has already leaked out about my space travel plans. I have even received death threats, most likely from people who don't like what I'm doing. While I realize, of course, that the growing volume of people enquiring into the possibility of escape will be impossible to hide, I would prefer the authorities not to get involved at this point in time.

"Secondly, we have already tested a prototype of our long-distance space vehicle – very successfully I might add. We are ready to go into full production and I have all the plans for constructing various types of space vehicles – some for transporting equipment and provisions, others for passenger transportation. We are going to need tons of very specific material from Baron Iron and Steel. My scientists have come up with an additive that will make steel plating virtually indestructible. I need to be able to work with you to manufacture the sheeting that includes this new additive. Are you prepared to become part of this deal?"

Seth was silent for a long while before answering. "While I still don't think it's possible to escape God's judgment by fleeing to a distant galaxy, I don't see any legal or moral reason for not supplying you with materials. Space travel is not illegal, even though I believe the motive for this particular venture is dubious, to say the least. If you send me the specifications for what you require I will gear up to get the material to you as soon as possible."

A look of relief came across Draco's face. "I knew I could rely on you. There are other sources I could have approached, but none as jacked up as Baron Iron and Steel. You won't be sorry you made this decision."

I sure hope not, Seth thought to himself as he and Draco shook hands.

CHAPTER 15

WASHINGTON DC, IN THE VICINITY OF THE WHITE HOUSE

Mike Cousins made his way from the White House, across Lafayette Square, then turned left and headed towards his nearby apartment. For a moment he reflected back on times before the advent of the Millennium when he and Mark Baron paid several visits to then president Lynton Granger in the White House. This was during the turbulent times of the Great Tribulation when many countries were under threat of invasion by the forces of the Antichrist.

The peace and tranquility of the late evening caused the big man's thoughts to wander back to his childhood. The eldest of six children born and raised in New Orleans, Mike could trace his family roots back to the cotton plantations of Baton Rouge where his forefathers had worked as slaves. He had followed the example of his God-fearing parents and, from an early age, was deeply involved with his church. He would probably have become a preacher had it not been for a particular incident when he was sixteen years old.

Left home alone with his younger siblings one night while his father rushed their mother to hospital with acute appendicitis, Mike was awakened in the early hours of the morning by the smell of burning. Smoke was filling the room he shared with his brothers, and through the doorway he could see flames coming from the kitchen. Being bigger and stronger than most sixteen year old's, he managed to carry his two young brothers through the flames to safety, then returned for his three small sisters, whom he also carried to safety outside. He then returned to the house and, using buckets filled with building sand from a heap in the garden, he doused the flames before too much damage had been caused.

The story of his heroic rescue efforts reached the local newspapers, and as a result of that the local fire chief offered him weekend work at the town's fire station. After that there was only one career that interested young Mike Cousins. Shortly after his eighteenth birthday he made his way to Washington where he joined the Washington Fire Department. It did not take long before his strength, endurance and courage made him one of the most highly decorated firemen in Washington.

Mike also vividly remembered his first meeting with the angel Raphael – or Rafe as he preferred to be called. It was at the beginning of the Tribulation when Mike was awakened one night by a stranger in his bedroom. On switching on the light, he was confronted by a short, powerfully built young man with a crewcut hairstyle who informed Mike that he had been chosen as one of the 144,000. This elite group had been selected by God and given supernatural powers designed to be of assistance to suffering mankind during the Tribulation. Mike was incredibly honored to be part of the team.

"Hey, big guy, I like that gold chain you're wearing. Must have cost quite a bit, but by the looks of your clothes I'd say you've got plenty of money. How about giving me that gold chain and then transferring some zenos over to my account?"

Mike snapped out of his trip to the past and turned. The man who'd spoken to him was in his forties, tall and thin with a mop of black hair. He had a scar on his face that extended across his right cheek. From the look of him he was no stranger to trouble.

"Why are you asking me for money?" asked Mike in amazement. "Why don't you ask your section leader to give you an advance, like everyone else does?"

"I did ask him and he refused. Says he doesn't like what I bought from one of my returnee mates."

"And what did you buy that he doesn't like?" Mike was curious.

"This," said the man, producing a foot-long dagger from beneath his jacket.

At that moment more men stepped out from behind a clump of trees, each brandishing a knife, a baton or some sort of club. Mike counted five in total.

"Better do as you're told," advised the largest of the group, a rough looking guy with a shaggy beard. "You might be pretty big, but count us; you don't stand a chance – we'll take you down easily. So get your gizmo out and make the zeno transfer like a good boy."

Scarface came up to Mike and grabbed the gold chain he wore around his neck; with a quick jerk he snapped one of the links and removed the chain. Mike did not resist, instead he asked, "And now what?"

"This might get me a few zenos on our back-street market," the guy said, pocketing the chain.

"Okay look, fellas, let's get one thing straight," said Mike, feeling the old familiar heat of imminent combat rise up inside him, a feeling that he had not experienced during the peaceful Millennium years. "There's going to be no money transfer. I'm going to take out my gizmo and summon the local security to come and pick you all up. Maybe a night in detention will make you see things differently. I've no desire to fight you. I don't even want my chain back; you can keep it."

"It's as I thought," said Scarface, "you're a huge big baby. But you're not gonna get away so easily. Once we get to work on you, you'll gladly give us your banking details."

Out of the corner of his eye Mike saw a man standing behind him start to swing a club towards his head. Although he was an immortal, he was not immune to pain or physical harm. He raised a massive forearm and blocked the blow then, grabbing the man by his arm, he pulled him off his feet and started to swing him around in a wide circle.

"You're breaking my ruddy arm," screamed the man. Mike let go of his arm, causing the man to fly into two of his friends, knocking them off their feet. Mike quickly took stock of the situation and saw that only Scarface and his big friend were left standing. The bigger of the two was about six foot six tall and probably weighed 250 pounds; this was considerably less than Mike's seven foot two frame and muscular 330 pound bulk. Mike was about to quietly subdue the man when he saw him take something off the back of his belt. To Mike's total disbelief he saw the glint of a short-handled battle axe.

"I was leader of a gang in Stockholm; they called me Axeman!" screamed the big man as he charged at Mike. "I'm gonna cut down that big body of yours before you even know what's happening!"

Mike stepped deftly to one side and lunged forward to meet Axeman's advance. His opponent tried to change direction and swing his axe sideways, but instead walked straight into Mike's right arm swinging horizontally into his nose. Mike could hear bone and cartilage crack under the impact. Axeman dropped to the ground, emitting an animal-like cry; he lay on his side, blood pouring from his shattered nose.

Mike looked around to see if any further threats were imminent from his attackers. Only Scarface was left standing, with two of the others painfully getting to their feet. Scarface threw his hands in the air as a signal that he didn't want to take the matter any further.

"Get down on the ground and check that Axeman can breathe," Mike ordered Scarface. "I'll check out your mates."

After seeing that no serious damage had been caused, save to Axeman's nose, Mike told the five to remain seated on the ground. He then ordered them to place any weapons they had on the ground in front of them.

"I'm assuming that you are all returnees," he said, "probably all belonging to the Shadow Brigade. Am I right?"

"Yeah; what of it?" demanded Scarface, looking sullen.

"Just this," said Mike. "If this little skirmish had taken place in my previous life, you might not have gotten off so lightly; you might not have survived at all. But that was then. I decided to change my ways and follow the king."

Mike made eye contact with each one in turn. "You are all returnees; do you know why you have been resurrected at this time?"

"To be chucked into the Lake of Fire, I guess," grunted Axeman. "Why else?"

"I'll tell you why else," said Mike. "Yes, you will be thrown into the Lake of Fire if you don't turn your lives around. This is precisely why you are here on Earth again – to be given another chance. This is your final opportunity to repent of your lives of robbing and killing. The last thing God wants is to destroy you forever, so He's giving you this one last chance. Time is short; the final judgment is very near. Don't mess around anymore. I can give you the contact details of the White Robe leader in this area, he will help you further. You can also gizmo me any-time you want – I'm Mike Cousins and I'm prepared to help at any time."

Mike gathered up the weapons lying on the ground and turned to leave.

"I'll dispose of these toys; you won't need them anymore. And don't take too long to make up your minds, time is short."

As Mike continued on his way towards his apartment, Scarface turned to his mates who were slowly getting to their feet. "Reckon I'll give it a try. I always thought the White Robes were a bunch of goodie-goodie creeps, but if there are more like him around, then I want to be on their side."

Axeman and the others nodded in agreement.

"I certainly don't want to come up against him again," said Axeman, his face still covered in blood. "When I arrived here I was told that this was our final chance, but I never believed it. As far as I'm concerned, let's do it!"

CHAPTER 16

OLD PART OF THE CITY OF JERUSALEM

The Shuk Mahane Yehuda, a large and flourishing marketplace a few miles north-west of the old city of Jerusalem, is an area that remained largely unchanged over the centuries. Despite the fact that construction technology made significant advances during the centuries of the Millennium, the elders encouraged property developers to maintain the character and ambiance of several areas of Jerusalem and the shuk was one of these.

Luke Baron had arranged to meet Mike Cousins at the Acropolis Grill Room, a restaurant in the shuk that boasted tasty Greek cuisine which was Mike's preference. When he arrived Luke spoke briefly to Alesandro, the headwaiter, and was shown to a secluded table near the back of the restaurant. Luke looked around and, not seeing Mike anywhere in the vicinity, he glanced at his watch.

"Apologies for being late, my friend, but I had to sort out some guys who got a bit mixed up with their priorities." The voice came from behind him, and Luke swung around in his seat to see Mike's huge frame striding towards him.

"Not at all," said Luke standing up and extending his hand. "I know that with your immortals' special mode of transport travel is no problem for you."

"Don't worry, my young friend," said Mike sitting down opposite Luke, "soon you too will be transformed into a spiritual body and be able to teleport – it's really quite useful, you know."

"I'm looking forward to it," said Luke realizing once again how close they actually were to entering the next phase of God's plan – eternal life in New Jerusalem."

"In the meantime," said Mike, bringing Luke back to the present, "you have something on your mind. Shoot."

Luke came straight to the point. "Recently Karen and I were accosted in the street by three thugs who we later learned are returnees. Fortunately two other returnees who seemed like pretty decent guys assisted us. It was rather a bad experience for both of us – we aren't used to people showing aggression like those two did. I guess you saw a lot of that during the Tribulation."

"Sure did, and it's not nice. I bumped into five of them before coming here, but we've been warned in the Word to expect this to happen at the end of the Millennium. I guess we're entering the dark period at the end of the Seventh Day of creation. We know now that Satan has been released from the abyss and is already gathering followers for his final revolt."

"But surely he has also read Revelation and knows that he cannot win this fight? He must realize that he and his followers are on their way to final destruction," Luke said, incredulous.

"Satan has always been extremely arrogant – that was his downfall right from the start. He knows scripture better than most, but he still thinks he can turn things around to get his way. I guess he must be the eternal optimist," smiled Mike sardonically.

"Or the most misguided being that ever lived. But if he's here on Earth now, have you any idea who he is? Has he taken on human form or is he drifting around in spirit form? You have connections with the Committee of Elders, do they have any idea who or what he is? Surely he can be stopped before he gets going."

Mike took a sip of hot coffee then sat back in his chair. "One thing you must never lose sight of is the fact that many things have already been decided. Scripture cannot be changed – it is the record of God's will and purpose, both past and future. God did not choose to destroy Satan when he first rebelled in heaven all those thousands of years ago; nor did He destroy him after he led Adam and Eve astray in the garden. He also did not destroy him at the end of the Tribulation; he merely locked him up for a thousand years. God chose to release Satan again at this point in time, at the end of the Millennium, in order to finally determine who his true followers are. Remember that everyone is given free choice – you either follow a path of righteousness or you follow your own desires which could lead you into condemnation when the final judgment comes around. That is the purpose of the White Throne Judgment, and we know how that is going to end for Satan. To answer your question: God will not change his mind and destroy Satan before the appointed time."

"Seems like we'll be having quite a tough time until Satan is finally destroyed," said Luke shaking his head sadly. "Pity about that, but who am I to question God?"

"Exactly," said Mike slapping a large hand on Luke's shoulder. "But remember the promise in scripture that although we now see in part, one day we will know fully why things are as they are. Be patient my young friend, it won't be too long now."

Luke turned the conversation back to the immediate reality facing them. "The problem we at the MMOD are faced with now, is how to keep track of mortal movements seeing that people are randomly popping up all over the world. Furthermore, there are no records of births to assist in the tracking process. We held an unofficial census last month and found that the world population had expanded more in nine months than in the past hundred years – and the numbers have been increasing exponentially since then."

"I'm afraid it's impossible to keep track of them," said Mike. "Bear in mind that every unsaved person who lived and died prior to Christ's Second Coming is being resurrected at this time. Not all at once, but gradually. We're looking at billions already on Earth and probably many more to come. Fortunately the planet can accommodate these numbers now because every square inch can be used for agriculture under our ideal weather conditions. Prior to the Millennium large portions of Earth were covered by oceans or arid deserts, and even areas that could be used were prone to all sorts of adverse weather conditions."

"That's true," said Luke, "but it sure will be a relief when we are all in New Jerusalem and the final judgment has been settled."

"Indeed, but patience is the key. Patience, with a good dose of faith – never lose faith. You've read the last chapter of the book, so you know how it ends. But to get back to the current action again, I'll pay a surreptitious visit to Draco's workshops and check what he's up to. If you, in the meantime, could try to keep track of what the returnees are doing it would help to complete the picture. I suggest that the MMOD doesn't worry too much about population numbers, rather keep track of what these people are up to. We know that Satan – in whatever guise he is masquerading – will start organizing some sort of an army of followers and lead them in a revolt against the king and his government. It would help immensely if we could pinpoint the main areas of his activities, and if we could get an idea of what he's planning, that would be a real bonus."

"Are you suggesting we place a spy in his midst – someone who could feed information back to us?"

"That would be the cherry on top, I guess," said Mike. "It would, however, be a very dangerous job. If Satan or his cohorts got wind of this person's intentions it would go badly for him or her."

"At our last MMOD meeting Martin Petrovic also offered to look into what Draco is up to. Have you met Martin yet?" asked Luke.

"So far only by reputation," said Mike, "but I've heard very good reports about him. Quite a whiz-kid on the quiet."

"He seems to be pretty efficient," Luke agreed. "The MMOD is using him as a consultant to good effect; he has a seemingly limitless chain of resources. Seeing that you will be looking into Draco's activities perhaps Martin could play the spy role."

"Sure, ask him," said Mike, "but you will have to make it clear that spying on Satan could be a risky business. Ah, here's our order, let's eat – I'm starving. By the way, how's Karen?" asked Mike with a sly smile.

"She's fine," said Luke, feeling his cheeks flushing slightly at Mike's pointed question. "Why do you ask?"

Mike smiled. "No reason really, but I did hear a few things lately. She's a bright young lady – and good-looking to boot, but I guess you've noticed that already."

"Okay Mike, you win," laughed Luke, "I'll admit I'm interested, but right now let's eat."

CHAPTER 17

MMOD, JERUSALEM

"Set myself up as a spy in Satan's organization? Well, I guess it's possible, but it would be extremely risky." Martin Petrovic stood up and walked over to the floor-to-ceiling window of Luke's twentieth floor office and gazed out onto the city below. He stood there for a while, deep in thought while Luke sat back in his chair, allowing Petrovic to think over the proposition. After a full minute Petrovic spun around and went back to his empty chair. He sat down, picked up his half-empty coffee cup, drank the remainder of the coffee, and then smiled at Luke.

"I'll do it. Sorry about the long delay, I was just considering different ways of getting into the organization, but now I've worked things out. It's a brilliant strategy and it can be done; count me in. There is one thing, though."

"What's that?" asked Luke, realizing that a man of Petrovic's intellect would be able to see pitfalls that lay hidden to most others.

"I want to have a female cohort go in with me. It's always easier for a team consisting of a man and woman to be accepted into a new organization than a man by himself."

"Okay," agreed Luke slowly, "any ideas on who would suit the role?"

"Yes; Maribeth Markham would be ideal. She's one of the finest electro-cyber engineers I know, and she's confident and has the ability to think on her feet. She would be my choice – if you and Karen can spare her."

"I guess you're right about a man-woman team being more readily accepted than a man by himself. I'll have a word with Karen, and then we'll need Maribeth's buy-in as well; after all, she'll be in the hot seat."

"Sure, do that," said Petrovic, getting up from his chair. "I must be on my way – another appointment unfortunately. But let me know what Maribeth thinks about the idea, and if she's in on it then we can start serious planning. And don't worry, I'll look after her."

"I'm sure you will," said Luke more to himself than to anyone else. *And I think she likes you too...*

CHAPTER 18

KAREN'S APARTMENT, JERUSALEM

"Tell us all you know about the returnees and their groupings," Luke asked Jed Rich as he, Karen and Barnaby sat together in Karen's apartment.

"The returnees have divided themselves into two distinct groups," said Jed. "They are as different as chalk and cheese. The group that Barnaby and I belong to is called the White Robes. It was given that name because the reason we have all been resurrected at this time is to prepare ourselves for the final judgment – the White Throne Judgment. We are an extremely diverse group, as you can imagine, with members from every race and creed, and also from totally different time periods. We do share some things in common, although most of the returnees have a lot of catching up to do. You can imagine what it's like to go to sleep in the twelfth century, for example, and to wake up in the Millennium Kingdom. Secondly, and most importantly, we all know that, for whatever reason, we lived apart from God in our previous lives but have now heeded the call of the king and our immortal section leaders and have turned over a new leaf."

"And the other group?" pressed Luke, keen to find out more about the group they needed to infiltrate.

"The other group call themselves the Shadow Brigade. They totally reject Christ's government and make every effort to subvert anything and anyone who submits to Him. In the last few weeks they have grown exponentially in number – no doubt because so many of the returnees are not prepared to change from their previous behavior patterns and still want to do their own thing."

"Who are the leaders of the two groups?" asked Karen, who had been taking notes on her gizmo.

"Our leader is an Australian woman by the name of Erica Merton. In her previous life Erica was one of the original group of English convicts sent to the Australian penal colony in 1788, specifically to a settlement called New Albion, which later became Sydney."

"I didn't know there were women among the convicts sent to Australia," said Karen in obvious surprise.

"Apparently there were nearly 200 women in the original group of settlers," continued Jed. "After serving her time as a prisoner Erica decided to use her beauty and charm to her own benefit and set up a rather exclusive brothel that was frequented by many of the army and navy top brass stationed out there, as well as other well-to-do civilian leaders. The fame of her 'business' was such that quite a number of young ladies came out from England to join her and make money off the wealthy locals."

"Wow," said Luke, "that's quite a past to live with. What is she like now?"

"Completely different," said Jed emphatically. "Erica realized that her previous life left much to be desired and that she died a sinner. Now she is using all her considerable energy to get other returnees to repent of their past lives and to accept the king. It's largely due to her efforts that the members of the White Robes have grown in number."

"What about the other group, the Shadow Brigade?" asked Luke. "Who is their leader and what do they get up to?"

"His actual identity is unknown," said Barnaby. "I don't think even his followers know who the leader really is. He goes by the name of Kratos, after the Greek god of strength and power. When he makes public appearances he is clothed in a black hooded robe and he also wears a mask – a totally featureless white mask with holes for his eyes, nose and mouth."

"Sounds ghastly," said Karen. "I wouldn't like to meet him on a dark night."

"It wouldn't be advisable," said Jed with a smile. "From what we've heard he's a real nasty character."

"Well, as we said earlier, it's his group that we plan to infiltrate," said Luke. "We need to find out exactly what they're up to and we thought you guys could give us some idea of how to go about it. We want it to seem natural to avoid suspicion, but we figure that we will need to get pretty deep into the hierarchy of the group to really get to the essence of what they're planning."

Barnaby gave a low whistle. "Wow! You realize that this could be a very tricky assignment, even for a skilled operative? There's no telling what Kratos will do to anyone that he finds spying on him. Who are you going to use for this job?"

"Martin Petrovic has agreed to take on this assignment, but he asked that Maribeth Markham go in with him as a female accomplice. He believes, and quite rightly I reckon, that a man–woman combination will be more acceptable than a man by himself."

"Could be," agreed Jed. "What does this woman Maribeth think of this – is she willing?"

"I'll contact her shortly," said Luke, "but I first wanted to get some background from you guys."

"Your big problem is that neither Martin nor Maribeth are returnees which will make them stick out like a sore thumb in the group," said Barnaby. "Or am I wrong – is Martin a returnee that I don't know about?"

"I know for a fact that Maribeth was born and bred during the Millennium and that she is definitely not a returnee, but as for Martin – well, he's a bit of a mystery. He never speaks too much about his past, but one thing's for sure, he's a top-class operative. He is the coolest, calmest and most efficient person I've met. If he says that he can do a job then I'll put my money on the job getting done quickly and efficiently. I did a lot of research into his previous assignments before I hired him as a consultant to the MMOD – the man is good at what he does."

"Let's hope so," said Barnaby. He quickly entered some data into his gizmo, then exclaimed: "Ah, here we are, the Shadow Brigade is holding a meeting tomorrow evening – but it's in London."

"That shouldn't be a problem," said Karen taking her gizmo from her handbag. "I'll call Maribeth right now and check if she's willing to go on this mission." After a brief conversation, Karen looked up at the others with a smile on her face. "Maribeth is overjoyed at being given this task – especially since it involves working closely with Martin. It's no secret – to me at any rate – that she really fancies him."

"Is she willing to infiltrate the organization in spite of the risks involved?" asked Luke, still concerned about sending one of his employees on a mission that could be dangerous.

"I assured her that Martin has had successful dealings with both groups of returnees and that she will be perfectly safe with him."

"Great! Sounds like the operation is a go then." Luke stood up and shook hands with Barnaby and Jed. "Thanks for filling us in on the returnees; I think we're in for an interesting time ahead."

"It's our pleasure," said Barnaby, "and may God be with you through whatever may lie ahead – I have a feeling we're going to need all the divine assistance we can get."

CHAPTER 19

MILLENNIUM SPORTS STADIUM, LONDON

On a cold January night about 150,000 members of the Shadow Brigade crowded into London's giant Millennium Sports Stadium, built on the site of the old Wembley Stadium. From the buzz around the stadium it was obvious that each person was waiting expectantly to hear the ground-breaking news that had been promised them in the communication each had received directly from Kratos himself. All eyes were on the temporary stage rigged up in the center of the sports arena. A number of less important speakers had already given their messages, mostly expressing their discontent with the king's government and the impending judgment, but they were just setting the stage for the main event.

Suddenly the music stopped and a multitude of spotlights focused their beams on a central point above the stadium. As the crowd watched, a figure appeared in the sky above and then slowly descended until it reached the stage. On recognizing the hooded figure with the white faceless mask, the crowd erupted into tumultuous applause. As one they began to chant "Kratos, Kratos, Kratos!" over and over again until the figure on the stage held his hands aloft and indicated that the applause should come to an end.

As the noise died down, Kratos moved to the end of the stage facing the largest of the grandstands. Holding his arms high he shouted, "I have come to bring you good news! Not one of you is to be thrown into the so-called Lake of Fire!" Immediately the crowd erupted in deafening applause which lasted for about two minutes until Kratos again beckoned for his fans to be silent.

"Apart from you wonderful people who have braved the cold tonight, there are millions and millions of people around the world listening to this broadcast," he continued. "I want to assure you once more that not one of you will perish in a lake of fire, for tonight our revolution begins in earnest. The so-called king and his forces have grown weak over the past thousand years, and the time has come for us returnees, and other like-minded members of the Millennium Kingdom, to rise up against this weak ruler and set up our own government on Earth."

Again the stadium erupted in applause and cheers. Kratos was in his element as he saw how the crowd was responding to him.

"I urge you all to join me in this final revolt against the king and his bunch of immortals that rule over us. We are preparing for war! We have already made advancements with our program to build weapons to take on the king's army; even his warring angels will be defeated. We must be prepared to fight for our freedom from this oppression that has been going on for the last thousand years.

"There is, however, an alternative and I won't stand in your way if you choose that option. My good friend and associate Gorgonius Draco is building a fleet of space vehicles capable of taking people to distant galaxies where you will be out of reach of any judgment that the king may try to impose on you. This may be an alternative for some, but the price of the space journey is high, and there will only be a limited number of people that can make the journey. The people remaining here on Earth will still be faced with the king's unjust judgment.

"Let us rather clean up the earth so that we can remain here under our own conditions and rules. I urge you to join me in this revolt against the king – we can do it; I promise you that my power is now greater than the king's. Together we can destroy his government and his followers, then I will be your leader and you will be my people; I will look after you and you will want for nothing.

"I will be communicating my planned strategy to all of you along with instructions as to what you must do to achieve our goals. This will be a combined effort; we will remove the king from Jerusalem forever!

"The time of our final victory is very close, and for this reason I will not be addressing you in a public meeting again until after we have defeated the king. The reason for this is that I am about to issue an ultimatum to the king, and I will support my ultimatum with a show of power that the world has never seen before. This will, of course, make me public enemy number one, and they will try to hunt me down.

"Although I won't be appearing in public again until after our victory, I will keep you updated via VisionCast which will be broadcast from various secret venues. Keep the faith, my loyal followers – the Shadow Brigade will soon rule the earth!"

Again the crowd erupted in tumultuous applause and began the chant "Kratos, Kratos, Kratos!" With his hands aloft Kratos began to drift upwards until he disappeared into the gloom of the icy night.

CHAPTER 20

DRACO ENTERPRISES' SPACE CENTER, WASHINGTON DC

Gorgonius Draco was standing high up on a gantry in one of the enormous sheds he used for the construction of his spacecraft. He looked with satisfaction over the endless assembly lines where teams of highly skilled workers were constructing multiple sub-assemblies that would soon be fitted together to make a fleet of the largest, most powerful spacecraft ever known to mankind; spacecraft that would be able to cover millions of light years at a speed never before dreamed of.

He smiled to himself as he recollected the data that his space probes had sent back to him over the light years from galaxies such as Andromeda, Triangulum and Centaurus. From that information his scientists had determined that unimaginable wealth lay in those galaxies waiting to be mined; natural resources that would enable him to become the most powerful person who ever lived. People would equate his wealth with that of King Solomon, only on a far greater scale.

Draco's thoughts were interrupted by the persistent buzz of his gizmo in his jacket pocket. He removed the device and saw that it was Kratos calling. "Kratos, how did your meeting go tonight?"

"They bought everything hook, line and sinker, my friend. I put in a plug for your space expeditions and I think many are considering that option. I have no objection to it; let them think they are going to a life of blissful relaxation in faraway galaxies."

"Yes, that is the message we must convey," agreed Draco. "There must be no hint that they are to be put to work as slave laborers on the mines. We need thousands of laborers to mine the riches of the galaxies, especially the xerlite deposits."

"While I will still have millions who will remain behind to do my bidding," enthused Kratos. "Once the king's government has been overthrown the universe will be ours! Things are working out, my friend."

Draco remembered a movie he had watched in his previous life. "To quote a fictional leader of yesteryear, 'I love it when a plan comes together'! We'll keep in touch, Kratos."

CHAPTER 21

MMOD OFFICES, JERUSALEM

There was an atmosphere of electrified expectation in the main boardroom of the MMOD offices in Jerusalem that Friday morning when Luke opened the meeting.

"At the conclusion of our housekeeping meeting today, the chairman of the Committee of Elders, none other than the prophet Daniel, will be joining us for a discussion on current affairs. Daniel is particularly interested in Martin and Maribeth's meeting with Kratos the other evening, so we will hold their report until Daniel joins us."

Luke continued the meeting with a feedback session on the previous week's action points. Maribeth reported on her attempts to obtain more information on the downing of the airliner by what were reported to be "strange creatures". Despite her efforts, nobody had yet been able to throw more light on the matter.

Luke then reported on his meeting with Mike Cousins, now a leading figure in the king's government in the eastern United States area. "Mike said he would look into Draco's affairs to find out if he is constructing weapons of any type. As you may know, my relative Seth Baron's iron and steel company is one of Draco's main suppliers, but even Seth doesn't know exactly what Draco is doing with the all the raw materials he obtains from him. I received a call from Mike shortly before our meeting today, and according to what he can make out, Draco is building a large number of spacecraft. He says they look like passenger transport vehicles that are too big and cumbersome to be any type of fighter aircraft. Mike saw nothing that could be construed as the manufacturing of weapons."

"And so the plot thickens," said Karen. "We all know that something evil is brewing somewhere, but as yet we don't seem to have any clarity on the matter."

At that moment Luke's gizmo vibrated urgently on the table. He picked it up, spoke briefly to the caller and then placed the device on the table again. "Daniel has arrived and will join us immediately," he advised his colleagues.

"I've never met Daniel before," Karen whispered to Maribeth. "Of course, I've seen him in hologram form and heard many of his VisionCast addresses to various groups, but I sure am excited to meet him in person."

"I can't believe it either," said Maribeth. The excitement of finally meeting the man who reported only to the king himself was obvious in her voice.

The conference room door opened and a tall, imposing man who looked to be in his late thirties swept into the room. Luke sprang from his seat and greeted the newcomer warmly. Then he turned to his colleagues seated around the table, "Colleagues, let us welcome Daniel, convener of the Committee of Elders." A warm round of greeting rose from the MMOD staff seated around the table; they still could not quite believe that Daniel was there in person. Daniel sensed the uneasiness and raised a hand as he smiled broadly at those in the room. "It's an honor and a privilege to be invited here today. Please be at ease, I'm a worker in the king's service like all of you." Then, with a mischievous smile, he added, "And I left my lions back in the den today so you're all safe."

The laughter around the table broke the ice and immediately everyone stood up and greeted Daniel as they would a long-lost family member. The women embraced him and the men shook hands warmly. Grateful that Daniel had completely changed the mood in the room, Luke called the meeting to order. "Colleagues, I'm glad that Daniel is present to hear first-hand what Martin and Maribeth have to report on their meeting with Kratos last Saturday evening. Martin, you first please ..."

"Thanks Luke." Martin moved around to the virtual screen that came alive as he pointed his finger towards it. "I have shared informally with some of you during the week, but let's start from the beginning. Last Saturday Maribeth and I attended a mass gathering of the Shadow Brigade in London. As you all know, the leader of this group is known by the name Kratos. I tried to contact Kratos before the meeting but with no luck. I got as far as his so-called chief whip, a red-bearded giant named Xantho, who listened to me with some interest and promised to convey my message to Kratos, but that was it."

"What did you tell him?" Daniel asked with interest, wondering what information Martin could have that would interest Kratos.

"The thing that Kratos wants more than anything else at the moment is information. Remember, he is not omnipresent and omniscient. He needs to know exactly what the king's government is up to and what plans we have to stop him and his organization. I therefore decided not to beat about the bush, but to use the approach that we are disgruntled government workers with access to highly privileged information. I thought Kratos might be interested in an exchange of information, and I was right. It was this approach that hooked him, and he invited us to meet with him."

"Tell everyone about the meeting," said Luke.

"At first I thought it wasn't going to happen. After delivering his address Kratos used the same method for exiting the stadium as he did for his entrance – he descends and ascends as though he has supernatural powers."

"Does he have supernatural powers?" asked Karen. "Is he an immortal, by any chance?"

At this point Daniel joined in the conversation. "As far as we can tell Kratos is either a returnee trying to somehow drum up enough support to overcome the king's government in order to escape judgment, or he is Satan himself in human form. Continue please; I presume that you actually met him the other night?"

"Yes," said Martin. "After Kratos' ascent Maribeth and I were about to leave the stadium feeling rather defeated when Xantho appeared before us and said that Kratos would meet with us. He led us to a private suite above the stadium administrative offices and there was Kratos, still wearing his smooth white mask."

"You said he wanted information," said Luke. "What did he want to know?"

"To start with he wanted to find out about me, my background and also that of Maribeth. He said he had heard of me and some of my previous work, but he really became very interested when he learned of my connections with the king's government and some of the people that I have contact with. As far as Maribeth is concerned, he seemed satisfied with the fact that she is closely connected to the MMOD and especially her working relationship with you, Luke. It seems that Kratos is also a technical boffin – he asked Maribeth some pretty in-depth technical questions, and he seemed more than pleased with her answers."

"Yes," continued Maribeth, "he was interested in all our connections, but what really sealed the deal was our apparent fervent desire to topple the king's government. He was also very interested in Martin's connection to Gorgonius Draco."

"Ah, yes – our other 'Satan suspect'," said Luke. "Did you get any clues as to Kratos' link with Draco?"

"In his address Kratos mentioned that Draco is building spaceships for the purpose of taking paying customers to the far reaches of the galaxy to avoid the White Throne Judgment. He did not seem to really support this alternative, but he offered it as another possibility. His real aim, however, is not to flee from judgment but to topple the king's government and set up something of his own."

"Our information shows that he is gathering millions of followers from all around the world," said Daniel. "This makes it difficult to take any form of forceful action against him. We get back to the old situation that arose with Adam and Eve in the Garden of Eden – if you take any drastic action against a person like this you immediately reinforce his claims that he is correct in all he says and that God is bullying him to keep him quiet. I fully support what you are doing here, and would appreciate feedback on how things progress with the infiltration process. While I realize that Kratos wants you to keep your contacts with the MMOD and with government, playing the role of double agents can be tricky. You will both need to take care in all your dealings with Kratos, and even with Draco. If they sense that you are a threat to what they are trying to achieve, they are likely to punish you severely.

"I am going to give you my personal contact details which you can use to call me in extreme circumstances," Daniel told them. "For routine reporting, though, I would appreciate receiving feedback from Luke via the usual channels."

With that Daniel rose from the table. "Brothers and sisters, I'm very impressed by what I've seen and heard here today. I have a meeting with the Committee of Elders in Washington in an hour's time, so I must be on my way. It's been an honor and privilege to attend this meeting with you. Martin, you and Maribeth are literally stepping into the lions' den – take care, and pray without ceasing."

CHAPTER 22

KAREN'S APARTMENT, JERUSALEM

Karen studied the data projected onto the virtual screen from her gizmo and shook her head. *It doesn't make sense to me,* she mused. *What is motivating so many of the returnees to rebel against the king and his government? I must be missing something. They have everything they could possibly need in the Millennium Kingdom. Conditions are perfect, everything is far better than they had in their previous lives on an imperfect Earth – why then do they need to join Kratos or Draco? Are they so afraid of the final judgment? Don't they realize that the whole purpose of them being resurrected prior to the judgment is so that they can follow the king unconditionally and turn from any previous wickedness? What more could anyone want?*

On impulse she flicked her gizmo to scan her recently received messages and saw one that had come in from Pete Barnaby. She opened the message and projected its contents onto the virtual screen.

Karen, I have some vital information that I must get to you and Luke as soon as possible. This information is too sensitive to send over the media; I need to pass it on in person. I've stumbled across a clue to the true identity of Kratos – if I am correct we could all be in danger. Let's meet as soon as possible. Barnaby.

Quickly she tried to call Luke, but his phone was engaged. Consumed with curiosity she ran up the two flights of stairs to Barnaby's apartment. She stopped before the door and was about to press the buzzer when she noticed that the door was slightly ajar. "Barnaby? It's Karen here, I got your message, can I come in?" No answer. Karen could hear soft music coming from inside, so she pushed the door open and poked her head inside. Looking past the entrance hall she could see the back of Barnaby's head as he sat in an arm chair in the living room, apparently lost in the music playing in the background.

Not wanting to startle him by making a sudden appearance, she called softly, "Barnaby, I'm sorry to disturb you. It's about the message you left on my gizmo." Slowly she approached the seated figure, but suddenly she realized that there was something strange about his posture. Barnaby's head seemed to be leaning to the left at an odd angle. Walking quickly towards the back of the chair Karen called out in alarm: "Barnaby, are you all right?"

On receiving no answer she put a hand out nervously and touched his shoulder. There was no response. She moved around the chair to be met by the unseeing gaze of her friend's half-open eyes. The front of Barnaby's shirt was covered in blood and it appeared as though his throat had been cut.

He was most certainly dead.

Karen's first reaction was to scream as loudly as she could, but then her better judgment clicked in and she realized that Barnaby's attacker might still be close – perhaps still in the apartment. Instead she reached into her pocket and took out her gizmo and spoke a name into it. Then in a hushed whisper she said, "Luke, it's me, Karen. I can't explain now – just get to Barnaby's apartment as soon as possible, and bring some security guys with you."

CHAPTER 23

BARNABY'S APARTMENT, JERUSALEM

For hundreds of years the elders had not found it necessary to maintain a large security force in any part of the Millennium Kingdom. Although petty crime did still exist, even in the absence of Satan, violent crime such as murder was unheard of.

Children born to those mortals who first entered the kingdom after the Tribulation still retained the stigma of original Adamic sin and were prone to make incorrect choices until such time as they made a conscious decision to put aside any sinful ways and to follow the path taught to them by the king, the elders and their immortal community leaders.

Since the resurrection of the returnees, however, violent crime was on the increase and, as a result, the elders were forced to increase the size of security forces worldwide. In many instances, mortals born during the Millennium were also being led astray by the wild promises of errant returnees and so the general state of lawlessness was gradually on the increase.

Luke arrived at the apartment at the same time as Jed Rich.

"Who could have done this terrible thing to a great guy like Barnaby?" asked Jed, tears welling up in his eyes. Karen immediately showed them the message she had received from Barnaby. "This is the work of the Shadow Brigade," said Jed angrily. "They know that Barnaby and I are actively involved with the White

Robes. I'm sure they are behind this terrible act of violence. I've notified our leader, Erica Merton, and she'll be contacting me later today to discuss the whole messy situation. Someone will pay for this!"

"Let's not get too hasty about planning any retaliatory action," said Luke, trying to calm the obviously distraught man. "Barnaby might have sacrificed his life for what is right and proper, but I'm sure he would already have had his final judgment and will now be rejoicing in Paradise waiting for us to join him. Remember, the Millennium has now passed and we all await our final destiny. Please don't do anything at this point in time that might get you into trouble on judgment day."

"You're right," said Jed dejectedly, "but it still makes one mad to think that a great guy like Barnaby should end up like this."

"But he hasn't ended up like this," added Karen helpfully, "as Luke said, he is now in Paradise – where we will all be soon." Jed smiled as Karen gave him a hug.

"Thanks guys, I know you're right – I must snap out of it. We'll leave it to the security guys; they should be here any moment now."

"Any idea what Barnaby could have meant when he said that he might have stumbled on the identity of Kratos?" asked Karen. "If that's true, where could he have got this information?"

"Well, although Barnaby has only been here a short time, he had a knack for building up a network of contacts very quickly," said Jed. "He was the type of guy people trusted. He never spoke about it too much, but he hinted at the fact that some of his more dubious contacts had connections to the Shadow Brigade. It seems impossible, but perhaps one of those contacts shared something that he probably shouldn't have and was then pressurized to get rid of Barnaby before he could share it with anyone else."

"Well that is one possibility," said Luke. "Whatever it was, it must have been pretty accurate information that Barnaby had, otherwise he wouldn't have been murdered."

"But why so brutally?" asked Karen, still shaken by the scene she had come upon.

"I guess it sends a message and a warning to anyone who finds out too much," said Luke. "I will definitely warn Martin and Maribeth that they need to be extremely careful in their dealings with the Shadow Brigade."

"Maybe we should pull them off that job," said Karen. "I'd hate this to happen to them."

Luke thought about this for a moment, then shook his head. "Remember Daniel's parting words at the meeting? 'Pray without ceasing.' Let's keep trusting that everything will work out according to his plan."

The trio was startled by a loud knock on the front door. Luke opened it and was confronted by one of the largest men he had ever seen; a man almost the size of Mike Cousins offered Luke his huge hand in greeting.

"I'm Captain Hugo Dimitrov of the king's security force in Jerusalem. You must be Luke Baron; I would recognize one of the Baron family anywhere."

Luke looked completely dumbfounded. "Hugo Dimitrov – my great uncle Mark has often spoken of you. Weren't you the manservant and bodyguard of the infamous Count Helmut von Meinhof – the Antichrist?"

"Yes, indeed I was, and although that may seem like a black mark against me, it was largely the reason that I sought the truth and a better way of living. The terrible things I did for Count von Meinhof were forgiven me when I turned to the king, thanks to guys like your uncle Mark and Mike Cousins who, by the way, is still the strongest guy I've ever met. But down to business..."

Quickly Dimitrov began to direct the team that was with him. One of the team politely asked Karen, Luke and Jed to leave the area and then proceeded to take four dimensional scans of the whole room. "We can pick up every hair and fiber in the room with this new scanning device," said Dimitrov. "We can also detect scents and aromas that even a trained dog would not detect. We then feed the information into a database that will enable us to link the findings to every person who has been in the area over the last six months. Much of the data will be irrelevant as Barnaby has only lived here for about two weeks, but nonetheless, the system will give us a complete picture, unless..."

"Unless the intruders are returnees that have escaped being recorded on the database?" suggested Karen, already seeing where the system could fail.

"Precisely," said Dimitrov. "One moment; I'm getting the results back now, and it's as I thought. Every person who has been in this room recently has been identified, except for someone who was in the room within the last three hours. This person is not on record – obviously an unregistered returnee."

"So where do we go from here?" asked Luke. "Do the perpetrators get away with this terrible crime?"

"Not if I can help it," said Dimitrov, slamming his huge right fist into the palm of his left hand. We now have on record details of the unknown's hair samples, fibers from his clothing and even the scent of his body odors. It is mandatory for all returnees to be scanned and recorded, and to date thousands have complied, but..."

"But those that have complied have probably been the 'good guys'," said Karen. The task was not going to be all that easy. "Many members of the Shadow Brigade have no doubt avoided being recorded."

"You've hit the nail on the head," said Dimitrov, "but never say never – we have newly-developed methods that I'm not at liberty to mention. It will only be a matter of time before we get to the bottom of this – and many of the other crimes that are spreading throughout the kingdom. Never forget who wins in the end ... and I've a feeling that end is not far away."

"Let's hope so," said Jed, taking a last look at the body of his friend being wheeled out of the room by the medical staff. "It can't come too soon."

CHAPTER 24

KAREN'S APARTMENT, JERUSALEM

Karen lay back on the couch in her living room and gladly accepted the cup of tea Luke offered her. Still shocked by the gruesome scene in the upstairs apartment, she kept mulling over the reasons behind such a terrible act.

"Whatever Barnaby had discovered about the true identity of Kratos is obviously the reason he was killed, but why cut his throat? I still can't believe that was necessary."

"It sure is cruel and messy," said Luke. "I remember my great uncle Mark telling me about the weapons they used in the previous dispensation, but only recently have we seen a resurgence of weapons being produced. I guess whoever killed Barnaby didn't have access to any new weapons, so he used a knife. In addition to keeping him from revealing the identity of Kratos, it also served to send a message to us."

"A message?" asked Karen looking up questioningly.

"Obviously it's a warning that we should stop investigating the Shadow Brigade or something similar could happen to one of us."

Karen looked shocked. "Do you really think they could come after us too?" Then, to Luke's surprise, she threw her arms around his neck and started sobbing on his shoulder. "Perhaps we should leave this whole thing to the security people; I would hate anything to happen to you. Seeing Barnaby like that was ... terrible ... if it was you..." Then, realizing that she had shown feelings that she had previously only felt deep inside – feelings she had hardly admitted to herself, let alone to Luke – she pulled away and looked sheepishly at the ground.

"Oh, I'm sorry, I didn't mean to..."

Luke placed a hand gently under her chin and lifted her face close to his. "No need to feel sorry," he said gently. "I was thinking exactly the same thing about you. In fact, I was seriously considering taking you off this assignment and placing you on something ... well, something safer."

"That's not what I want." Karen put her arms around Luke's neck again and looked into his green eyes. "I was only afraid of what might happen to you and ... of ... of losing you. I'm not afraid for myself. If there's a danger to be faced I'll face it with you. Besides, we know what the future holds for both of us and we needn't be afraid of anything or anyone."

"So that's settled then; we go after Barnaby's killers even if it means we confront Kratos and his cronies?"

"Definitely," Karen agreed. "We're not alone in this – we have the full might of the king and his government behind us, so let's get to the bottom of this as soon as possible. I'm sure there are thousands of returnees that are still bewildered as to why they have been resurrected at this time. We need to assist the White Robes as much as we can to win them from Kratos and his Shadow Brigade. Let's make these remaining years of the Millennium a victory for good over evil! Where should we begin?"

"I think we should get together with the 'good guys' first. I'll contact Erica Merton, the head of the White Robes, and arrange a meeting with her and we should definitely take Jed along, as he is our liaison person here in Jerusalem." Luke took out his gizmo and made the call.

CHAPTER 25

TOOWOOMBA, QUEENSLAND, AUSTRALIA

The city of Toowoomba lies eighty miles west of Brisbane, the capital of Australia's Queensland province. The road from the airport to Erica Merton's neat suburban home passed through lush rolling countryside, leaving Karen and Luke in no doubt as to why Toowoomba was nicknamed "The Garden City".

"I've visited Erica a number of times in the past on Society business," said Jed, "and every time the beauty of the place amazes me."

"It's certainly different from Israel," agreed Karen, completely astounded by the range of vegetation and colors that flashed by the window of their high-speed, driverless anti-gravity taxi. "Not that Jerusalem isn't a beautiful city, but it's a different kind of beauty. In Jerusalem you can't help but feel the greatness of the city's past and all that it stands for, but this has a new freshness about it – it's like being on holiday on a tropical island."

The taxi drew to a halt in front of a large house set back in a breathtaking display of colorful blooms of every hue. "Wow," exclaimed Karen, "this must be where the Millennium Kingdom merges with Paradise itself."

"It certainly is a beautiful garden," agreed Luke, helping Karen out of the vehicle. "I can't wait to meet Erica; she must have especially green fingers."

They made their way up the path and were half way to the house when the front door burst open and a tall, athletic looking woman in blue jeans and a white T-shirt emerged. She stopped for a moment then ran the remaining twenty yards. On reaching them she threw her arms around Jed and kissed him on both cheeks. "It's so good to see you again," she said in a broad Australian accent. "I was devastated to hear about Barnaby – it must have been such a shock to you."

"It sure was, but it was Karen here who found him first." Stepping back, Jed beckoned his companions closer. "Erica, let me introduce you to two very special people – Luke Baron and Karen Leigh." They exchanged greetings, then Erica invited them to go inside her house. "I'm sure you must be famished after your journey. After you've freshened up we'll have tea and cake, then I think we have to get down to some serious discussion."

After tea they adjourned to the cozy sitting room. "It's no coincidence that Barnaby was killed soon after telling me he had a clue to the identity of Kratos," said Karen. "The fact that he believed we're all in danger could mean that Kratos is masquerading as someone we know; he could even be in our group of close acquaintances."

"That's a scary thought," said Erica, "but have you any suspects in mind? Surely you would have had a feeling about someone as evil as Kratos; how could he keep himself under wraps right under your very noses?"

"Because he is not only cruel, but also extremely clever," admitted Luke. "Bear in mind that he is probably the embodiment of Satan himself – the original deceiver; he could make himself into anyone or anything he wanted and we wouldn't know."

"This is why we need to listen carefully to the prompting of the Holy Spirit more than we ever have before," said Jed, bringing them back to the reality of the changing mood prevailing over Millennium life. "Although I am also a returnee who was not born into the Millennium, I soon realized that prior to this latter-day resurrection, people who were born into the Millennium arrived with far less baggage."

"What do you mean by that?" asked Karen, intrigued by a subject she had never really thought much about. "How did you 'arrive' in the Millennium – if you don't mind such a personal question?"

"Not at all," said Jed with a smile. "I'm sure it's different for everyone – and possibly Erica could share her experience as well – but in my case I woke up in an apartment in Chelsea, London. I had no idea where I was or why I was there. I remembered driving my BMW sports coupe at extremely high speed along the A2 motorway between London and Dover in the early hours of July 20th, 2025. It was after midnight and I had been to a party; I was extremely drunk and didn't see that a large truck had stopped ahead of me. To cut a long story short, I piled into the back of the truck and woke up two days later in hospital. I overheard a doctor telling my sister that I had broken nearly every bone in my body and had massive internal injuries."

Karen was fascinated with Jed's account of how he left his previous life. "Is that when you died?"

"No, that was about two weeks later – two weeks of hell, I can tell you. I actually prayed for death. Death came eventually, and I knew nothing until I woke up in the apartment of another returnee, an artist by the name of James Callan. He was expecting me and was kind enough to tell me where I was and why I was there."

"You mean God actually arranged your transition from 'death' to resurrection in the Millennium Kingdom to be as smooth as possible?" asked Luke, hearing for the first time what it was like for someone to die and be raised into an entirely different environment. "Did you realize immediately that you had been raised to face a final judgment, or did that have to be explained to you by someone else?"

"God is truly amazing," said Jed, smiling at the memory of how things happened. "I actually knew deep inside why I was back on Earth again, even though I hardly ever set foot in a church during my previous life. There were gaps in my knowledge, of course, but God put me with James Callan for a reason. I only found out later that each and every returnee arrives back on Earth as an adult, but always in the care of a guardian who has been specially assigned to help that person through the transition. I was blessed to mentor our late friend Pete Barnaby when he was resurrected, but that's another story."

"So James was specially assigned to you?" Karen was spellbound as she digested this latest proof of God's endless love for all mankind – even those who had gone completely off the rails in their previous lives. "Why then do so many returnees still reject God, even though they are given a guardian to explain matters to them? You'd think that they wouldn't want to repeat the same mistakes again."

"That's exactly why our group is called the White Robes," said Erica, standing up to attend to the kettle that was on the boil. "We all recognize the fact that we went wrong in our previous lives and need to put on the 'white robe of righteousness' – we don't want to mess up again. That's why our society desperately reaches out to all returnees."

"But why do so many still not see that?" probed Karen, the urgency evident in her voice. "Do they really want to be eternally condemned?"

"They once again fall for the lies they are fed by the likes of Kratos and his followers," said Jed. "Kratos has scared so many with his lies about the final judgment, in particular the lie that only condemnation will result from the judgment. That's why he's calling for a revolt against the king and his government. We know now that he has promised that once the king has been overthrown, and he, Kratos, is supreme ruler, there will be no judgment except for his own judgment over those he chooses to dislike. Many believe he can actually pull it off due to the sheer force of numbers he has on his side."

"Don't forget what Martin told us about Gorgonius Draco's plans," said Luke. "He is building special spacecraft capable of transporting people to distant galaxies with the promise that, once away from Earth, they will be free of the final judgment. So it seems many returnees have decided not to change their ways and are placing their hope instead in either joining Kratos or escaping with Draco."

"It's a sad state of affairs," said Erica, "but let's have lunch, and then we can come up with a strategy for combining our efforts."

CHAPTER 26

Luke sat back in his chair, a look of contented satisfaction on his face. "That was an amazing meal, Erica, are you prepared to share the secret of your recipe?"

Erica laughed, "I'm glad you enjoyed it, and of course I'll share the recipe with you. I'll give Karen a written copy, but briefly it is a favorite Aussie traditional dish known as venison steak-frites. You probably noticed that the potato frites were especially thinly cut – actually sliced using a laser cutter – and the steak was on the rare side."

"Couldn't have been better," echoed Jed wiping his mouth after finishing his steak. "Do you think we could introduce it in Israel, Luke?"

"I'm sure it'll be a hit anywhere," commented Luke, reaching into his pocket to retrieve his vibrating gizmo. He glanced quickly at the caller's name. "Excuse me for a moment, folks, it's Martin – could be important." Luke hurriedly left the room and went onto the verandah. "Martin, what's up? Are you and Maribeth okay?"

"We're fine, and we seem to have been accepted by the Shadow Brigade hierarchy. Maribeth has made a big impression on Xantho, Kratos' big red-bearded assistant. But the reason I'm calling you now is to tell you of a worldwide VisionCast broadcast that Kratos will make in three hours' time. From what we can gather, his address to his people will have huge ramifications.

He will not be speaking at a public meeting, but will be broadcasting from a secret venue."

"Any idea what the theme of his broadcast is to be?"

"Expectations within the Shadow Brigade are that it will be a call to arms, so to speak. His followers are getting increasingly anxious about the impending White Throne Judgment and they want action before any such judgment takes place."

"Do you think that is what Kratos will do today – declare war on the king and his followers?"

Martin was silent for a moment, then said, "Yes Luke, I think things will be getting extremely hot from now on."

CHAPTER 27

THE ULTIMATUM

Three hours later – at 7:50 p.m. in eastern Australia and 10:50 a.m. in London – Luke, Karen and Jed were seated with Erica in front of the VisionCast virtual screen in Erica's living room. She switched on the screen and within a few minutes the morbid tones of the ancient *Funeral March* by Chopin began playing.

"Martin tells me that the *Funeral March* has been adopted by Kratos as his signature background music," said Luke.

"How morbid," remarked Karen with a shudder.

Suddenly the figure of Kratos appeared before them, wearing not his usual black, but a full-length shimmering white robe with matching hood along with his characteristic white faceless mask with slits for his eyes and mouth. He was standing in front of a wall-mounted flag depicting a dragon's head breathing fire across a multitude of cowering figures.

"I can't get used to these virtual hologram images that appear from nowhere," said Erica with a shudder. "Especially when the image is of this guy; he gives me the creeps."

"I thought he only wore black, hence the Shadow Brigade name," said Karen.

"He's full of surprises," replied Jed wryly. "I guess he's making some sort of statement."

The music faded and Kratos raised both hands above his head. "Fellow citizens of the Shadow Brigade, and all those who support the ideals of a society free of the tyranny of the king and his government, this is a sad day in our history; a day that I had hoped might never happen." He paused to clear his throat, as though the words he was speaking were choking him with emotion.

"I have tried to be reasonable with these self-righteous people, especially with the so-called 'immortals' who consider themselves a cut above everyone else," he continued. "I have tried in vain to point out how unjust it is to try to impose the will of a select few onto millions of other people whose beliefs are a bit different to theirs. These people arrogantly declare that their king will bring a judgment against us and will condemn us to destruction in a lake of fire. Why, I ask you – why should that group decide that they have the sole right to existence?"

Kratos paused, then his voice became softer, "I will tell you why: it is because they envy what we have. They are bound by all sorts of rules and morals imposed on them by their god. History has shown how cruel and thoughtless those 'godly' beings really are; look at the Great Tribulation a thousand years ago, for example. That loving king of theirs rained down chaos and destruction on them until there was virtually nobody left, and then he threw some good solid leaders into the Lake of Fire. Some love.

"But I have never tried to impose onerous restrictions on any of my followers; I have always shown love and respect for all people. I have tried to reason with the king to change his 'grand plan' of judgment and destruction, but he seems hell-bent on destroying me and all you wonderful people who believe in me. But that is about to change."

Kratos paused for a moment and looked straight into the camera, his eyes glowing like two coals on fire. "Today I issue an ultimatum to the king and his government, including his army of angels who are no longer any threat to me. I am giving you seven days – your own magical number – to rewrite the book of Revelation so that it no longer makes any mention of a final judgment or of anyone being thrown into a lake of fire. You will, of course, ask 'why should we comply with this demand?' – well this is where my little demonstration comes in."

Kratos raised a remote control he had been holding in his left hand and pressed a button. Immediately a video screen behind him came to life, showing what appeared to be the image of a planet. "Many of you more informed viewers will recognize this image to be the planet Jupiter. Jupiter is the largest of the planets in this solar system and has a total of sixty-nine moons orbiting it. Ganymede is the largest of the moons measuring nearly 3 500 miles in diameter." The image before them changed to reveal a close-up image of Ganymede. "This is Ganymede," said Kratos. "What you are about to see is an actual live demonstration of the power that I have harnessed – a power that that I will unleash if my demands are not met."

Kratos raised the remote in his hand once more, and pressed another button. Immediately the image of Ganymede disappeared in a blinding ball of fire. "Yes, my friends, your eyes are not deceiving you. What you have witnessed is the complete destruction of one of the moons of Jupiter. Your scientists and astronomers will soon verify what I am telling you. I can repeat this demonstration whenever and wherever I choose. Right now, my promise to the king, his government and whomever else is aligned with him, is that in exactly seven days' time I will destroy your beloved city of Jerusalem – and all in it – if my demands regarding the book of Revelation and any attempts to harm any of my followers are not met. Jerusalem will be but the beginning of the chaos and mayhem that I will rain down on this puny little planet. You have seen the power that is now at my disposal; I will not hesitate to use it. Today's demonstration was merely to show what I am capable of, not to harm you – not yet, at any rate. The seven-day count begins at midday today, Jerusalem time ... the ball is in your court."

CHAPTER 28

GOVERNMENT HEADQUARTERS, WASHINGTON DC

Daniel surveyed the select group before him. "It seems that everyone's here, so let's get started; we have urgent matters to deal with today."

Alongside Daniel on the stage sat the other eleven elders, and before them the audience consisting of the immortals in charge of each country. Other key figures had also been invited to attend, including Mike Cousins, Luke Baron and Karen Leigh from the MMOD in Jerusalem and Hugo Dimitrov, head of security in the king's government in Jerusalem.

"To make sure we're all on the same page, I am going to replay Kratos' worldwide address." Daniel pressed a button on a remote control and immediately the VisionCast image of Kratos appeared on the stage. The audience listened carefully to the threats made by Kratos, and watched as he demonstrated his ability to destroy Ganymede at the touch of a button. The replay ended and Daniel leaned forward in his chair.

"As you may well guess, Kratos is now the most wanted man on Earth. We have every resource in our worldwide network searching for him. Although we have constantly monitored his meetings and public utterances in the past, up till now he has not done anything to warrant bringing him in. But that has all changed now. If he carries out his threat against Jerusalem, who knows where it will end. Many think the man is crazy – I personally have a theory about him that even I thought impossible at first, but since his little demonstration, I may be closer to the truth than I thought."

"And your theory is...?" asked Luke.

"Firstly, that Kratos is actually Satan released from the abyss, in line with Revelation 20 that prophesied the return of Satan at the end of the Millennium. Secondly, that Kratos is merely a stage name – used when he appears in public with his robes and mask. I believe that Kratos has the ability to adopt a human appearance and is walking around among us, looking like any one of us, but with all the guile and evil powers that he has gathered over the ages." Daniel looked across the worried faces in front of him. "Any questions at this stage?" Several hands were raised. Daniel pointed to Reuben Chait, immortal in charge of Russia.

"Do we know what Kratos used to blow Ganymede out of existence? Has he developed some new technology or is he using some dark spiritual power?"

Hugo Dimitrov rose from his seat. "I can field that one, Mr. Chairman. We believe that this 'new' power is linked to the theft of documents containing the details of weapons used immediately prior to the establishment of the Millennium Kingdom. These documents included details on the making of nuclear bombs, which it seems were used to destroy Ganymede. Although the bombs used 1,000 years ago were extremely powerful, we have reason to believe that Kratos has several scientists in his ranks who are quite capable of applying modern Millennium science to the weapons of the past. We know too that a number of brilliant nuclear scientists from the past are among the returnees. Assisted by modern technology, they could easily have improved the old weapons to the extent we witnessed this morning."

"Scary stuff," said the chairman, "but the king's orders are clear; there is to be no compromise on any of Kratos' threats. The king is not prepared to rewrite any part of scripture – the very idea is ludicrous. In addition, the White Throne Judgment will take place at the appointed time."

The apostle Thomas, sitting in the front row of the audience, tentatively raised his hand. "I doubt if this is going to have a good ending for us," he said hesitantly. "How can we ignore Kratos' ultimatum and still stop him from destroying Jerusalem in seven days' time? We have seen what he can do. Our scientists have confirmed the fact that Ganymede has been destroyed. If Kratos has the power to annihilate moons at the touch of a button, how can we doubt that he will do the same to Jerusalem – and possibly to the whole earth – at the end of this week? Shouldn't we be at least a little bit worried?"

A smile came to Daniel's lips. "Thomas – still the 'doubter' I see. In this case, however, there are probably many others who harbor similar uncertainties after seeing Kratos' demonstration, so let me tell you what we have decided. As I said earlier, I suspect that Kratos is either Satan who has been released from the abyss, or he is someone working under the direct control of Satan. We also believe that Kratos is merely a *nom de plume*, or a stage name, if you like. This means that in everyday life there is no person called Kratos, but instead the person we see addressing the Shadow Brigade on VisionCast could be your friendly next-door neighbor. For this reason we already have two special agents who have successfully infiltrated Kratos' organization and are in regular contact with Luke Baron and Karen Leigh of our Mortal Movements and Occurrences Department. Feedback to date is that the real identity of Kratos is closely guarded, but our people are making steady progress to win favor in the organization. We are trusting for a real breakthrough very soon."

"Once we know who Kratos is, what type of action is intended against him?" asked Dimitrov, eager to get to grips with the person who was threatening their very existence. "My suggestion would be to arrest him and his immediate henchmen and put them on trial."

"Bear in mind that he doesn't plan to make public appearances anymore, and we haven't been successful in tracing the origin of his VisionCast broadcasts, so his whereabouts are not yet known to us," Daniel replied. "He could be anywhere in the universe.

Feedback from our two infiltrators suggests that even his closest henchmen receive their orders indirectly. As to his final fate, we will leave that up to the king to decide. If Kratos is indeed Satan, as we suspect he might be, then his fate is sealed in accordance with scripture. We cannot, and will not, change anything. But if it turns out that Kratos is one of Satan's underlings, we will certainly take action against him."

"What about Gorgonius Draco; have we anything to fear from him or from the plans he is putting into effect?" The question came from Nancy Goodchild, a representative of the Women's League of America.

"As we all know, Draco is building spacecraft with the capability of reaching other galaxies," said Daniel. "He too has a team of top scientists working for him, and he has already sold out quite a number of flights, mainly to returnees who, for their own particular reasons, are hoping to get as far from Earth as possible before the White Throne Judgment. Of course we know that any such attempts are futile. Even if they reach another galaxy, the king is the master builder who created the whole universe – distance is no deterrent to him. Although Draco has close ties with Kratos, we don't anticipate that he will be a threat to anyone; he seems too engrossed in his space program to worry about anything else.

"To bring this meeting to a conclusion, the message we would like you leaders to take back with you is this. Nobody has any reason to panic; the Committee of Elders, under the guidance of the king, has things under control. We have set plans in motion and are expecting results very soon."

"Are we going to evacuate Jerusalem before the seven-day ultimatum expires?" Thomas asked.

Daniel smiled tolerantly. "You walked the sands of Israel for three years with the master; did he ever let anyone down or were his words ever in vain?"

Thomas gave a sheepish smile, "No Mr. Chairman, he never let anyone down – I guess I must stop thinking out aloud."

Daniel stood up and raised his hands above his head. "Go in peace, and may the peace of the Lord go with you."

CHAPTER 29

DARTMOOR, DEVON COUNTY, ENGLAND

Dartmoor Prison, in the county of Devon in England, was originally opened in the pre-Millennium year of 1809 to house French prisoners of war resulting from the Napoleonic wars. With the conclusion of the Napoleonic wars in 1815, the establishment was converted to a prison for British offenders, in which capacity it was used until the end of the Tribulation period.

With the advent of the Millennium, and the period of peace and calm that followed the confinement of Satan in the abyss, the need to maintain prisons fell away. Part of the Dartmoor complex was kept as a museum in remembrance of its checkered history, while most of the prison cells were leased to farmers who were allocated land in the area. Some of the cell blocks were converted to relatively smart living quarters while others were used for the storage of farming equipment.

It was to this establishment that Xantho, Kratos' giant, red-bearded right-hand man had been sent soon after the entire precinct was purchased by Blue Ray Electronics, a front for the Shadow Brigade. On paper Xantho was the owner and director of Blue Ray, while Kratos remained a mystical figure in the background. In fact, nobody knew anything about Kratos' personal life – if indeed he had a personal life at all. Whether or not Kratos existed under a different name remained a mystery.

Even Xantho, who was closer to him than anyone else, had only ever seen him in his robes and mask.

Kratos had been looking for a suitable location in England to set up his headquarters, from where he planned to organize and direct his growing worldwide army. Xantho, who had become increasingly attracted to Maribeth Markham, had asked her to accompany him to assist with the logistics of equipping the establishment with state-of-the-art communications and other electronic hardware.

"What happens if the king's security people inspect the facility?" asked Maribeth. "We all know they are searching high and low for Kratos; if they find this place with all its advanced equipment, won't they close it down and arrest everyone working here?"

Xantho smiled down at her. "Kratos is way ahead of the game. This facility is registered as an electronics research and testing business and we have a host of genuine customers to back that up. We can prove that we have tested, and are still testing, a variety of electronic components and modules that are used in many different industries. You won't believe the talent that has emerged from the host of returnees who have joined our ranks. Some of the best brains that ever lived in the past are with us now."

"Will Kratos be joining us here soon?" asked Maribeth, still hoping to get to the bottom of the question regarding Kratos' true identity. "I hope he'll be impressed with the set-up I've installed in the main ops room."

"You did good with the comms, Maribeth, that's why you're here, but a word of advice – don't try to get too familiar with Kratos, he doesn't appreciate anyone scratching around in his private affairs. In fact, he only communicates directly with a handful of chosen leaders, and then only when he is wearing his robe and his mask. I have never seen his face. For your own sake, do your job and nothing more than that."

"I wouldn't dream of prying into his private affairs," Maribeth lied, "but you've been working closely with Kratos for some time now, what do you know about him?" Maribeth knew she was pushing her limits by approaching Xantho on the topic of his boss, but she also knew that time was running out, and if they were to make any progress on stopping Kratos' plan to destroy Jerusalem, she and Martin would need to come up with something concrete soon. There were only five days left before Kratos would carry out his threat against Jerusalem.

"As I said, Kratos only communicates directly with a chosen few, those being his leaders in each country and with me, his right-hand man," said Xantho, with more than a little pride in his voice. "But even I haven't been privy to the details of Kratos' private life."

"And your own life?" Maribeth had been wanting to find out more about this rough giant with, from what she could deduce, a rather tender heart.

Xantho looked sternly at her, then his face softened. "All I know is that in my previous life I was a professional fighter who went through some bad times. Being of Greek origin, I became a member of the Philadelphia Greek mafia way back in the 1970s, and I was executed for murder. I didn't consider my actions murder because we were at war with the Italian mob at that time. They cornered a group of us at the docks one night and opened fire on us. They killed some of our guys and, to give you the short version, I took out a couple of them – with my bare hands, mind you; I never really took to guns. Anyway, I happened to be caught, tried – if you can call it that – and executed. After I was resurrected into the Millennium Kingdom Kratos found me and, probably due to my size and fighting skills, took me in and made me his bodyguard and chief assistant. Since then I have served him full-time. I sure wasn't looking forward to any final judgment that the king had in mind, so I fully support Kratos' plans to stop the king in his tracks. I take it you're as excited as the rest of us about what's going to happen in five days' time?" Xantho studied Maribeth's face for some sign that she might not approve of what he had told her.

"Isn't that why we're all in the Shadow Brigade?" asked Maribeth, realizing that Xantho was testing her once again. "I too have not lived a perfect life. I've hired out my computing skills to clients for a variety of dark purposes – even for my own enrichment," she lied. But from what you've told me about yourself, you haven't committed any serious crime – nothing you couldn't repent of and be saved from final judgment."

"What about my killing those guys?" asked Xantho. "Isn't that serious?"

"Yes, it is. But as you explained, it wasn't premeditated murder for your own personal gain; it was more in the way of a soldier taking the lives of enemy soldiers. But I'm not God, I can only say it the way I see it. In my view, if you repented of some of the things you were involved with, there would be nothing keeping you from being judged fit for eternal life instead of eternal damnation. But again that's just how I see it."

Xantho was quiet for a long while, then he said, "I guess I've come this far with Kratos and he has been good to me. I doubt if I could really change the way I am."

"That's up to you," said Maribeth softly, "but I still think you could avoid punishment if you really wanted to."

Xantho was again quiet for a while, as if dealing with serious conflicting alternatives. "What's your next task?" he asked, obviously trying to change the subject.

"Well, I was working with Martin on finalizing the comms systems in the main control room, but the last I heard from him was that he had been sent on a high-priority assignment by Kratos himself. No matter, I have the comms systems well in hand."

"Good. Anyway, I must go check on some work down in the C block, so I'll see you later. What about having dinner with me tonight?" Xantho asked.

Maribeth hesitated a moment as she had been hoping that Martin would return in time for dinner, but realizing he was probably well and truly tied up with Kratos, she said, "Sure, that would be great."

"I'll pick you up at seven," said Xantho, obviously pleased that Maribeth had agreed to have dinner with him. "We can't have a pretty lady like you wandering around Dartmoor by herself with all these returnee workmen in the area."

Maribeth watched as the big man walked away. *I wonder what your real motive is for wanting to see me again tonight. On the one hand I feel like you really have a desire to seek forgiveness for your past, but on the other hand your loyalty to Kratos is very apparent. Have you realized that I am actually a spy in your midst and perhaps you want to get enough evidence to tell Kratos, or are you genuinely interested in being with me? I had better be on my guard tonight.*

CHAPTER 30

PRINCETON VILLAGE, DARTMOOR

The small village of Princeton, situated a few miles south-east of the old Dartmoor Prison complex, is traditionally a farming hub where local farmers gather for both business and pleasure. The Millennium years had not brought about much change to the local way of life, a fact that suited the hard-working farmers who, although making use of the most modern technology to ensure maximum crops, still relished the same quiet country life that their ancestors had enjoyed for years.

The Princeton Lodge is a neat traditional inn in the center of the village, the pub being a favorite meeting place for the locals on a cold winter evening. Xantho and Maribeth were met at the door by Dan Timmins, the proprietor, a cheery rotund little man with a warm smile. "Good to have you Blue Ray guys in the area, and always good to see you personally, Mr. Xantho. Who's the pretty lady with you tonight?"

"Good to be here on such a cold night, Dan," said Xantho shaking the proprietor's soft little pink hand in his enormous grasp. "And, by the way, it's Xantho, and not 'Mister' Xantho. But meet Maribeth Markham, she's new with us – one of our electronics experts."

"Delighted, Maribeth," said Dan, "I've reserved a special table in a cozy side room – nice fire, candlelight, just right for the head of Blue Ray and his lovely partner."

They were shown to a cozy little room with a warm fire burning in one corner. A waiter entered and took their orders.

"You know, Maribeth, you're the first girl I've really spoken to – one on one, so to speak – since my ... my..."

"Since your resurrection?"

"Yes, since coming into the kingdom. Of course, there were lots of women in my old life; too many, in fact. But none that I ever wanted to get serious with."

"And by 'getting serious' you mean ...?"

"Yeah, all of that," said Xantho, blushing so deeply that even his ruddy complexion couldn't hide his awkwardness. "I never even got close to a woman, even though there was no shortage of women in the gangs. My family was very traditionally Greek, and we grew up in a traditional community."

"By traditional you mean there was no dating, or anything like that?" asked Maribeth, fascinated by the vulnerability of the big man in front of her.

"Dating, yes, but always with a chaperone. My parents even selected a wife for me ..."

"You were married ...?"

"No, never got that far. The girl who was selected for me was just a kid, and I was not in the least bit interested.

"So what did you do?"

"In a nutshell, I left home and became a prize fighter."

"You mean you were a boxer?"

"At first, yes, but then I moved on to cage fighting and then to the 'no rules' type of fighting. Made quite a name for myself among the wrong types. Then I got involved with a Greek gang – and you know the rest."

"You killed a man."

"Two men, and I'm not proud of it. If I could have it all over ..."

"But you can have a new start. This is what I was telling you earlier." Maribeth reached over and took his huge right hand in hers. "This is why you have been resurrected at this time; you have the opportunity to choose all over again."

Xantho looked into her dark green eyes, and hesitantly moved a lock of raven hair that had fallen across her right eye; then he took both her hands in his. "I really like what you're saying, but this leaves me with one worrying question – one I don't even want to think about. Why are you here, Maribeth? Why are you part of the Shadow Brigade, and yet you sound like a White Rober?" For a moment they looked into each other's eyes, and then he averted his gaze. "I think I know what's going on," he said slowly, "and I don't know what to say or think at the moment. I thought you were one of us, and now ... now.... Oh, Maribeth, please don't do this; don't try to spy on Kratos. Just leave and go back to where you came from."

"I can't," she said softly. "He has got to be stopped. If you have any feelings for me, and I think you do, please take this chance and help me bring Kratos to justice before he goes too far."

Xantho let go of her hands. "Kratos has been my whole existence, till now. He told me that a murderer like me cannot escape the Lake of Fire, and my only hope was with him."

"He's a liar and a deceiver," said Maribeth calmly. "It's never too late to turn your life around."

"This is all new to me; give me time to think it over," said Xantho. "But in the meantime, Maribeth, if you stay on here, please be careful. Be very, very careful."

CHAPTER 31

Back in her room Maribeth took out her gizmo and tried to call Martin again. After her third call went onto voicemail she left a message for him and, almost as an afterthought, she included Luke and Karen on the same message: *Hi guys, I'm making progress with Xantho, but from what he's told me so far I really don't think he knows too much about Kratos' private life or his origins. He is basically only a trusted worker and not a confidante; I guess we must look elsewhere. Seeing that Kratos is away from Dartmoor at the moment, I will try to do some snooping around in his private quarters tonight. Please call me and let me know if any of you has made any progress – we only have five days left.*

Kratos' quarters were located on the top floor of a house situated to the right of the main gate; according to old historical records, the house was originally the residence of the prison governor. Xantho resided on the bottom floor, thus providing effective protection for his master in the suite above.

Shortly after the tower clock struck midnight Maribeth, clad in a black tracksuit, moved silently past the door of Xantho's ground floor apartment and made her way up the stairs to Kratos' apartment entrance. Having spent many days working on the communications systems that linked the apartment to the main operations room, Maribeth had an electronic code on her gizmo that would open the door. She stopped for a moment outside the apartment and listened; hearing no sound, she activated the code and when the door opened with a slight "click", she entered.

Maribeth crept past the communications systems she had set up in the large room that served as Kratos' secondary command post and, using a small flashlight to illuminate the room, made her way into what seemed to be a study. A variety of personal communication devices took up most of the space on the main work area, but Maribeth knew that Kratos would never store any vital information on the machines themselves. All his personal and other top-secret data would be stored in his heavily protected virtual storage locations in cyber space. She was hoping to find something far more personal that would give a clue as to his real identity – perhaps family photos or a personal note from someone other than his work acquaintances.

The next room Maribeth entered was a bedroom which contained a large wardrobe. Reasoning that some people kept items of a personal nature in their wardrobes, she opened the cupboard doors and shone her torch inside. Immediately she stifled a cry as she stepped back in shock. Looking back at her from inside the wardrobe were three faceless masks; their hollow eyes and mouths seemed to tell her she was in a place that she shouldn't be. Two of the masks were glistening white while the third was ebony-black; Maribeth had seen Kratos wearing a white mask before, but never a black one, and for a brief moment she wondered when he wore that one.

Forcing her breathing to slow down, she shone the torch to the left and saw the familiar hooded robes; two were black and one was white. Maribeth decided that he must mix and match according to either his mood or the audience he was addressing. There didn't seem to be any personal items there, so she closed the cupboard and turned towards the dressing table on the other side of the room. Suddenly she froze...

The tall figure of a man was standing silently in front of the large windows on the southern side of the room. Silhouetted against the bright moonlight outside, he stood still, his arms folded. Maribeth shone her torch in his direction and instantly recognized the long black robe and the white faceless mask glinting in the torchlight.

"Kratos!" she gasped.

"Yes, it's me."

CHAPTER 32

LUKE BARON'S APARTMENT, JERUSALEM

Luke's gizmo buzzed in his pocket. "Luke, this is Martin. Did you and Karen get Maribeth's message? I see she copied you both on the message she sent me last evening."

"You mean the message in which she informed us that she was going to scratch around in Kratos' apartment?" Luke asked.

"Yeah, that one. I only saw the message this morning, and I've heard nothing from her since then. I tried her quarters here at Dartmoor, but there's no sign of her. We were supposed to meet at eight this morning to carry on with some installations, but she didn't pitch, so I wondered if she had contacted you or Karen."

"Neither of us has heard from her today. Have you checked with Xantho? It seemed like he and Maribeth were working closely together on the comms systems."

"I saw him at breakfast, but he hasn't seen her since last evening when they had dinner together at a local restaurant. I don't mind telling you I'm worried."

"Where is Kratos at the moment? I know that he only communicates via Xantho, but perhaps Xantho knows something that could be helpful."

"Xantho is not permitted to divulge any information or whereabouts regarding Kratos, but he hinted broadly that Kratos is in the US at the moment, making war plans with his leaders there. He also hinted at a possible meeting between Kratos and Draco."

"Interesting," said Luke. "I think I'll give Seth a call and see if he can do some scouting around our friend Draco. Seeing that Draco is his best customer, perhaps a friendly visit will be good for business, if you know what I mean."

"Good idea," Martin commented. "Let me know if anything comes up. I'll keep you informed about Maribeth – hopefully she'll show up soon with a perfectly good explanation."

"Let's hope and pray that we make a breakthrough soon," said Luke looking at his gizmo, "time's running out fast."

CHAPTER 33

DRACO ENTERPRISES' ESTATE, WASHINGTON DC

Seth Baron sat in Gorgonius Draco's sumptuous reception area and accepted a cup of coffee from his petite secretary. Noticing that the name on her ID tag read "Leinani" he said, "Pretty name, Leinani, what's its origin?"

My mother is Polynesian and my father is an American who lived in Hawaii most of his life. The name means 'beautiful child', which I normally don't mention to avoid being teased," she smiled.

"Well the name certainly suits you – no need for teasing," said Seth with a chuckle.

"Still chatting up the pretty girls, I see. I thought at your age you would have given that up already." Seth swung around as Draco entered from the corridor, smiling broadly. "If you've come to book a trip to a distant galaxy on one of my intergalactic spacecraft, you're in luck – the first ten spacecraft have come off the production line and are almost ready to go. The seats are already fully booked, but I always reserve a few places for special guests, which you are seeing that your iron and steel made the whole venture possible. Let's go into my office and we can talk."

In Draco's office Seth was shown to an armchair in a section of the room that resembled a plush lounge. Seth saw an opening to introduce the reason for his visit. "You mentioned that your space project will be ongoing; have you forgotten about our friend Kratos' demonstration the other day and his threat to carry out more destruction in a few days' time?"

"Ah, Kratos, yes," Draco took a long sip of coffee. "He came to see me yesterday and we discussed several issues."

Seth was immediately interested but did not want to appear too enthusiastic for fear that Draco might close the conversation. "Did you discuss his threats against Jerusalem? Is he still serious about his intention to destroy the old city and anything else that gets in his way?"

Draco stood up and walked slowly over to the window. For a moment he stood still, as though he was enjoying the view of his estate, then he said, "Kratos will never destroy Jerusalem – he loves it too much. Jerusalem is an obsession with him. He does, however, fully intend to overthrow the king's government and set up his own government in Jerusalem.

"I guess I shouldn't be telling you these things; after all, you are of the Baron dynasty and many of your extensive family members hold office in the king's government. But I have always considered you differently, especially in light of our business interests. So, to answer your original question, yes, Kratos will continue with his plans. They will begin with Jerusalem but will definitely spread further afield. However, by then I – and many of my clients – will be on the way to a distant galaxy. As I have said, you and any of your family members are welcome to join me. I would even invite you to enter into a little business venture I have started – a very lucrative venture, at that."

Seth considered this new information for a moment; something didn't add up. "If Kratos isn't going to destroy Jerusalem with some type of a huge bomb, how does he plan to capture it? Jerusalem is the seat of the king's government and is well protected by security personnel; granted, they don't have many weapons as such, but the king can call on a multitude of warring angels..."

"The warring angels will be no match for what Kratos has in mind. Do you know how many people have joined his army?

There are thousands upon thousands – mostly returnees, who see the overthrow of the king as their last hope of avoiding destruction. They have been receiving training and weapons – oh yes," he added when he saw Seth's surprise, "Kratos has been producing weapons at several different locations. These weapons are based on pre-Millennium weaponry, but they have been greatly improved."

"Will he take his forces to Jerusalem, and if so, how will he transport them?"

"Once again, I suppose I shouldn't be telling you this, but even if I do there is nothing you or anyone else can do to stop Kratos. He has built up of a fleet of high-speed anti-gravity troop carriers, and he'll use those to transport his forces. Exactly how he plans to organize the whole event, even I don't know. All I can say is that Kratos has power, or powers, that even I don't understand. He can do things that nobody else has ever done. Trust me, he will overthrow the king's government, exactly as he says he will."

Draco sat in his armchair once again, and crossed his long legs; his eyes burned into Seth's. "But there's something else worrying you, I can tell. We have chatted about many things, but we haven't got to exactly why you came to see me today, have we? What's really on your mind?"

"A young lady who is a close associate of my great nephew, Luke Baron, has gone missing. She has been ... connected ... to Kratos' group for a while, working on specialized communications equipment for Kratos. Anyway, she has not been heard from for about two days. We heard that Kratos was visiting you this week and wondered whether he mentioned anything about a certain Maribeth Markham?"

Draco smiled knowingly. "And why would the Barons be interested in one of Kratos' workers? Without knowing what the situation is, I can guess that this Maribeth Markham was working as some type of double agent, otherwise why would one of Luke Baron's technical people be working with Kratos?

"But to answer your question, he did mention that he had uncovered what he termed 'a spy'. Exactly how he has dealt with the matter he didn't say, but I can imagine he would deal harshly with anyone who tried to infiltrate his organization. As you may have heard, Kratos is a very secretive person; nobody – not even me – knows his true identity. As far as I know he never even takes his mask off. Whether this Maribeth is still alive or not, I cannot say. All I know is that I wouldn't want to be caught trying to infiltrate the inner circle of the Shadow Brigade – things wouldn't go well for such a person."

Realizing that was the most he could expect to learn from Draco regarding Maribeth's fate, Seth changed the subject. "When we met recently you wanted to meet at a deserted sports stadium because you believed someone was trying to steal certain secrets from you and might even try to kill you. You seem more relaxed today."

"Let's say I've dealt with that situation," replied Draco dismissively. "There was a group of returnees that bore a grudge against me for various reasons, but they have been ... sorted out."

"By 'sorted out' you mean...?"

"Exactly, but that's not a matter that need concern you. Let's just say that it was them or me." At that moment the light on Draco's desk communicator flashed brightly. Draco quickly answered, spoke briefly, and then turned to Seth. "You will have to excuse me now; I have a meeting with my construction heads in twenty minutes. It's been good chatting to you, though, and if I hear anything further about the missing lady I'll certainly call you."

Seth rose and extended his hand. "Thanks for your time," he said, "I too have another meeting to attend, so must be on my way. I'll make sure that the rest of your order is dealt with immediately, but ..." Seth hesitated for a moment, then decided to say what was on his mind regardless of what Draco might think. "I still believe that your best plan of action would be to repent of anything you've done that might be held against you, and to remain here in the kingdom. Once you've asked for forgiveness for past ... indiscretions, you needn't fear the judgment. There is nothing that can't be put right, no matter what you've done in the past."

Draco took his hand. "It's a bit late to try to convert me, Seth, but I appreciate the thought. Remember, some people still believe that I am Satan himself, in which case conversion would be impossible. Anyway, I hope you find your missing lady – but tell Luke that going after Kratos is playing with fire; he could get burned."

"I'll bear that in mind," said Seth. To himself he thought, *that's nothing compared to the fire awaiting you if you throw your lot in with Kratos and his cronies.*

* * *

As soon as he arrived home Seth put a call through to Luke in Jerusalem. "Luke, Seth here. Are you awake?"

"Well, I wasn't a moment ago – it's one thirty in the morning. What's up?"

"I've just had a meeting with Draco – you'd better wake up and listen."

Luke listened.

CHAPTER 34

LUKE'S APARTMENT, JERUSALEM

As soon as he'd finished talking to Seth, Luke contacted Karen. "According to what Draco told Seth, Kratos has probably discovered that Maribeth is working for us and is, in effect, a spy in his camp. It would seem that he has somehow taken her out of circulation."

"What do you mean by 'taken her out of circulation'?" Karen sat up, suddenly fully awake and rubbed her eyes. "Do you mean he has ... murdered her?"

"Probably not; the last I heard from Martin, who was with her at Dartmoor, is that Maribeth had an admirer in the form of Kratos' right-hand man, a huge fellow named Xantho. While I realize that Xantho could not go against the wishes of his master, he may have had enough clout to protect her in some way from Kratos' wrath – if that's what has happened. At this stage it's all speculation."

"What do you plan to do?" Karen asked. "I was told that Daniel and the Committee of Elders have already put all their resources into finding Kratos."

"My starting point will be the last place Maribeth was seen – Dartmoor. I'm trying to get hold of Martin to meet up with him there, but for some reason he's not answering. He could be tied up with Kratos at the moment, which means he can't speak freely. The Dartmoor establishment is registered as an electronic equipment testing facility, which we are sure is a blind for Kratos' main communication center. I'm leaving for Dartmoor in an hour."

"Not without me, you're not," declared Karen. "Although you're overall in charge of the MMOD, Maribeth reports directly to me, so she is my responsibility. We knew this was a dangerous mission and I am not going to shirk my responsibility."

"And if I, as your direct boss, order you to stay, then you must obey."

"Is that what you're doing; are you ordering me to stay?" Karen challenged him.

"No, I won't order you to stay, although I would prefer it if you remained safe." Luke replied. "Anyway, I know that with or without me, you wouldn't merely sit at home knowing Maribeth is missing. Let's meet at the office in half an hour – I want to call Mike Cousins and run the situation by him before we leave; he always has valuable insights that we might miss."

"Good idea, Luke; I'll see you at the office soon."

CHAPTER 35

CITY OF TIBERIAS, WESTERN SHORE OF SEA OF GALILEE

The sun streaming through an open window woke Jan Vogel from a deep sleep. For a moment he wondered if he was back on the farm in South Africa, then he remembered leaving his home country to become a mercenary to the highest bidder. From a young age he had been a fighter; in fact, he was generally known as someone with an enormous chip on his shoulder. His general attitude was "my way or no way".

A phenomenal shot with a rifle, he had hired himself out as a sniper in the endless wars in Africa and the Middle East, then in 2036 he'd joined what seemed like the winning team at the time – Count Helmut von Meinhof's Union Army. Some people saw only evil in Von Meinhof and even went as far as calling him the Antichrist, but he was a great military strategist which was what Vogel admired most. With the Union forces he had fought in Europe and the Middle East, ending up in a final thrust against Israel following Israel's revolt against the Union in 2038.

Still trying to get his bearings, Vogel wondered if he was still in Israel's Jezreel Valley at the height of what was known by the troops as "the Battle of Armageddon", but looking around he saw only a small room with a cupboard in one corner, a table and chair and a window overlooking a large courtyard. Surprised that he was lying on a bed, he surmised that he had been wounded in battle and had been taken to a field hospital. Instinctively he felt for his prized prototype sniper's rifle, then his memory slowly returned. Israel had been part of Von Meinhof's Union, but due to interference from other countries, mainly the United States, Israel had rebelled against the Union in early 2038. Von Meinhof had moved a large army into the area in order to teach Israel a lesson. As an expert sniper, Vogel had been positioned on a high point to fire his high-velocity exploding shells into any Israeli military vehicles moving through the Jezreel Valley.

He remembered hearing a strange loud blast of a trumpet, followed by a searing light that had split the afternoon sky. The last thing he remembered was the strong conviction that this was not some enemy you could come against with normal weapons; this enemy seemed to be coming out of the sky, but not with conventional aircraft. He remembered too his desperate attempt to stow his precious rifle in its steel casing; after placing it in a hollow made by an exploding mortar, he covered it with some very large stones on the hilltop where he had been positioned. The last thing he'd wanted was for his weapon, a top-secret prototype developed by Von Meinhof's vast military workshops, to fall into an unknown enemy's hands. If he got into trouble he would use his short range side arms – a sub-machine gun and a Glock handgun.

Vogel forced his mind back to the present. Slowly he stood up and made his way to the door, then out into a long corridor. "You look a bit befuddled, mate, don't blame you, you've been asleep for a long time." Vogel swung around to see a short, wiry man smiling at him. "The name's Bennie Johnson," he said, "don't worry, there's a whole bunch of us returnees living here – you're not alone."

"This might sound stupid, but where the hell are we?" Vogel asked.

Johnson laughed. "That's a question we all ask when we arrive, 'cos we don't all arrive in the same place. There must be a reason why you were resurrected here, but come with me and I'll explain everything to you."

An hour later, over coffee and biscuits, Vogel learned that he was in Tiberias, a city on the western shore of the Sea of Galilee, and that he was one of thousands, maybe millions, resurrected to await their final judgment. After hearing Johnson's explanation of the current situation in the Millennium Kingdom, and the impending judgment of all those resurrected into the kingdom, he jumped to his feet. "Nobody's going to judge me!" he declared. "I'm going to get my weapon back and then I'll join anyone fighting for freedom."

"Weapon?" asked Johnson. "Nobody has weapons anymore except maybe that madman Kratos and his cronies. Why don't you join the king's people and sail through the judgment?"

"Like I said," answered Vogel, "nobody judges me; when I'm looking down the sights of my rifle I'll do the judging. I remember where I left my rifle and it's not too far from here. I'm going to get it and then I'll join Kratos or anyone else who's against being judged."

"Whoa there!" cried Johnson, raising a hand in protest. "I've been commissioned to tell you all about your new surroundings – you can't simply leave without knowing what's going on around you."

"I'll find out as I go along," snapped Vogel heading for the front door. "I can live off the land if I have to. I don't need anyone or anything."

With that he was gone.

CHAPTER 36

DARTMOOR, ENGLAND

Posing as tourists visiting historical places in England, Luke and Karen booked into the Princeton Lodge, a neat little inn that had retained an atmosphere of peaceful country living. Over a beer in the busy pub Luke asked Dan Timmins, the proprietor, about the Dartmoor museum, and whether it was still open to visitors.

"Why sure it is," said Dan, giving his grey handlebar moustache a tweak. "Every morning I deliver sandwiches and other snacks to the museum for them to sell to their visitors – been doing that for the past 600 years. They run a small coffee shop on the premises, but have limited resources to prepare their own food. Anyway, my sandwiches are the best in the county, so naturally they would prefer them to making their own." Dan puffed his chest out so that his braces stretched over his considerable girth. "You folks planning a visit?"

"Yes, we thought we would pop around there tomorrow," said Karen. "I love visiting places of historical interest."

"I know what you mean," said Dan, "although nothing too exciting has happened during the Millennium years. It's always interesting to go back to the old days – especially the Tribulation period when things were really hot; not that I would want that chaos again. Peace is good." Dan ran his hand through his thick grey hair and said in low voice, "Be careful, though, part of the old prison has been taken over by a new bunch called Blue Ray Electronics, and from what I've heard they're a pretty weird bunch."

"How so?" asked Luke. "What have you heard about them?"

Always ready for a bit of gossip, Dan leaned over and said confidentially, "Well they don't like strangers poking about on their premises and they keep pretty much to themselves. Some say they are part of this Shadow Brigade that's been in the news recently – those fellas that've been causing some trouble for the king's government. There's even a rumor that they want to bomb Jerusalem, although whatever for beats me." With that Dan shook his head and moved off to serve two newcomers at the bar counter.

"What do you make of all that?" asked Karen when Dan was out of earshot.

"Could be an interesting visit tomorrow," said Luke. "Dan is right, though, seeing that we know that Kratos is in charge there, we need to be very careful."

CHAPTER 37

An icy wind had swept in from the south overnight, and Luke and Karen shivered as they left the warmth of the Princeton Lodge and made for their hired vehicle. Although the hire company offered a wide range of vehicles, ranging from large space cruisers to small road-bound vehicles, Luke had chosen a road vehicle. He reasoned that a space cruiser was not appropriate for the short trips he and Karen would undertake, and it would be an opportunity to view the unique countryside of the Moors.

Luke held the passenger door open for Karen; just then Dan Timmins came running out after them, his face red with both the cold air as well as the unaccustomed effort of having to break into a trot. "Wait up, you two," he gasped as he approached them. "I've got a message for Karen Leigh – is that you, Miss?"

"Yes, I'm Karen Leigh," said Karen climbing out of the vehicle again and looking expectantly at Dan. "Who's the message from?"

"It's from a Maribeth Markham – she said it's very urgent."

"Well, what did she say?" asked Luke.

"She says to meet her as soon as possible on the steps of the town hall in Yelverton. She sounded pretty excited."

"Yelverton – that's a village near here, right?" Luke asked, recalling that he had seen road signs on their way to Princeton.

"Yes, a fairly large village 'bout twenty miles south-west of here," Dan confirmed.

"Did she say why she's there and where she's been for the past few days?" Karen was anxious to know what had happened to Maribeth.

"No, she just said to meet her there as soon as possible – that's all I know," said Dan, turning to go back into the warmth of the lodge with its very effective central heating which was operating at full strength.

"How on earth did Maribeth know we were here, and why call the lodge and not one of us directly?" mused Luke. "Let me try and call her again." Luke removed his gizmo from his pocket and directed a call to Maribeth. After a while he rang off and placed the device back in his pocket. "Very strange; there's no answer ..."

"All we can do now is go to Yelverton and meet up with her," said Karen moving towards their vehicle again. She's a very capable and intelligent woman; there must be something wrong."

"I sure would like to know what's really going on and why she went off the radar for so long," said Luke climbing into the driver's seat and programming their destination into the vehicle's auto pilot. "Let's get to Yelverton asap."

CHAPTER 38

ON THE ROAD TO YELVERTON

Luke and Karen traveled in silence for a while. "Penny for your thoughts," said Luke.

"I'm thinking about ... us," said Karen, knowing that this discussion would lead somewhere Luke might not want to go.

"What about ... us?"

"Probably more questions than answers at this stage." Karen was defensive and not quite sure where to take the conversation. "What I mean is ... where do you see us, say, five years from now."

"My guess is that we'll be happily settled in New Jerusalem; this world would have passed away and there'll be a new heaven and a new Earth." Luke saw her face cloud over and quickly continued. "I realize that we've only known each other a short time, but for me it's been long enough to know that I can't imagine a future without you. Does that make sense to you?"

"Well, if this is some sort of a proposal it needs a bit of polishing up," smiled Karen.

"I was hoping for the right time and place to broach this subject," replied Luke, "but our world as we know it might end any day now; who knows what's going to happen when Kratos' ultimatum expires. Will he really destroy Jerusalem? If so, will he stop at Jerusalem or will he attack the rest of the world too?

We've seen what he did to that moon of Jupiter, so he has it in his power to do enormous damage on Earth."

"You're forgetting something," said Karen, "the final chapter has already been written, and it's Satan who gets destroyed. But I know what you mean, times are very volatile at the moment."

Luke reached out and took Karen's hand in his. "This one thing I promise you: I want to be with you forever. I don't care where it is, but I want you with me."

They had traveled about fifteen miles along the small road linking the two villages and were climbing a long hill when they noticed a large vehicle coming towards them. "That huge truck takes up most of the road, it's enormous," commented Luke, making sure that his headlights were on to make them clearly visible to the oncoming truck. "If he stays on his side we can perhaps squeeze past." The vehicle's auto drive, sensing danger ahead, slowed the vehicle almost to a standstill and moved over to the edge of the road.

They were about thirty yards from the truck when it veered onto their side of the road and made straight for them.

"What the ...? He must be out of control – hold tight," Luke shouted as he flicked the switch that placed the vehicle back under his control. Frantically he gunned the accelerator and spun the steering wheel to the right, causing the small car to veer onto the other side of the road as the truck reached them. There was a screech of tearing metal as the truck caught the rear left hand side of their vehicle, causing it to spin off the road and into the grass on the other side. Luke fought hard to correct the spin and keep the car from rolling, and eventually the car came to a stop as it made heavy contact with a large bush. For a while they sat still, saying nothing, then Luke regained control of his wits.

"Are you alright?" He leaned across towards Karen. "You're bleeding."

"I think my head hit the window when the car spun around. Apart from that I don't feel that anything is broken, but I'll probably have bruises to show for it in a few days. Thank goodness you swerved to the right instead of trying to go further over to the left; that truck would have hit us head on."

"That guy must be crazy," said Luke, "we could have been killed! What on earth was his problem? It seemed like he was deliberately trying to hit us."

"If he did hit us that huge truck of his would hardly even have felt the bump, but we would have been mincemeat," replied Karen, trying to open her door. "This door's jammed, can you open yours?"

Luke pushed against his door which opened with a grating noise. "Only just opens; we must have caught that bush pretty hard, I can see it's bent out of shape." Slowly Luke climbed out and made his way to the passenger side. He tried the door but it wouldn't budge. Seeing a heavy piece of metal lying nearby, he picked it up and used it as a lever to prise the door open far enough for Karen to climb out.

"No sign of that truck anywhere; the blighter didn't even have the decency to stop," said Luke. "I didn't manage to see his number either, everything happened too fast."

"Neither did I, but there can't be too many trucks that size around here," commented Karen, "hopefully we can trace the owner and the driver."

Luke removed the gizmo from his jacket pocket and checked to see if it was still working. He was about to call the MMOD office in Jerusalem when the screen lit up with an incoming call. "It's Mike Cousins," he said in surprise as he answered the call. "Mike – where are you?"

"Still in Washington DC. I had a strange feeling that something was up with you; am I right?"

"You're spot on, my friend. We've still been unable to locate Maribeth and today we heard she wanted to meet us in a village near Dartmoor in England – a place called Yelverton. We were on our way to Yelverton when someone deliberately tried to take us out – a huge truck came straight for us. I managed to swerve in time, but the truck caught the side of our vehicle and spun us off the road into some bushes. We are both 'okayish', but we sure would appreciate some help. We're about fifteen miles out from Princeton. As I said, we got a message that Maribeth was in Yelverton and wanted to meet us on the steps of the town hall. We were on our way there when this happened."

"Hold tight, I'll be there in half an hour. Do either of you need medical attention?"

"No, we're a bit shaken but no serious damage done. Come as soon as you can; in the meantime I'll try and contact Maribeth again."

"Still can't get her, I'm afraid," said Karen, "I've been trying to call her with no luck. I left another voice message, but I've got a strange feeling that something has happened to her – the same way something nearly happened to us."

"You mean whoever tried to wipe us out has done the same to Maribeth?" Luke was voicing the same growing unease that Karen felt. "Mike will be here shortly. Let's hope we can get this sorted out soon; Kratos' deadline is coming up fast!"

CHAPTER 39

About ten minutes later Mike Cousins appeared before them.

"Wow, that was quick," said Karen.

"I have a great mode of transport," the big man chuckled. "But seeing as your vehicle is a bit of a mess and you guys still need physical transport, let me shoot through to Yelverton and rent a high-speed anti-gravity vehicle. Then we can go to Yelverton together and look for Maribeth."

Twenty minutes later Luke, Karen and Mike made their way to the front steps of the Yelverton town hall. "So much time has elapsed since Maribeth asked us to meet her here that I guess she would have moved off long ago, thinking we weren't coming," said Karen, scanning the area.

"I've got a bad feeling that Martin Petrovic could also be in trouble," said Luke. "I haven't heard from him for about two days; he usually contacts me daily."

"Unless he's somehow tied up with tracking Maribeth," said Karen, not wanting to imagine the worst. "Maribeth informed me of the state-of-the-art electronic devices that Kratos has acquired – perhaps Martin doesn't want Kratos to pick up his communications until he has completed what has to be done."

"Let's hope they're both safe and sound," said Mike. "In the meantime you two had better be on your guard. I have a feeling that your accident was no coincidence."

Having seen no sign of Maribeth in the vicinity of the Yelverton town hall, Karen suggested that they split up and do a walk-about of the area, then meet back in front of the town hall in an hour. "I don't like the idea of you being by yourself when we don't know who our enemy is; anything could happen," said Luke protectively.

"Don't be silly, Luke, I'm a big girl; I can look after myself." Karen sounded indignant, but deep down she knew Luke was right.

"I agree with Luke," said Mike, "let's stick together until we have more clarity about Maribeth and Martin. I really believe we're dealing with the devil himself here, so we can't take chances."

After walking around for an hour they made their way back to the hired vehicle. "I didn't really have much hope of seeing her around here," said Luke. "I doubt very much now that Maribeth was anywhere near Yelverton; I think that call we received asking us to meet her here was merely a ruse to lure us out onto the road so that that truck could finish us off."

"I think you're right," said Mike. "For some reason Kratos – and I do believe he's behind this – doesn't want us sniffing around the Dartmoor area. It's getting dark now, I suggest we get on back to Princeton and then tomorrow we pay a visit to Blue Ray."

"I agree," said Luke, "in the meantime I'll send a message to Martin to let him know what we're up to, in case he gets back and looks for us."

CHAPTER 40

BLUE RAY ELECTRONICS, DARTMOOR, ENGLAND

The sign above the entrance gate read "Blue Ray Electronics" in large gold letters set against a bright blue background. Mike, Luke and Karen presented their universal access identification cards – issued to high profile persons in the king's government – to the guard at the gate, who looked totally unimpressed. "My orders are to let nobody in without a Blue Ray card passing my recognition scanner."

"We have business with the CEO of Blue Ray; could you please tell Xantho that we need to see him urgently? Tell him it's about Miss Maribeth Markham." Luke was counting on his suspicion that Xantho was more than a little taken with the raven-haired Maribeth.

The guard disappeared into an adjoining room while a second guard watched that nobody slipped past the gate. A few moments later the first guard reappeared. "Xantho will meet you here; please wait."

About two minutes later a vehicle pulled up outside the guard-house and the huge red-bearded figure of Xantho squeezed itself out. He looked suspiciously at the three waiting to see him, then came directly to the point. "So you're asking about Maribeth; do any of you know where she is? I've been looking for her since yesterday – what's your connection with her?"

Not knowing how much Xantho knew about Maribeth and her mission to find Kratos, Luke decided to assume that he knew her only as a freelance electronics engineer. "Maribeth did some work on our systems in Jerusalem a while back and we urgently need them to be updated; that's why we are trying to locate her. We can't raise her on her gizmo, so we came here personally."

The explanation seemed to satisfy Xantho and he visibly relaxed. Extending a huge hand to Luke he said, "Xantho's the name; and you are...?"

"I'm Luke Baron, and these are my associates – Karen Leigh and Mike Cousins."

Xantho shook hands with Karen then, looking Cousins up and down, he said "It's not often I meet a man my own size – you've been in the fight game, haven't you? I can see it in your eyes."

"Long ago," said Mike with a smile, "but those are days I prefer to forget."

"Same with me," said Xantho, releasing Mike's hand. "Maybe we can exchange stories someday. In the meantime, let's go inside and see if we can figure out what's happened to Maribeth."

CHAPTER 41

ON A ROOFTOP OVERLOOKING THE PREMISES OF BLUE RAY ELECTRONICS

Jan Vogel cradled his sniper rifle in the crook of his arm as he opened the small box containing his "spotter" kit. This device gave him precise information on ambient temperature, wind speed, wind direction and distance to the target. Ideally a sniper would have an accomplice with him to relieve the shooter of the task of testing ambient conditions, but the transportable box enabled him to work alone. He studied the readings, then made adjustments to his rifle.

Vogel had been extremely relieved to find his rifle where he had buried it, high on a hill in the Jezreel Valley. The airtight steel casing had preserved the weapon in good condition, but it still took him many days of cleaning every part in order to return the rifle to its original condition. His box of ammunition was also intact, and after testing the weapon in a deserted valley he was confident that it was as good as new and the ammunition reliable. Vogel knew that nobody would have anything like his weapon on Earth at the moment because weapon production had ceased at the beginning of the Millennium.

For many months Vogel had sought out the leaders of the returnee revolt against the king and his government. Eventually he had seen an advertisement by one Gorgonius Draco offering passage to a distant galaxy in order to escape any final judgment that might take place. He visited Draco and learned of his plan to build spaceships capable of reaching distant galaxies, but escape was not part of Vogel's make-up. After a while he won the confidence of Draco who trusted him enough to put him in contact with Kratos himself.

"Here is a man with the same vision and dedication that we have; I'm sure he would be an asset to your army," Draco had told Kratos. "He also possesses enormous skill with a weapon that can do immense damage at a great distance, which I'm sure could prove useful in many circumstances." Kratos was interested, and after a meeting with Vogel and having seen his skill with the rifle, he invited him to join the Shadow Brigade as part of the inner group hierarchy. Kratos found it both useful and amusing to have someone who loved killing as much as he did, especially when it came to the elimination of specific targets that Kratos found annoying.

It was for this purpose that Jan Vogel had placed himself on the roof of a twenty-floor apartment building overlooking the Dartmoor campus. Vogel's range finder had placed the target at a distance of 5,000 yards, a distance that would have been ludicrous to anyone except Vogel. He had hit targets at 8,000 yards in practice and was confident he would get a kill on this occasion.

Vogel heard the vehicle approaching before it appeared from behind the surrounding buildings. His two-way radio came to life: "*Hulle's op pad, Jan.* (They're on their way, Jan.) It's Luke Baron, the Leigh woman and some black man that I don't know."

"*Dankie* (thank you) *Piet*," he said in Afrikaans to his trusted South African accomplice. "*Ek's reg vir hulle.* (I'm ready for them.)"

Vogel watched as the vehicle stopped at the entrance to the compound and eventually he saw Xantho going to meet the trio. He watched the greetings that took place, and then took aim. Once his targets were clear of the vehicle Jan took a quick estimate of their walking pace as they made for the main entrance of the building. He calculated that the high-velocity round would take three seconds to reach the target, but that wouldn't matter since he was directly behind the man. The sniper drew in a slow breath then, with the target centered in the cross-hairs, he gently took up the pressure on the trigger.

CHAPTER 42

Mike had an uneasy feeling about the whole situation, but knowing that Xantho was as keen as they were to locate Maribeth – although for different reasons – he didn't allow his anxiety to get the better of him. The big man kept scanning the environment and could see nothing untoward, but before entering the main door of the building he felt a strong prompting to cast a glance behind him. As he turned he saw the sun glint on a small piece of glass. Without fully knowing why he did it, he dived at Luke, knocking him off his feet. At the same moment he felt a searing pain in his left shoulder. "What the...?" gulped Luke in surprise as Mike's huge form knocked him to the ground.

"Quickly, into the building, everybody!" yelled Mike, springing to his feet and grabbing Karen. He shoved her roughly through the door and pushed Luke in after her. Xantho was still looking around trying to assess what Mike was seeing and then there was another faint crack from the distant rooftop. Mike grabbed Xantho and hurled him bodily through the door, slamming the door shut as he himself dived through, but not before he felt another searing pain between his shoulder blades.

Xantho was not used to being thrown around by anyone, and was surprised by the apparent effortless ease with which Mike had bundled him into the building. Luke and Karen also couldn't understand what had got into the big man. "What's going on, Mike?" demanded Luke. "What did you see outside that made you act like that?"

"I've been shot twice," said Mike, removing his jacket and unbuttoning his shirt. "You will probably see the marks on my shoulder and my back, and there are holes in my clothes." He turned around to reveal a long red welt on his shoulder where the bullet had hit and glanced off, and another one between his shoulder blades. "I think these bullets were meant for you, Luke, and possibly for Karen too. The second bullet could easily have hit Xantho as he got between you and the shooter."

Xantho looked completely flummoxed. "But if you've been shot, how come you're still walking around with only two marks on your back to show for it?"

"Because I'm an immortal," said Mike. "I could feel the bullets sting when they hit me, but they cannot penetrate my skin." Seeing the puzzled look that remained on Xantho's face, Mike realized that, as a returnee in Kratos' service, Xantho had probably never been exposed to immortals. "The resurrected body is like a spiritual body, except that it's solid and we can do things like eat food, and have the sensations of touch and feelings. That's why I felt the bullets sting my skin without the skin being penetrated."

Xantho merely shook his head. "I've heard about immortals, but I've never seen one this close. All I know is that I sure wouldn't like to have met you in the ring during my fighting days, immortal or not. The way you threw me through the door .... But let's get to the bottom of who's trying to shoot us."

"I saw the glint of what was probably a telescopic lens a second before I heard the shot being fired from the roof of that building across the road," said Mike. "I'm going back now to see if I can find the shooter."

Xantho took out his gizmo and made a call simultaneously to four of his men. He explained that they had been shot at and gave the last known location of the shooter. "Be careful, men, he's armed with an old-fashioned rifle, but he knows how to use it."

"I'll go with them," said Mike, hurrying outside to meet up with Xantho's men.

"So, you and Karen have come to find out what's happened to Maribeth," said Xantho to Luke. "You may or may not know it, but Maribeth and I were ... we were getting to know one another; at least I was trying to get to know her better." The big man actually was blushing beneath his tough exterior. "I'm also worried about her and want to get her back."

"What do you know about Kratos?" asked Luke. "Is that his real name? Where does he come from? Do you think he's involved with Maribeth being missing – and Martin too?"

"Although I work for Kratos and consider myself one of his trusted employees, I really don't know anything about him. Nobody – but nobody – gets that close to him. I do know that he has powers that I've never seen before, but where he gets them from I really don't know."

Just then Mike returned with the news that the roof where the shooter had been positioned was empty. "Whoever he is he knows his job. The rooftop was clean as a whistle – no cartridge shells left lying around; not even a piece of paper that might give him away. He must have planned his escape beforehand, probably with an accomplice or two."

"Whereto from here?" asked Karen.

"I'm not expecting Kratos back till tomorrow evening," said Xantho. "He said he had preparations to make in Israel."

"Probably to do with his threat to destroy Jerusalem," said Luke. "Do you think he will carry it out?"

Xantho took a deep breath. "I wish I knew for sure. On the one hand he is fanatical about his hatred for the king, yet on the other hand he truly loves Jerusalem and he is serious about wanting to rule the world from that city. Whether he will destroy it or not, only he knows."

"We've heard that he has a worldwide army of thousands of troops; surely he won't bring them all across to try and take Jerusalem," said Mike.

"I'm not sure whether it can be called an *army*," said Xantho. "Put it this way, he now has millions of *followers* worldwide. Some of them are those born into the Millennium Kingdom who have decided to exercise their free-will choice and not follow the king, but most of his followers are returnees like me. These are people who will eventually face the White Throne Judgment and be denied entry into New Jerusalem. For this reason they will try anything to avoid judgment. The first prize would be to overthrow the king and his government, which is what Kratos is promising them.

"As far as an actual army is concerned," continued Xantho, "Kratos has about 10,000 'troops' trained to use the new weapons he is developing. He got hold of the records of all weaponry used prior to the advent of the Millennium Kingdom, and he has laboratories and factories in Russia and China that are in full-time production reproducing them. He is using many returnees who were scientists in their previous lives, especially those trained in weapons development. And that's quite apart from his army of warring demons who, from what I've heard, are the meanest critters imaginable."

"Which tends to prove that Kratos is actually Satan," commented Luke.

"I don't think there's any doubt about that," said Xantho.

"And you're telling us all this ... why?" asked Karen, suspicious of Xantho's motives.

Xantho gave a huge sigh, "I guess it's all back to Maribeth again. When we last met she tried her best to get me to change."

"Change?" Karen pressed.

"Yeah – she wanted me to leave Kratos and go over to the king's side. She seemed to think that I could avoid a bad final judgment, that the things I've done could be forgiven."

"And, what do you think?" Karen asked, more as a challenge than a question.

The big man blushed again. "I've never met anyone like her before," he said. "I will do anything to find her before harm comes to her."

"Do you think Kratos is behind her disappearance and also that of Martin?" asked Luke, anxious to find his two missing colleagues.

"If he has got something to do with it he never mentioned it to me; not that he tells me everything he does, of course. As I said before, he plays his cards pretty close to his chest. As for Martin also being abducted, if that's what happened, I really can't say. Although Martin and Maribeth were working broadly on the same projects, they weren't working that close together most of the time. Martin often left the premises to get his things sorted out; he seemed to be on a different mission, if you know what I mean."

"Martin operates on a broader and more strategic level, while Maribeth is more hands-on – a real technical boffin," explained Luke.

"That's exactly how I saw it," said Xantho.

In the meantime Mike had been standing to one side and speaking into his gizmo. Eventually he signed off and put the device back into his pocket. "I just sent Daniel and the Committee an update," he said. "I'll probably hear back from them soon. In the meantime we must get cracking on finding Maribeth and Martin, and locating Kratos, of course. There are only three days left, and if Kratos is still hell-bent on carrying out his threats against Jerusalem, we must find him and stop him."

"I can tell you now, you won't find Kratos if he doesn't want to be found," said Xantho. "That man can virtually blend into the walls if he wants to."

"Well then we must knock the walls down," said Mike, slamming one enormous fist into the other. "From tomorrow there are only two days left."

"I have an idea that may or may not work, but it's worth a try," said Karen. "Seeing that Kratos probably now sees Xantho as being 'contaminated' by his obvious attraction to Maribeth, and his present contact with us, we need to find someone who has greater credibility with Kratos to find out where he is at the moment, and to pass that information on to us."

"And where would we get such a person? If he doesn't fully trust me anymore, who will he trust?" asked Xantho, not believing that anyone could have been closer to Kratos than he was.

"Kratos is no fool, of that I can assure you. He will see right through any ruse we can come up with."

"The person to use is Draco; he and Kratos seem to be good buddies and on the same wavelength," suggested Karen. "If we could put pressure on Draco to use his network of devious contacts to find Kratos, we might come up with something."

"I think you're onto something there," said Luke. "And I know who we can approach to put pressure on Draco. I'll call him right away."

CHAPTER 43

KRATOS' UNDERGROUND DETENTION FACILITY

Maribeth opened her eyes and blinked a few times. She felt groggy, as though she had woken from a long drug-induced sleep. *What on earth did he give me to make me feel like this?* she wondered as she looked at her surroundings. *And where the heck am I?*

She was lying on a bed in a room about five yards square with a small barred window high up on the wall behind her. The door to the room was closed and, she supposed, locked. Standing up on the bed Maribeth hoped to be able to see out the window but it was too high. She tried to jump up and hold on to the sill to pull herself up, but soon realized that her legs were still too shaky to try something like that. She crossed the floor and was about to try the door when it opened and a tall woman with long black hair stood there looking as surprised to see her as Maribeth was to find someone opening the door. The woman quickly entered the room and shut the door behind her. Maribeth noticed that the woman had not locked the door after her which meant that if she could subdue her somehow, she could escape.

"So, you're awake at last," said the woman. "You slept for about ten hours."

Deciding that shock tactics would be her best strategy to escape, Maribeth grabbed the woman by her jacket and tried to spin her off her feet. To her surprise the woman lifted her off the ground as though she was a small child and hurled her bodily onto the bed, where she hit her head hard against the wall. It took Maribeth nearly a minute to regain her senses.

"Who are you?" she stammered. "You could have killed me."

"Don't try that again, sweetie pie; next time I won't be so gentle with you," the woman growled.

"Where am I? Why have I been brought here?" Maribeth demanded as she lifted herself slowly off the bed and tried to stand up. Quickly she sat down again when she realized that she was still very groggy.

"You're in a place where you can't contact anyone else. Kratos himself brought you here last night and placed you under my ... *care.*"

"Who are you, and how did you manage to lift me up and throw me like that?" Maribeth was desperate for answers. She remembered going into Kratos' living quarters at the Dartmoor facility and being confronted by ... by....

"I'm Anastasia, a high-ranking demon and head of all the women who work closely with Kratos. As to how I did what I did to you, well, that was only a warm-up. If you give me reason to I will show you exactly what I'm capable of. All I know is that you've displeased Kratos and that's a bad thing to do. No doubt he will visit you shortly and that, I'm afraid, may not go too well for you." With that Anastasia turned on her heel and left, locking the door behind her.

Maribeth sat back on the bed and gently rubbed her aching head. "Now what?" she said under her breath. "I sure hope Luke and company can get me out of this before...." Suddenly Maribeth recalled the moment in Kratos' bedroom when she turned around and saw him standing behind her – the evil and hate she saw in his eyes, which seemed to be glowing behind the white mask, was the most frightening thing she had ever seen. Nothing compared, however, to the instant he lifted his mask and she realized that she, and everyone she was connected to, were in dire trouble.

CHAPTER 44

ESTATE OF GORGONIUS DRACO, WASHINGTON DC

Draco rose to his feet and looked with satisfaction at the faces around the conference table in his "war room".

"As you know, each person sitting around this table represents the interests of hundreds, even thousands of people who are willing to buy a passage to a distant galaxy in order to escape the unfair judgment the king has planned for us. As you are also aware, my exploratory spacecraft have found two planets in the Andromeda galaxy that are similar to Earth, where mortals can survive without having to use artificial breathing apparatus, and where there is water and vegetation.

"The fact that Andromeda is 2.5 million light years from Earth has pros and cons. On the up side it is far enough away from Earth to escape the final judgment, while on the down side the journey there, using my new hyper-drive spacecraft, will take roughly two Earth years. My original exploration teams didn't have it as good as you travelers are going to enjoy. Their biggest gripe about the journey was being confined to the small cabin of the spacecraft for that length of time.

"Of course this won't be the case for our paying customers who make the journey with us. My first ten passenger craft have been completed, and my workshops are gearing up for the production of the next ten craft. Each craft can carry 5,000 passengers in luxury. There are parks on board as well as sporting facilities and gymnasiums. Best of all, my new spacecraft will simulate Earth's gravity so there will be no experience of weightlessness that is so debilitating. Work on the next ten spacecraft will begin as soon as the raw materials have been delivered; we are hopeful ..." Draco stopped in mid-sentence as the red gizmo that he kept for emergency calls started buzzing on the table in front of him. He glanced at the caller identity and saw that the call was coming from Seth Baron.

Turning to the people around the table Draco said quickly, "Ladies and gentlemen, I must take this call. In the meantime I have asked Professor Joel Lipton, my leading expert on the chosen Andromeda planets, to give you a presentation on what life would be like on these glorious places of refuge. Professor Lipton...."

A short, scrawny man in his late fifties rose from the table and moved to the front. "Ladies and gentlemen, you have made the right choice. As you know, your destination is a planet in the solar system known as 103, which is one of the many solar systems in the Andromeda galaxy. Andromeda is, of course, the closest galaxy to our Milky Way. If you thought that conditions in the Millennium Kingdom resemble Paradise, wait until you see the planets we've chosen in 103. What Mr. Draco has told you so far is but a taste of what you can expect when you get there; have a look at these pictures ..."

In the meantime Draco had moved out of the conference room. He pushed a button on his gizmo; "Seth, what's up?"

"I'm afraid a bit of an emergency has come up, Draco."

"Nothing that will hinder the delivery, I hope."

"It may or may not have an influence on your order – it all depends."

"Seth, you're speaking in riddles; what's the problem?"

"I need to urgently locate Kratos and I thought you might be able to assist."

"Me? Kratos? How should I know where Kratos is? All I know is what you know – in two days' time Kratos is going to carry out his threat against Jerusalem. He's probably gone to ground till that's all over. I imagine everyone in the king's government is looking for him to try and stop him. What made you think I would know where he is, and why should this stop your production of my metal?"

"Remember I told you recently about one of the MMOD ladies who has mysteriously disappeared."

"Yes, I do remember, and I told you that anyone trying to infiltrate Kratos' network can only expect the worst to happen to them. Has something happened now?"

"She is still missing, that's why we need you to help us locate Kratos," said Seth, a ring of desperation apparent in his voice. "We are extremely worried about her and will do anything to get her back."

"Including threatening to disrupt my space program," Draco shouted, his face turning red.

"We know that you are probably the only person that Kratos trusts, and that with your network of, shall we say 'devious contacts', you have the best chance of locating him. We are trying every means at our disposal, but so far have come up with nothing."

"So you decided to threaten me to get me to do your dirty work – Kratos' whereabouts in exchange for my metal! Do you realize that this is out and out blackmail?" Draco was furious.

"I'm not trying to blackmail you, Draco, but these are desperate times. There are only two days to go before Kratos carries out his threats, and very likely he won't stop with Jerusalem. As you know, the Committee of Elders has declared an emergency situation until Kratos has been located and dealt with. For obvious reasons they need to locate Kratos before he carries out his threats, and from my side I would very much like to rescue young Maribeth from whatever Kratos has planned for her."

"That's if she is still alive," said Draco grimly. "From my dealings with Kratos you don't fool around with him. He has enormous resources and great power over thousands of people, possibly millions. You get in his way and you're tickets, I'm afraid."

"That's precisely why we can't waste any time. If we can locate Kratos we can hopefully kill two birds with one stone – find Maribeth and put a stop to his weekend plans."

There was silence on the line for a while, then Draco said, "I'll get back to you shortly, however your threats to delay my production could seriously jeopardize our business relationship. I realize that you are probably being placed under pressure to contact me with this 'request', and at the end of the day I *am* probably your best hope of locating Kratos; maybe in your position I would have done the same. Tell me honestly, would you really stop production of my metal if I refused to help you?"

"Yes, I would."

"I'll get back to you as soon as I have some news."

CHAPTER 45

BLUE RAY ELECTRONICS, DARTMOOR, ENGLAND

Xantho sat alone in his apartment and contemplated Luke, Karen and Mike Cousins' visit to Blue Ray. It worried him that a sniper had been ordered to kill Luke, and possibly Karen as well. If Kratos was behind the attack – which Xantho increasingly believed to be the case – then Maribeth, being their colleague, was certainly in grave danger. If Kratos had taken her captive, she might already be dead.

He tried to call her gizmo, but there was no response. In that moment he knew he had to find her – if it was not already too late. Xantho was about to storm out of his apartment and start tearing the campus apart when his gizmo buzzed and he saw the caller was Kratos. He answered quickly.

The instruction was brief: "Xantho, come to my apartment immediately." Before he could respond, Kratos had terminated the call. Firmly resolved to confront Kratos on the whereabouts of Maribeth, Xantho took the stairs three at a time up to Kratos' apartment which was directly above his own living quarters. He was about to knock on the door when a voice from inside called out, "Come in."

On entering, he saw Kratos standing in front of the large window overlooking the campus, clad as usual in his black hooded robe and white faceless mask. To the left of the front door stood a tall woman with long black hair whom he recognized as Anastasia, a she-devil. To the right of the door stood a tall, powerful-looking man with short cropped black hair and a neatly trimmed beard.

"Xantho, you know Anastasia," Kratos nodded in the direction on the woman, "and this is Zolas – he commands my warring demons." Kratos waved a hand in the direction of Zolas who offered nothing except an icy stare. Xantho could sense that he was being analyzed by a man who had vast experience in sizing up opponents. Xantho judged Zolas to be about seven foot tall, which was roughly his own height, and equally as broad and muscular. If the rumors about Zolas were true, however, it was generally understood that he, like many of the senior demons, possessed dark spiritual powers far in excess of what little power the lower ranked demons could muster. Kratos came straight to the point.

"What's this I hear about you conniving with my enemies?" His voice was low and menacing.

"I know nothing about conniving." Xantho decided to play open cards with Kratos, despite the dangers of this approach. "When I joined the Shadow Brigade you convinced me that there was no hope for me and that I would be thrown into the Lake of Fire at the final judgment. I have now met someone who has given me a different hope altogether; hope of a future in which my past transgressions will be forgiven and ..."

"And you can live happily ever after," Kratos finished the sentence for him. "I never took you for a fool who would be taken in by a mortal woman. Did you really believe her lies? Do you really think the so-called God and his son will spare you from the Lake of Fire just because you apologize for your past transgressions and say you believe in their deity? If you believe that you're more stupid than I thought possible. I took you in and I put you in charge of my operations here in Dartmoor. Now I find that you have turned traitor and are giving your allegiance to my enemies. This I cannot forgive."

Feeling the anger rising up inside him, Xantho advanced on Kratos. "What have you done with Maribeth Markham? If you have harmed her in any way I'll rip you apart." He made a grab for Kratos' mask and was about to rip it off when a blow from behind knocked him to the ground. He rolled over and looked up to see Zolas towering over him. Xantho made a grab for Zolas' legs and was about to lift the demon off his feet when he suddenly went numb all over. Try as he might, he could not move. In full possession of his mental capabilities, he realized that Zolas had used some dark spiritual power to render him immobile. All he could do was collapse onto his back as the numbness spread throughout his body. He glanced up to see Kratos standing above him, pointing at his head.

"You had your chance to join me in my glorious new kingdom, but you chose to follow the lies of a woman. You mortals are all the same. You will now join your other White Robe friends for the special party I've arranged for you. This is one party you are not going to enjoy."

For a moment Xantho struggled again in a vain effort to get to his feet, then everything went black.

CHAPTER 46

MMOD, JERUSALEM

Luke Baron, Karen Leigh and Mike Cousins sat at a table in Luke's MMOD office waiting for the final seconds to pass before their scheduled link-up between themselves and Daniel in Washington. At exactly eight o'clock Daniel's face appeared on the screen before them.

"To start with, a quick update from my side," began Daniel. "We have reports of large contingents of people, mainly, but not exclusively, male returnees gathering in various locations throughout the world. News on the ground is that they are followers of Kratos waiting to be transported to Israel, particularly the Jerusalem area, probably to assist with carrying out Kratos' threats against Jerusalem. Most of them seem to be armed with derivatives of the old weapons used during the Tribulation."

"Can't they be stopped and their weapons confiscated?" asked Karen.

"We could arrest some of them, but bear in mind that we have a very small security staff – far too few to be of any real effect – and we have not been building up a stock of weapons like the Shadow Brigade has. We *have* strengthened the security in the Jerusalem area under Hugo Dimitrov, but we still have no idea how Kratos will carry out his threat – if at all. By the way, what news do you have on Maribeth and Martin?"

"I am expecting to hear from Seth Baron pretty soon regarding the whereabouts of Kratos, then perhaps we'll get more information on our two missing colleagues," said Luke. "We believe, however, that..."

At that moment the door to the conference room burst open and Martin Petrovic stumbled in, looking as if he had just lost a street fight. The team around the table stared in horror at the cuts and bruises on his face, his right arm wrapped in a makeshift bandage.

"What on earth happened to you?" stammered Luke, taken completely by surprise by Petrovic's unexpected entrance.

"Where have you been – were you with Maribeth?" asked Karen. "Was Kratos ..."

"Whoa – give me a chance and I'll tell you everything." Martin tried to smile but the pain any facial movement caused was obvious. Then he noticed Daniel's face on the big screen on the wall. "Good morning, Daniel, I'm glad you're already in conference as I have unbelievable news for you all.

"I can see that you need medical attention," said Daniel, "but time is of the essence. If it's okay with you, please go ahead and fill us in on what happened to you, then get yourself off to the medics."

"First things first," said Martin. "Maribeth and I were both taken prisoner by Kratos, but by a sheer stroke of luck, and some running battles with Kratos' heavies, I managed to escape."

"Did you manage to find out who Kratos really is?" asked Luke.

"Yes, I did. Hold onto your hats – you're not going to believe this. Kratos is none other than our friend Gorgonius Draco."

"Draco, but that's impossible," said Mike. "If that's the case, why is he selling tickets for trips to other galaxies to escape final judgment?"

"That's all part of his bluff," explained Martin. "He's actually taking them to some very distant planets where he will put them to work in the xerlite mines he has started there. As you may know, xerlite is the new wonder metal used in strengthening all other metals to a point where the metal becomes virtually indestructible. Draco has been using this metal to build up his armament in preparation for the final battle."

"Final battle?" queried Luke.

"Yes. He firmly believes that he can defeat the king and take over, not only Jerusalem, but the whole world."

"Was it Draco who attacked you and caused all these injuries? What actually happened?" asked Karen.

"As you know, Maribeth and I were working together at Kratos' headquarters in Dartmoor. Maribeth was assisting with Kratos' communication systems and I was working with his logistics staff preparing to carry his troops from all around the world to the Jerusalem area and other key locations that he'll use when his final attack takes place. I will give you all the details I have shortly."

"Is he still aiming to carry out his threats this coming Saturday?" asked Daniel.

"That was his plan when we last met with him, and I doubt if anything will make him delay his plans," replied Martin.

"At what point did he turn on you and Maribeth?" asked Karen.

"I'm coming to that. Maribeth had carried out a search on Kratos' apartment in Dartmoor and discovered that he is Draco. Unfortunately Kratos – or Draco as we now know – came in and caught her in the act. I had just returned from the job he gave me and went looking for Maribeth so that we could catch up on each other's progress and then contact you, Luke. As I passed the block in which Kratos' apartment is located, I heard a scream coming from the upstairs window that I knew was part of Kratos' suite, followed by a woman's voice that I was sure was Maribeth's. The front door was locked, but I kicked it down and charged up the stairs. Draco must have been waiting for me. As I burst into the main bedroom something struck the back of my head and I went down like a sack of potatoes.

"When I came around again Maribeth and I were tied up in a locked room somewhere. We were alone for ages with no food or water, then after about ten hours a woman named Anastasia came and gave us some bread and water. I use the term 'woman' very loosely here, because if ever there was a she-devil, she's it. We demanded to know what was going on, and she broke the news to us that we were being kept for Kratos' huge feast planned for the eve of his attack on Jerusalem."

"Why on earth would Kratos invite you to a feast?" asked Luke.

"Because we were to be the guests of honor; Kratos planned to sacrifice us both on an altar in front of all his other guests – a type of entertainment for everyone. Although my hands and feet were cuffed, I thought that I could somehow catch Anastasia by surprise and overpower her so that I could get the keys to our handcuffs. Fortunately my hands were cuffed in front of me, so when she came close I grabbed her from behind and tried to throttle her with the handcuffs. It was then that I realized she is no ordinary woman. She broke my hold around her neck and lifted me up like a rag doll, then she threw me across the room. I must have hit my head again, because when I came around Anastasia had gone and it was only Maribeth and I in the room."

"We must get Maribeth out of there as soon as possible before something happens to her," said Mike. "Where is this place and how did you get away?"

"I think the place where we were being held is in an underground facility very close to the Temple Mount. Maribeth and I were locked up together in a small room, then this she-devil I told you about, Anastasia, came in again and said I was wanted for questioning. She left my hands cuffed but removed the cuffs from my feet and told me to follow her. We climbed a long flight of stairs and came out in the daylight on a large piece of open ground. She led me to a small building, and when we went inside there was a long steep flight of stairs that seemed to go pretty far underground. When Anastasia stepped ahead of me onto the top step I took my chance. Although my hands were bound, my feet were free, so I kicked her as hard as I could in the back, and as she lurched forward down the stairs I turned and ran. It's not for nothing I was once an inter-college sprinter; I must have covered the 200 meters to the main road in about fifteen seconds. I found a service station where a mechanic removed my handcuffs with a bolt cutter and then I came straight back here.

"Wow, what a lucky escape!" Karen exclaimed. "Can you find your way back there? We must rescue Maribeth immediately."

"Yeah, let's go get 'em," growled Mike, crashing one large fist into the other. "I can't wait to mix it with some demons. Even Kratos himself, or Draco as we now know. Can you get us back there?"

"I sure can," said Petrovic, "let's get Dimitrov and his security guys and we'll go right away."

"I'm on it," said Luke, his gizmo already in his hand. After a quick call he placed the gizmo back in his jacket pocket. "Dimitrov will meet us outside with his security team in about five minutes. We'll use one of their high-speed personnel carriers. Let's get Kratos, Anastasia and his whole evil bunch behind bars as soon as possible."

CHAPTER 47

Martin led the contingent back through the almost deserted streets of Jerusalem to a small building on the far side of the open piece of ground where he said he had escaped from Anastasia's grasp. Just as he'd said, they entered the building and were confronted by a long flight of stairs leading below ground level.

"This is where I booted Anastasia down the flight of stairs," said Petrovic.

"Karen peered down into the dark. "Do you think she's still lying down there somewhere?"

"Not a chance," Petrovic replied. "She may have fallen a short distance, but then she came flying up after me. I reckon if I hadn't run so fast to get away she would have had me. But we need to proceed very carefully; we don't know what's down there."

"Let me go down first along with Mike," suggested Dimitrov. "We're immortal, so meeting up with some demon woman doesn't scare us in the least – in fact, I look forward to it."

"Me too – I can't wait," echoed Mike.

Slowly they descended the steep flight of metal stairs; Dimitrov and his ten security guards had their recently-issued combination of impulse rifles and ultra-high voltage stun guns at the ready. The stairs ended in a narrow corridor, dimly lit by a source that was not immediately visible. Before long they came to a T-junction.

"If I remember correctly we go left here and carry on for about a hundred yards to get to the room where Maribeth and I were held captive," Petrovic told them.

"Let's hope we find her and that she's okay," said Karen.

The sound of footsteps approaching from further down the passage caused them to stop. "Could be the guards coming back," whispered Luke, "let's be quiet."

As one they flattened themselves against the walls of the corridor; they waited, scarcely breathing. A group of four men in battle fatigues, armed with impulse rifles and side arms appeared around the bend in the corridor.

Immediately Dimitrov challenged them. "We are the king's security detail; drop your weapons immediately and lie face down on the floor."

"And we are the new king's demon warriors!" one of the men declared. "Your weapons cannot hurt us, just as our weapons cannot kill the immortals in your group. But I can tell that you have mortals among you who would suffer pain and death if we used our impulse rifles, so your whole group better surrender."

Dimitrov turned to Luke behind him. "What he says is true. On the one hand we are days, perhaps hours, away from being resurrected into New Jerusalem, so even if a mortal does die now it won't be for long. But you could suffer much pain in the process, so I'm not prepared to take a chance with any of you being injured."

Dimitrov turned back to his guards, all of whom were mortals. "Men, do as he says; drop your weapons."

For a moment the guards looked hesitant, then they obeyed.

"Wise decision," said the head of the demon guards. "Now let's see who we've got here. I'm sure Kratos will give you all a warm welcome."

The guard took out a powerful flashlight and shone it over the faces of the group. Suddenly he froze, switched off the flashlight and shouldered his rifle. "I see no problem here; you may continue." He and his men did an about-turn and hastened back down the corridor from whence they had come.

Dimitrov turned to his group. "And that? What made them beat such a hasty retreat?"

"Perhaps he received an urgent telepathic message from somewhere – perhaps even from Kratos himself – to leave us and to report elsewhere immediately," suggested Petrovic.

"Could be anything," said Luke, "but the fact that they left us all unharmed is pretty amazing. They could have killed all us mortals and probably stunned the immortals too, depending on their power. But let's rescue Maribeth and then get out of here before something else happens."

"I agree," said Karen, "this place gives me the creeps."

CHAPTER 48

They made their way slowly down the corridor until they reached a green metal door.

"This is it," said Petrovic, "this is where we were locked up."

Dimitrov tried the door and, finding it locked, called out, "Maribeth, are you in there?"

A faint voice from inside replied, "Yes, who's that?"

"It's Luke, with the security guys," said Luke. "Can you move?"

"Yes, they removed my handcuffs, but the door is locked."

"Yeah, we know," said Dimitrov. "Get right over to the side of the room; I'm going to blow the lock." Once Maribeth confirmed that she was up against the wall to the left of the door, Dimitrov placed a small, magnetized box against the metal door's locking mechanism, then he removed a remote activator from his pocket and indicated to everyone to move away from the door. When he pressed a button on the remote there was a dull thud as the charge exploded inwards, bursting the lock. Dimitrov quickly entered the room, followed closely by Luke and Karen. Maribeth jumped up from the corner of the room where she had taken refuge from the blast, and threw her arms around Luke's neck.

"Have you seen him? Is he here with you now?" Maribeth sobbed.

"Whoa, slow down; you're safe now," said Luke, holding the obviously distraught Maribeth in his arms. "Who are you talking about?"

At that moment Dimitrov's gizmo buzzed urgently. He moved out of the room to take the call, returning a few seconds later. "There's a hostile crowd building up outside the king's headquarters," he said "I've sent my security guys to the scene immediately but I'll stay with you until we're safely out of here."

"You must hear what I have to say," said Maribeth, the anxiety in her voice blatantly apparent. "Where is Martin Petrovic?"

"Martin? He was here with us a moment ago," said Luke. "He told us how he was locked up in here with you, and then how he escaped from a woman named Anastasia."

"He's lying ... he fooled you ... he fooled us all," Maribeth could hardly get the words out of her mouth. "Martin Petrovic is Kratos – he is the devil himself!"

Karen raised her eyebrows and gave Luke a little nod, then stood next to Maribeth and put her arms around her. "You've had a tough time, my darling, you're not thinking straight at the moment. We'll get you home, put you in a nice hot bath and then let you sleep for as long as you want. When you're feeling stronger you can tell us what happened."

"But ... you've got to believe me! Petrovic has fooled us all! He wormed his way into our midst so he could keep tabs on what we were doing, but now that he's on the eve of his onslaught against the king, he doesn't care anymore. It was Petrovic who caught me searching his apartment back in Dartmoor; he knocked me out, drugged me and brought me here. Believe me, Martin Petrovic is Kratos!"

"Then why did he come back to MMOD headquarters and tell us exactly where to find you?" asked Luke. "Why would he have led us directly to his lair if he's against us?"

A voice came from behind them. "What better way to get you all together in my 'lair', as you correctly put it. It was even worth pretending to be a bit beaten up to achieve my goal. Look, my wounds have miraculously healed. And here you all are; I was getting tired of you poking your noses into my business, now it's all over for you."

They swung around to see a tall figure clad in a black cloak, wearing a white featureless mask, enter the room, followed closely by a tall woman with long black hair and two burly henchmen. With a flourish the figure removed the white mask to reveal Martin Petrovic standing there, a smile of triumph on his face.

"Martin, is this some kind of sick joke?" demanded Luke, still not believing what he was seeing and hearing. "Tell me exactly what's going on here!"

"The joke's on you, Luke. Why do you think the security guard did such a quick about-turn in the corridor a few minutes ago? I sent him a telepathic message that he recognized as coming from me and told him to leave immediately. My people obey me without question, and you will too from now on. You're all my prisoners, and you'll enjoy front row seats to my capturing of Jerusalem. Is that exact enough for you, Luke?"

"Have you gone mad?" spluttered Karen. "Earlier on you told us that Draco is Kratos, or Satan, now you say it's you?"

"Oh Karen; so beautiful yet so stupid. Don't feel too bad; I've been deceiving people for thousands of years. I love it – especially deceiving women; they're so gullible."

"I'm still confused," mumbled Maribeth. "Martin was with me in London that night we met Kratos after his live appearance. How could there be two of you together in a room?" she asked.

"Highly advanced cloning," explained Kratos. "I can instantly clone myself to look like anything or anyone, but you wouldn't understand – you mortals are so ... puny and so stupid. But I must admit that you, Karen, and Luke have been extremely lucky so far."

"What do you mean by that?" Luke was still trying to get used to the idea that their former colleague was actually Satan himself. "Why have we been lucky?"

"While I was still organizing my followers into a reasonable army, I didn't appreciate you and your MMOD crowd snooping around, so I planned to get rid of the two of you."

"Now I see what's been going on," said Luke. "The attempts on our lives in England – the huge truck running us off the road, and the sniper taking shots at us ..."

"At last you're getting clever," Kratos sneered. "I've been fooling you all right from the start. I even did you a few good turns in the beginning, but merely to worm myself deeper into your organization. Remember those trade union leaders I took care of and those rival gangs I got to stop their gang fights...?

"Yes, how did you do all that?" asked Luke.

"Simple; I merely showed them my real self and told them I'd roast them alive if they didn't do as I told them to."

"Your real self? What do you mean by that?"

"Watch and learn," smirked Kratos.

Before their eyes Kratos grew in size until he was about ten feet in height. He raised his hands to face level and they gasped as they saw his hands turning into hairy claws with long curved nails. Then, to their horror, his face began to change into a grotesque hairy mask. The creature towered above them; his eyes turned red and tongues of fire issued from his mouth. Karen screamed and jumped backwards, crashing into Luke who stood there dumbstruck. Then, in an instant, the creature resumed the familiar form of Martin Petrovic.

"Do you blame those gang leaders for being too scared to disobey me after seeing that?" he grinned. "I should have killed you two earlier, but you both got lucky. If this big lout of a fireman had not gotten in the way of my sniper you would both be unpleasant memories." Kratos pointed directly at Mike. "No matter, I've got you where I want you now. After allowing you to witness my little show tomorrow I'll finish the job myself. Then you will all be ... terminated; rather painfully, I'm afraid."

CHAPTER 49

While Kratos was showing off to the others, Dimitrov had been sizing up his chances against the enemy immediately present in the room. Kratos had brought two henchmen with him – one was short with shoulders almost as broad as his length, the other was tall and swarthy with long black hair and bushy sideburns. Dimitrov decided to go for Shorty first, feeling confident that Mike would join the fray. Slipping his stun gun from his pocket, he gradually edged closer to Shorty who was nearest him. When he was about three feet away, he grabbed the man by the arm and rammed the stun gun into his back, activating the trigger. Shorty screamed and collapsed to the floor. Almost immediately Mike crashed his huge body into Bushy, throwing him to the floor. Dimitrov turned to see if Luke and Karen were safe, and in that moment Shorty took advantage and struck his wrist, causing him to drop the stun gun. Before the king's man could react Shorty had fastened his hands around his throat.

Remembering his days of "no rules" fighting, Dimitrov grabbed his opponent by both wrists, then placed his left foot in the man's stomach before rolling backwards and sending his opponent flying to the floor behind him. Dimitrov sprang to his feet and jumped on top of Kratos' henchman. Shorty, however, quickly wrenched one wrist free from Dimitrov's grasp and, with a twist of his body, gathered up the stun gun and placed himself on top of the other man. As Dimitrov struggled to prevent the man from jamming the gun into his neck, he saw Luke's lithe body eluding Anastasia's grasp and executing a textbook blow to the back of the man's neck. Shorty grunted, then collapsed on top of Dimitrov who pushed him off and sprang to his feet to take on Anastasia and Kratos.

In the meantime Mike had dealt Bushy a blow to his jaw that would put him to sleep for a week. Seeing that Dimitrov was dealing with Shorty, the fireman turned to take on Kratos himself; to his surprise their arch enemy was nowhere to be seen. Realizing that the opportunity to capture Kratos must not be wasted, he charged to the door and peered out just in time to see Kratos' black cloak disappear at the far end of the corridor. Mike immediately took off in pursuit.

In the meantime Karen nudged Maribeth and pointed to Anastasia who, seeing that her accomplices had not fared very well, was about to join the fray. "Let's get her out the way," she said softly. Before Maribeth could warn her that Anastasia was no ordinary woman, Karen sprang at Anastasia, grabbing her around the neck from behind. In an instant Anastasia wrenched Karen's arm away from her neck and twisted it behind her. Then she lifted Karen into the air and flung her in Maribeth's direction. "Your little friend hasn't learned any manners yet," she hissed. "I'm sure you haven't forgotten what happened to you the last time you tried your luck with me?"

The impact of Karen being flung into Maribeth sent them both sprawling to the floor, and when Dimitrov saw what had happened to Karen he realized that this was the she-demon that Petrovic had told them about earlier. He knew that, as an immortal, he himself could not be killed, but understood that the power of a high-ranking demon could not be underestimated. As Anastasia turned from dealing with Karen, Dimitrov delivered a powerful blow to her left cheekbone. Anastasia, stunned for a moment, turned and smiled. "So you're the 'great' Dimitrov that I've heard about – the Antichrist's bodyguard and now head of the king's security force. I've never mixed it with an immortal before, so let's see how this turns out."

Anastasia assumed a stance similar to that of a cat about to pounce on an unsuspecting bird. Then, like a spring uncoiling, she sprang straight at his face, using her long fingernails to gouge at his eyes. Although Dimitrov had not had a serious fight since unwittingly killing a man in the ring during a professional fight way back in the pre-Tribulation days, his sixth-sense for combat had not left him.

Quick as a flash he swept Anastasia's clawing hands to one side and applied a headlock around her neck, but he struggled to hold her and soon grasped that her strength was greater than his. As he attempted to gain a chokehold on her she shouted something in an unintelligible language. As if she had called upon some evil force for help, she broke loose from his grasp and swung him around. Then, placing her arms around his considerable girth, she proceeded to apply pressure until Dimitrov felt himself losing consciousness due to a lack of oxygen. In his previous life Dimitrov had fought professionally in both the legal and the dark illegal arenas of the fight game. It was while pursuing the darker side of the game that the fatality had occurred, and Dimitrov would have found himself in jail had it not been for Count Helmut von Meinhof, the Antichrist, who singled him out to be his personal bodyguard.

Although Dimitrov had fought men of great strength in his previous life, he quickly understood that he was now up against a demon who had access to dark powers, no doubt given to her by the Prince of Darkness himself. Gradually he felt himself losing consciousness as Anastasia applied more pressure to his solar plexus. Realizing that Cousins was not there to help him and that Luke would be powerless against the demon, in his mind he cried out, "Lord, help me!"

"Release him and go from this place; your judgment is at hand!" The command rang out in a voice that Dimitrov vaguely recognized from his distant past. He felt the grip around him instantly released, and he shakily stood upright, tenderly feeling his ribs. Before him stood a newcomer: a shortish man with a blond crew cut hairstyle. Although the man was at least a foot shorter than Dimitrov, there was no doubting the strength in his bulging biceps and barrel chest. "Remember me?" the newcomer smiled as he extended his hand.

Dimitrov grasped the outstretched hand of the angel Raphael, or Rafe as he preferred to be called, second in charge to Michael, leader of the warring angels. "Rafe, I can't believe it's you. Boy, am I glad you showed up. What did you do to Anastasia – where is she?"

"Anastasia and I have crossed swords in the past and she has always come off second best. She won't try to tackle me by herself, so she's probably gone to recruit some help, but don't worry about her, let's get you all out of here."

Luke had helped Karen and Maribeth to their feet, and after checking that there was no serious damage resulting from Anastasia's attack on them, he came over and shook Rafe's hand. "I can't believe I'm actually meeting you," he said, an unmistakable note of awe in his voice. "I grew up on tales of the old Tribulation days from my relatives Mark and Britt Baron, and you featured prominently in many of them. Did you really turn missiles with nuclear warheads around in mid-flight?"

"Well, not by myself, but my legion of warring angels and I accomplished many things during those dark times. But back to the present: you've probably noticed that our friend Kratos has made himself scarce while everything else was going on here."

"I was planning to go after him once I had dealt with Anastasia," said Dimitrov, "but it didn't turn out the way I planned."

Just then Mike came back into the room. Remembering Rafe from the Tribulation days, he let out a shout and the two shook hands warmly.

"I take it Kratos eluded you," said Rafe.

"I nearly had him, but he somehow disappeared before my eyes. Even I, as an immortal, can't do that. I really thought I had him!"

"Just as well," said Rafe grimly. "Kratos is, as you've probably all guessed by now, none other than Satan, the devil himself.

He's a very difficult customer to deal with and that's best left to the king. It is written that King Jesus will throw Satan and his cronies into the Lake of Fire after judging them, but certain things must happen before that. In the meantime I'm going to get you all out of here. As you know, tomorrow's the day that Satan has threatened to pull all his tricks out of the bag, so let's get back and prepare for the final battle. There's a great deal to be done before tomorrow."

CHAPTER 50

MMOD OFFICES, JERUSALEM

Luke, Karen and Maribeth made their way back to the MMOD offices, where they immediately contacted Daniel and brought him up to date with events in Jerusalem.

"I'm glad that you're all safe," said Daniel, "those were some dangerous enemies you were up against."

"Are there any plans to evacuate the large cities?" asked Karen, "Jerusalem, for example."

"Not at all," said Daniel. "In any case, where would the people go? We understand Kratos has missiles programmed to target all the major cities of the world, each armed with revamped nuclear warheads that would destroy a city like New York and the surrounding areas for miles around. They make the old pre-millennial weapons look like fireworks."

"From what we heard at Dartmoor," Maribeth added, "Kratos may destroy other cities that oppose him, but he plans to take Jerusalem using only his ground troops – and there are enough of them. He sees Jerusalem as being his future capital, so he wants as little damage done as possible."

"That is my understanding as well. Tomorrow will be a significant day in the history of mankind," continued Daniel, "second only to the resurrection day of our Lord. As you know, the outcome of tomorrow's conflict has already been decided and recorded in scripture, but the details have not been filled in yet. The Committee of Elders has been addressed by the king, who has given instructions directly to Michael as head of the warring angels.

"Tomorrow's battle will go strictly according to Revelation Chapter 20, and we know that doesn't bode well for our friend Kratos. He has, however, recruited a huge army worldwide, mostly returnees who have hardened their hearts and remained totally unrepentant – his so-called Shadow Brigade. He also commands a large contingent of warring demons who, according to Michael, are best left to the warring angels to deal with. Although Jerusalem will be his main target, the Shadow Brigade, led by demon commanders, has already surrounded most of the major cities throughout the world, and they are armed with advanced versions of the old weapons used at Armageddon."

"Who would have thought that Martin Petrovic, who wormed his way into our midst, was actually Kratos – the devil himself," said Karen, shaking her head.

"Don't beat yourselves up about that," said Daniel. "Remember that Satan has been deceiving mankind ever since the Garden of Eden, but all that comes to an end tomorrow. By the way, I will be joining you, along with the rest of the elders. We will all be in Jerusalem for the festivities that are planned after the defeat of Kratos and his minions."

"Will New Jerusalem really be coming down from the heavens – and will we be entering our final destination the near future? I can't believe it's that time already!" exclaimed Maribeth, not quite believing that the old Earth would be ending soon.

Daniel chuckled. "Don't start sounding like our friend Thomas now, Maribeth. By the way, where is that young man who was with you at Dartmoor? What's his name again – Xantho, wasn't it? From what I heard he was quite keen on you. I'm sure you'll succeed in winning him away from Kratos. Anyway, I must be on my way, see you all on the morrow; over and out for now."

Maribeth blushed at the mention of Xantho. Her gizmo had been removed from her when she was taken prisoner by Kratos, and she had not yet acquired a new device. She realized that Xantho might have been trying to contact her, but he was probably still part of Kratos' Shadow Brigade and his freedom might have been restricted. Although she felt certain that Xantho wanted to leave Kratos' group, he still had many things to work through and he might have decided to stick with Kratos, especially once she had been removed from the scene.

Sensing what was on Maribeth's mind, Karen took out her gizmo and handed it to Maribeth. "Here, see if you can get hold of him." Then she added, "But don't be too surprised if Xantho has already decided to go in with Kratos."

"No, I'm half expecting him to decide to follow Kratos; after all, we had made no real commitment. At first I was quite keen on Martin Petrovic, but I soon realized he was not interested in a relationship; just as well! It was such a difficult time under very challenging circumstances. But thanks, I do want to hear what he has to say, even if it comes to the worst."

Karen touched her arm gently. "Go out onto the verandah and see if you can get hold of him. No matter what happens in the future, Luke and I are here for you – never forget that."

"Thanks Karen," Maribeth replied with tears welling up in her eyes. "I know he's a rough diamond, but underneath his tough exterior ... well ... I think I've fallen in love with him."

CHAPTER 51

A SMALL ROOM IN THE LABYRINTH BENEATH
THE TEMPLE MOUNT

Bakkus was a small, wiry man with a shock of black hair and a large hooked nose; his shaggy eyebrows seemed to meet in the middle, forming an unruly arch above his nose and a protective cover above his pitch black eyes. He stopped in front of a steel door and opened a small hatch; in one hand he held a tray of food, in the other a small, stubby stun gun. "I don't know why they bother to feed traitors," he yelled through the door, "but I'm coming in with some grub for you. Any nonsense out of you and I'll put you out for the rest of the day and you won't get anything more to eat – ever."

A voice from inside the room called for him to enter. Xantho lay with his huge body on a small bunk that was designed to hold a person half his size. Despite his natural ruddy complexion, red welts were clearly visible on both cheeks and a recently acquired scar ran across his left cheek, with dried blood still obvious below the scar.

"How the mighty have fallen," sneered Bakkus. "From being the boss's right-hand man to being my captive – that'll teach you to disobey Kratos."

Xantho shook his head in an effort to clear the cobwebs that had resulted partly from the drugs they had pumped into him, and partly from the subsequent beating that Bakkus and two of his demon cronies had dished out while he was still semi-conscious. The big man cast his mind back to what he could remember of the circumstances leading up to him being a prisoner. He remembered Maribeth telling him that she was going to search Kratos' apartment while he was out and he had seen her slipping past his apartment door back in their Dartmoor accommodation on her way up to Kratos' apartment. Although she had been up to the apartment many times while installing the communications and control systems that Kratos required, this time it was at midnight and she had no business being there. Fortunately Kratos was not expected back until the next afternoon.

Xantho knew that Maribeth had a double agenda and that she was an agent for the king's government, but he couldn't deny the strong feelings that he had begun to have for her. Whenever she was around him it seemed that the world was a brighter place. Then there was the fact that she had told him many times that the supposed "sin" that was keeping him in the Shadow Brigade was not unpardonable, and that he could easily be forgiven the bondage that had been plaguing him for so long. On the other hand, life with Kratos was quite comfortable. Kratos seemed to accept him as he was, and his size and strength made him the ideal right-hand man – even more so than any of the minor demons that fawned around Kratos, vying for his attention. He knew that even Kratos could not trust a demon, and the fact that he, Xantho, was physically stronger than most of the lesser demons, made him an ideal foreman. Physical force was the attribute these lesser demons understood.

It was his position of power within Kratos' group that made Xantho very unpopular among both the demons and the returnees working closely with Kratos. However they all respected his no-nonsense approach and, of course, the fact that he reported directly to Kratos – and nobody dared challenge Kratos or question his motives.

Going back to the night of his capture, Xantho remembered the visit to Blue Ray by Luke, Karen and Mike, and he remembered that a sniper positioned outside Blue Ray had taken shots at Luke, only to be foiled by Mike. That event, and his growing concern over Maribeth's continued absence, had led him to confront Kratos directly about Maribeth's disappearance when summoned to Kratos' apartment. He had challenged Kratos about the whereabouts of Maribeth and was about to rip Kratos' mask off when Zolas, Kratos' warrior commander, used his dark powers to render him incapable of movement. His last memory was Kratos pointing a finger in his direction before he blacked out.

When he came around again he was in this cell, bound hand and foot, with Bakkus and two of his demon cronies sneering at him. Bakkus held a large syringe filled with a yellowish liquid, which he plunged into Xantho's arm. The effects were almost immediate – he couldn't move a muscle; then the three demons set about beating him with steel truncheons.

That's about as much as he could remember. Xantho knew that if he could only get free of the cords that were binding his hands and feet, he could easily deal with Bakkus – and his two mates, for that matter. Although they possessed some demonic powers, he felt certain that his years of honing his fighting skills would enable him to overcome them. The red-bearded man was feeling stronger already, but he decided not to make that known to Bakkus. Instead he stood up from the bed on which he had been lying, but immediately collapsed again to the floor.

"Must be tough to be so weak and helpless," sneered Bakkus. "Why don't you have a bite to eat, it might make you feel better."

Xantho groaned and lifted his head, then held onto a small bedside table for support as he struggled to his feet. "Thanks for the food; I guess I should eat something, but I feel too weak to even get the food to my mouth. In any case, I can't eat with my hands tied up like this."

Bakkus considered this for a moment, then decided that as Xantho could hardly even stand on his feet, he would be no threat for quite a while yet. He removed a knife from a sheath on his belt and cut the cords on Xantho's wrists. "I'm keeping your feet tied up, but at least you can eat. I'll give you ten minutes to eat, then I'll be back to tie you up again. Can't have you trying to escape now, especially seeing as Kratos has planned such a nice party for you and your friends tomorrow." With that Bakkus left, locking the door behind him. Xantho could hear him cackling with mirth all the way down the passage.

Working swiftly on the cords binding his ankles, Xantho untied his feet, but left the cords positioned loosely around his ankles so that it looked as if he were still tied. He ate some of the tasteless gruel and drank some water, then he deliberately spilled some of the gruel on the table and positioned himself on the bed to look as though he had passed out while eating. He closed his eyes and waited for Bakkus to return.

A few minutes later he heard the quick, sharp footfalls belonging to Bakkus, and then the sound of the door opening. "What the hell happened to you – are you sleeping or have you flaked out again? For a big guy you sure are fickle." Bakkus flicked the switch on his stun gun to the "on" position and aimed it at Xantho's rib cage. Quick as a flash Xantho pivoted his body and, with his left arm, knocked the stun gun from Bakkus' grasp. Using all his energy he sprang from the bed and crashed a huge fist into the side of Bakkus' head. The demon screamed as the initial impact of the blow struck him, then he crashed to the floor like a puppet whose strings had been cut.

"I always wondered what would happen if I hit a demon really hard," said Xantho. Stooping down he picked up Bakkus' stun gun and slipped it into his pocket. "Well, good night, my evil friend; I'm not sticking around for the party tomorrow – I'm out of here!"

CHAPTER 52

STREETS OF JERUSALEM

Maribeth left the MMOD offices and made her way towards her apartment. Overhead she could hear the constant drone of the troop carriers as they cut their powerful high-speed propulsion and changed to cruising mode to await their landing instructions from Kratos' ground crews. She looked up, but could only see heavy rainclouds forming, bringing the occasional peal of thunder that followed a flash of lightning across the dark sky.

I still can't believe that Martin Petrovic turned out to be Kratos, she pondered as she entered a convenience store. *To think that I actually fancied the two of us together at one stage – he seemed so ... decent, and so capable. But as Daniel pointed out, Satan always has been the ace deceiver. I'm not the first to fall for his lies.* She wandered through the empty store and saw old Hymie Glass behind the counter. "The place is deserted, Hymie, guess everyone is anxious about tomorrow."

"Yeah, well, not me," said the old man with a chuckle. "I read the last chapter of the good book, so I know what's going to happen tomorrow. I ain't scared. Call me a crazy old fool if you like, but I'd look that Kratos fella straight in the eye and tell him to get out of my shop. And you, Miss Maribeth, you all by yourself today?"

"At the moment, yes. Karen did invite me back to her place after work, but I must give them some space to themselves."

"Ah, young love is in the air ... and you ... you must have plenty of young fellas after you; in fact, if I were a few hundred years younger ..."

"You're very sweet, Hymie. I *am* interested in someone, but we were living on opposite sides of a chasm – I won't go over to his side, and he can't make up his mind to come over to my side."

"Sounds like you have a bit of a problem there, Miss Maribeth, but I know which side you're on – the same side as me. If you're saying what I think you're saying, the guy you fancy is still with the Shadow Brigade, and with what could go down tomorrow he's running out of time to make up his mind."

A new voice came from behind her: "Thought I saw you coming in here. Believe me, my mind's made up; I'm firmly on your side, and that's a fact."

Maribeth swung around and looked straight into the chest of Xantho. She shrieked with joy and, jumping up, threw her arms around his neck. "What happened to you, where have you been? I was so worried." Then, looking at his face, she added, "Who did this to your face, was it Kratos?"

"No, not him. I had a run-in with some of his demon buddies, but I later found out that they too are highly susceptible to a right hook to the jaw."

At that moment Maribeth realized that she had never before openly shown affection for Xantho, but she had to admit to herself that it felt very natural – and very good. She gathered her purchases from the counter. "Let's get you back to my place so that I can patch those cuts – and we have lots to discuss. I'm sure Kratos won't be pleased you've left the Shadow Brigade; he'll probably try to get back at you somehow."

"He'll have to do it himself then," said Xantho, "I've already shown him I can handle his demon buddies. Anyway, from now on he'll have his hands full organizing his little show tomorrow. What news have you heard from your friends at the MMOD?"

"Dimitrov and his security team are spread thinly around the city, but we all know they can only offer token resistance. According to Daniel, the king will be taking personal command tomorrow, so nobody on the MMOD team seems too anxious. But still, we don't really know how everything will go down.

"You and I have worked inside the Shadow Brigade, so we know more about Kratos' organization and his capabilities. What worries me are the vast supplies of revamped missiles he has planted all over the world, all of them with enhanced nuclear warheads, each with enough explosive power to make the old weapons used in the Tribulation look like kiddie's fireworks. If he gets to setting those things off – well, it could look bad for us all."

When they entered Maribeth's apartment she told him to sit on a stool in her small kitchenette and she brought out a first aid kit that contained the latest antiseptic medications. "What did they hit you with?" she asked.

"I'm not sure because they injected me with something to knock me out. If it wasn't for that I would have ripped them apart. They also had my hands tied behind my back. I gave one of them a good hiding, but I sure would like to meet the others again."

"Maybe you will tomorrow. Tell me something else; do you still believe that you can't be forgiven for causing the deaths of those two gang guys you killed way back in your past life?"

"I've given that a lot of thought," said the big man, running his hand through his red curly hair.

"And?"

"I finally got peace that what happened was not intentional, and it was me or them – and the fact that my mom and little sister would have been next if they put me out of the picture. I guess I had no choice. I did what had to be done. While I was lying locked up in that room I actually closed my eyes and asked for forgiveness for my part in their deaths. For the first time I got a feeling that the account had been cleared, and I felt a weight lift off my mind."

Maribeth took both his large hands in hers and for a moment their eyes locked, then she moved away. "Come on," she said, "we need to get some sleep before tomorrow; you can sleep here on the sofa."

Without saying a word Xantho bent down and lifted her off her feet, then he turned and flopped down onto the sofa with her on his lap. Maribeth snuggled in close to his chest and closed her eyes; before long they were both asleep.

CHAPTER 53

KAREN'S APARTMENT, JERUSALEM

Karen and Luke stood on the balcony of Karen's twenty-fifth floor apartment and looked out over the city of Jerusalem. The air was filled with the drone of powerful airships as wave after wave of troop carriers moved over the city to offload Kratos' troops in preparation for the taking of Jerusalem. Although Dimitrov had all his resources stretched out around the city, they both knew that the king's security detail could only offer token resistance against the huge army surrounding the city. It was now impossible to get in or out of Jerusalem because of the blockade, and even air transport had been grounded for fear of being shot down.

Karen shuddered as another huge troop carrier made its way overhead. "Can we really survive this?" she asked, throwing her arms around Luke for comfort and burying her head on his shoulder. "Even David had better odds against Goliath than we have against Kratos."

Luke held her close and looked into her eyes. "Do you really doubt what God can do?"

"Well, no, I don't doubt what God can do, but why has he let it go so far? Why hasn't he sent the warring angels to rip these troop carriers out of the sky? Dimitrov has only about 300 men against thousands – maybe millions – and they have been producing weapons for the last two years while we have only a few simple weapons ... but ...."

"But God," Luke finished the sentence for her. "We know the victory will be his and not ours. We have read that fire will come down from heaven and devour them; it won't be up to us at all. In any case, why do you think King Jesus has waited this long and not taken action immediately?"

"Why indeed! I'm not being funny or disrespectful, but why wait so long? Why didn't he stop Kratos long ago?"

"Because he wants to give everyone a fair chance to choose him and not evil," said Luke, taking her by the hand and leading her inside. Together they sat down on the semi-circular sofa in the corner of the room. "How many returnees do you think have repented of the mistakes they made in their previous lives – mistakes that could have meant death in the Lake of Fire?"

"According to the stats we got from Erica Merton recently, she now has billions on record who have joined her organization," replied Karen.

"Exactly. Now if God had decided to shut Kratos down immediately, those billions would not have had a chance to redeem themselves and make the correct choice. Their names could never have been entered into the Book of Life, and we know from Revelation 20 that if your name is not in the Book of Life, then you're a candidate for the Lake of Fire. It's as simple as that."

"I guess I know all that, but thanks for being so strong." Karen twisted around and kissed Luke passionately for the very first time. Immediately she drew back, "I'm sorry – bad timing. I was letting my fears defeat my reason. You're right, of course, everything was decided long ago. I guess it's difficult for me to get my mind around it when I see Kratos' troops flooding in to take the city."

"Why do you think I secretly call you my 'left-brain chick'?" Luke asked, a huge smile creasing his handsome face.

"You do? I guess you're referring to me as a logical, rational thinker and not some airy-fairy girl ruled by emotion instead of logic. I'm assuming that's a compliment?"

"Exactly, and I wouldn't have you any other way. At least I know that my children will be brought up by a mother who is a sound thinker and not some dumb pushover they don't respect."

"Mr. Baron, if that's yet another proposal then it's the most devious proposal that any girl has ever been offered! Here you are talking about children on the strength of one little kiss. Remember, I'm a left-brain chick – I don't fall for snippets of nonsense that I'm thrown. You'll do it properly or not at all."

"You mean like now?"

"Only if you're being serious."

Luke got down on one knee and took her right hand. "Karen Louise Leigh, will you be my wife? We can have one of the first weddings to take place in New Jerusalem once all this is over."

Karen was still not sure whether Luke was being serious or whether he was pulling her leg. "Are you being serious now?"

"Very serious," said Luke. Standing up he took her in his arms and kissed her on the lips. "Are you convinced yet?"

"I guess a glimmer of belief is forming in my left brain," she said smiling. "But are you sure there'll be weddings and marriage in the life to come? Isn't it written that there is no giving in marriage in heaven?"

"That only applied to conditions in heaven before the Second Coming and not to life in New Jerusalem when we'll all have glorified bodies. Of course there will be marriage on the new earth. Why would God institute marriage in the perfection of the Garden of Eden, allowing man and woman to be companions for each other, and then not continue with marriage in the perfection of New Jerusalem? Wouldn't make sense, would it?"

"No, I guess not, Mr. Logical Left Brain. Don't tell me we're two left brainers getting together – the poor kids."

"I'm sure they'll manage," laughed Luke.

"Strangely I'm not scared anymore," Karen commented.

"Me neither. It's like I was given a glimpse into the spiritual realm and could see the hordes of angels surrounding Kratos' army."

Karen snuggled close to Luke on the sofa. "Will you stay with me till morning?"

"Only if you behave."

"I'll try."

"You'd better; goodnight." His only answer was the sound of Karen breathing deeply...

CHAPTER 54

TOOWOOMBA, EASTERN AUSTRALIA, TWO DAYS EARLIER

Erica Merton awoke from a deep sleep when she heard her name being called. She glanced at the time on the gizmo: two thirty in the morning. She had heard this voice many times – the voice that spoke deep within her conscious mind and yet was as real as if someone was in the room with her. She whispered, "Speak, Lord, I'm listening."

The message was brief and to the point, and she knew she had to act on it without delay. She picked up her gizmo and instructed the device to place a call to a Professor Joel Lipton in Washington DC. Professor Lipton, converted returnee and leader of the White Robes in the Washington area, was a space research scientist who occupied a key position in Gorgonius Draco's research team. Although he did not agree with Draco's theory of avoiding judgment by moving to another galaxy, he had made an agreement with Erica that he would remain in Draco's organization for the purpose of influencing other scientists who were fearful of the final judgment, to join the White Robes.

It was late morning in DC. "Joel Lipton, here; hello Erica?"

"Yes, it's me. I have an urgent message for you, can I continue?"

"Message from...? Oh, of course, one moment, I'm with some colleagues right now – I'll move to another room." Thirty seconds later he continued: "Okay, let's have it."

"Joel, Draco's story about taking his customers to a new wonderful home on the planets of a distant galaxy is not true at all."

"What do you mean? I've spoken to the leader of the team that has already moved machinery and equipment to some of the planets of solar system 103 in the Andromeda galaxy; he says the living conditions are even better than on Earth and the living accommodation and other amenities are nearly ready."

"That may be the case," said Erica, "but those people are not being moved there to take up a wonderful new life – Draco's plan is to use them as slave labor in his mines where they're mining some new wonder mineral called xerlite. They will be put to work under the supervision of Draco's security guards – I have been told their lives will become such hell that the Lake of Fire will seem a better alternative."

"But, that's crazy! It can't be true!" Lipton thought for a moment. "On the other hand, I have wondered about some of the equipment that has already been moved up there – things like heavy duty drilling equipment. I thought it was to bore for underground water, but xerlite ... I know we've been using xerlite on the metal sheeting of our spaceships to strengthen them, but I had no idea what Draco's plans are for mining the mineral.

"What now ... should I tell the others? I can tell you this, if what you are telling me is true, Draco's customers will not take the news sitting down. Guys like Barend Barnes and Greg Madison who have been made group leaders by Draco were brutal murderers in their previous lives, and they haven't changed very much since then. They, and many others like them, were counting on escaping the judgment. If they find out that Draco wants to make them his slaves, they'd rip him apart."

"When is the first group scheduled to leave?" Erica asked.

"Tonight. Draco has planned a huge farewell starting at three this afternoon. There will be bands playing, a slap-up dinner, speeches, the works."

"We need to stop them before they take off."

"Well, if we spill the beans to guys like Barnes and Madison, then I guarantee Draco's future will be pretty bleak – guards or no guards."

Erica thought for a moment, then said, "Let me get hold of Seth Baron before you do anything. He has had ongoing contact with Draco, and as his main supplier I'm sure he'll be attending the launch. I'll get back to you soon."

"Sounds like a good plan; Seth has a great deal of influence in many places," said Lipton. "In the meantime I'll do a bit of probing myself. If Draco is intending to sell off large supplies of xerlite he must already have established suitable markets for the stuff. I have seen for myself how xerlite can be used to strengthen metal, it won't be long before everyone wants it. Till later."

CHAPTER 55

DRACO'S SPACE LAUNCHING SITE, TEN O'CLOCK ON THE MORNING OF THE LAUNCH

While Erica was talking to Joel, Seth Baron was passing through the security point at the entrance to Draco's launching site. At Draco's request he had arranged to be there on the morning of the launch to ensure that any last-minute requirements could be attended to by him personally. Later that day he would return as Draco's guest of honor at the dinner to be attended by Draco's team leaders and the leaders of the different traveler groups on board the spacecraft. While the dinner for the leaders was in progress the rest of the passengers would be on board the spacecraft settling in and preparing for the launch of the five enormous spacecraft that towered above the surrounding landscape.

"Well, do you think we've put your iron and steel to good use?" Draco asked, rubbing his hands together gleefully as they stood together at the entrance to the platform that would carry passengers up to the main entrance foyer of Gorgo I. Draco had named his ten ships Gorgo I to Gorgo X, a shortened version of his own name.

"Most impressive, I must admit," answered Seth. "I might not agree with your motive of trying to escape any future judgment, but I must admit that you and your team have built some mighty impressive spacecraft." Seth's gizmo buzzed in his pocket. "Please excuse me for a moment, I must take this," he said to his host.

"Go ahead," said Draco, "I have a few matters to deal with myself. I'll meet you in my office in half an hour's time. With that he moved off to meet a group of excited customers.

"Hello Erica, what's up?" Seth asked.

"Where are you at the moment?" the leader of the White Robes asked in reply.

"I'm at Draco's launch site, so the background is rather noisy, but please go ahead."

"Listen carefully," said Erica, "the information I'm about to give you is guaranteed accurate. You will need to act quickly, but judiciously because Draco will definitely not want this news to get around among his passengers. Your own life could be at stake if he knows you are aware of what I'm about to tell you."

"Good heavens, are you serious? Shoot, I'm all ears."

CHAPTER 56

"Seth, have you decided to join us on our journey to Andromeda?"

Seth swung around to see Greg Madison approaching him, and quickly put his gizmo in his pocket. "Er, no Greg, not yet, at any rate." Seth had met Madison and his sidekick Barend Barnes on a previous occasion. Contrary to what one might expect, having heard of Madison's reputation for violence, in the flesh the man could pass as a small mild-mannered school teacher. His balding head and round steel-framed spectacles added to his scholarly appearance. Barend Barnes, on the other hand, was a giant with pitch black hair, a long unruly beard and tattoos covering most of his body. Yet even Barnes, for all his size, recognized that behind Madison's mild demeanor lay a cruel, calculating killer who would not hesitate to terminate an opponent for the slightest reason. Barnes, however, found it beneficial to attach himself to the smooth-talking leader of the North American contingent of travelers seeking a new life far away from the king's judgment.

"I guess you don't need to escape judgment," chuckled Madison. "I hear the Barons are still in the king's good books."

"Everyone has the right to make their own choices in life," said Seth with a smile. "You, or anybody else, could confess any past indiscretions right now and there would be no need to escape from here. By the way, have you any idea what you'll be doing on the planets of solar system 103?"

"Pretty much the same as I was doing in my previous life on Earth – setting myself up in a position of power from where

I will exploit gullible idiots who are only too willing to do as they're told by someone they're terrified of. I make no excuses for it; I enjoy power."

"Have you discussed this with Draco yet?" asked Seth. "Does he mind if you set yourself up in a powerful position on a planet that he probably considers his domain?"

"Sure I've discussed it with him. Draco and I have very similar ideas and ambitions, except that his intention is to roam between the habitable Andromeda planets and not set himself up in any one particular place."

"What about the huge security force Draco is taking over with him; has he told you what he plans to do with so large a force?" Seth probed.

"Well, you know as well as I do that most of us traveling to 103 are doing so because we're a rough and ready bunch of bastards who will think nothing of separating fools from their money – or from their lives if it comes to that. Draco, of course, has his own interests he needs to protect at 103 and other solar systems. In any case, I intend to employ as many of his 'heavies' as possible to work for me. Once things get settled he won't need all that security, and as my own businesses grow I will need a small private army to protect *my* interests. I've met the guy Draco has put in charge of his security team and I don't like him at all. Calls himself 'General' Zurlich. He's a real arrogant piece of work who thinks he knows everything but actually is all mouth. When I get settled my good friend Barend Barnes will head up my security teams, and believe me, he's very good at what he does. Anyway, why all the questions?" Madison finally asked.

Seth thought it an opportune time to fill Madison in on some home truths. It was becoming obvious to him that Greg Madison did not consider himself subservient to Draco, and he was not the type of man who played second fiddle to anyone. He decided to leap in with the bad news.

"Do you know Professor Joel Lipton, one of the boffins on Draco's team?"

"Yeah, sure I do," said Madison. "What about him?"

"Just this; according to Lipton, Draco has been taking loads of mining equipment to the 103 planets, in fact, I have been told that of the ten spaceships due to launch today, two of them are loaded only with heavy mining machinery. Have you any idea what he's planning to do with all that equipment?"

"Well, I know there's drinkable water below the surface, probably some other minerals as well. What of it?"

"Ever heard of xerlite, that's X-E-R-L-I-T-E?"

"Can't say I have. What is it?"

"It's a mineral found recently on the 103 planets by Draco's geologists. When mixed with most metals, the strength of that metal is increased almost a hundred-fold. In fact a sheet of metal the thickness of tissue paper becomes virtually unbreakable. Draco has used xerlite extensively on the ten spacecraft due to leave tonight. Think of the possibilities for something like that, and how much it would be worth to someone who holds the monopoly on its production. Of course mines need labor, and that's where you and your fellow travelers come in."

"Are you saying that Draco will recruit a lot of returnees to work the mines?"

"Yes, but not as paid workers – as slave laborers, and that would include you and Barend."

"You're joking; that's impossible."

"Not when you've got a huge well-armed security force to police it. That is why Draco hired a heartless bully like Zurlich to run his security team. Think about it; once you are all up there, there's nobody to turn to for help."

Madison grew red in the face. "Who told you this?"

Unwilling to stretch Madison's capacity to understand spiritual truth to the limit, Seth answered, "From very reliable high-level sources inside the king's government. But you should really put this information to the test yourself."

Madison removed his steel-rimmed spectacles and rubbed them furiously. "Nobody makes a slave out of me. I'm going to find out if what you're saying is true, and if it is..."

"You'd better find out fast; it's only a few hours before take-off. How are you going to go about finding out?"

Madison took out his gizmo and barked the name "Barend". Looking at Seth while he waited for Barend to answer the call he said, "Barend and I will pay Zurlich a visit, and believe me, if he knows anything about this, we'll make him sing like a canary. That space fleet won't go anywhere till we get to the bottom of all this."

CHAPTER 57

MMOD AUDITORIUM, JERUSALEM

The MMOD boardroom was too small to host the war-council that was scheduled for eight o'clock that morning, so instead the large auditorium on the fifth floor was used. Daniel and the entire Committee of Elders had arrived early and had enjoyed breakfast together in the main dining hall. Contrary to what might have been expected under the circumstances, the atmosphere was light, and banter between the groups of friends and colleagues was almost frivolous. The group resembled individuals who had come together for a party instead of world leaders preparing for war against a fearsome and merciless enemy whose forces gathered against them outnumbered them almost a hundred-fold.

It was obvious from the general conversation that any concerns about Kratos and his threats were far outweighed by the expectation that, according to prophecy, the end of the Millennium was imminent, to be followed by the final judgment. It was almost as if the whole group had gone forward in time, witnessed the positive result of the battle to come, then come back to the present with the certain hope of a glorious victory. Still, every person there knew that the path to victory was often strewn with casualties, and exactly how that would turn out was anyone's guess.

Daniel took up position at the head of the large conference table in the middle of the auditorium's stage. Five of the elders sat to his left hand side, and six to his right. Seated in the front row of auditorium seats were Luke and Karen, Xantho and Maribeth, as well as Hugo Dimitrov and three of his divisional heads. The remainder of the auditorium was filled to capacity with the White Robe leaders from every part of the globe, all eager to hear what final plans had been made to counter the immediate threat of Kratos and his hordes.

Daniel opened the proceedings. "Beloved friends, it warms my heart to be with you all today. I have called all the main role-players together for this briefing; the only person still missing is Mike Cousins who is tying up some loose ends and will join us shortly.

"The excitement in the room is obvious, and rightly so, for we know that the fulfillment of the promises we have anticipated for so long is now imminent. We know that this earth, which has been the home of mankind since the beginning of creation, is soon to be replaced with a new heaven and a new earth. Although none of us has yet seen New Jerusalem, we have heard the king describe it on many occasions, always with the qualification that it is going to be even more wonderful than we can imagine. Following the natural deaths of believers in the past ages and our subsequent resurrections, we have all experienced the wonders of heaven, but even heaven will be surpassed by the glory of the new heaven and the new earth, with the pearl in the center being the city of New Jerusalem.

"But in the meantime we have to contend with our friend Kratos and his threats against all of mankind, with Jerusalem as his primary target. This being the case, I would like to ask Captain Dimitrov, head of the Jerusalem security group, to give us a detailed report on the operational capability of Kratos' forces, as well as our plans to counter them. Captain Dimitrov."

Dimitrov rose quickly from his seat and ascended the stairs to the stage, his speed of movement belying the size of the man. He spoke into his gizmo and a huge virtual screen appeared. He then highlighted several outlying areas where Kratos had positioned his forces around Jerusalem.

"As we all know, some time ago Kratos got hold of digital records detailing the weapons used prior to the Millennium. They included complete details of the construction and use of every weapon known to mankind at the time of the Great Tribulation, including what were known at the time as nuclear weapons. Since then he has used every returnee he could who had a knowledge of physics, chemistry and advanced technical know-how to improve upon these weapons and to come up with an arsenal of weaponry such as the world has never seen before.

"As inhabitants of the Millennium Kingdom we never deemed it necessary to arm ourselves – until recently when the increase in crime due to the unrepentant returnees started to become a factor. Even then we limited our production to small hand weapons, giving preference to non-lethal weapons. Reports received from our sister security forces around the world are that Kratos' forces in most other countries and major cities worldwide, seem to be favoring non-nuclear weapons, except for New York, London and Beijing where low-impact tactical nuclear weapons are on standby. Of course, exact details of Kratos' capabilities are difficult to obtain. All we have are best-effort estimates.

"As far as Jerusalem is concerned, our information is that no nuclear weapons of any description are evident. Instead Kratos is relying on his huge infantry to take the city using mainly small-arms. This is a clear indication that he wants to preserve Jerusalem for his future seat of government, should he defeat our forces."

"That will never happen!" The confident declaration came from the main entrance to the conference room where the doors swung open and two figures entered the room. All eyes turned to the door. The two newcomers were totally different in size and appearance. One was a very large African with shoulders that would not fit through a standard sized door unless turned sideways. The other was more than a foot shorter, but almost as broad as he was tall, with a blond crew cut. He wore a bright red T-shirt that fitted snugly enough to reveal his biceps, the size of which suggested the man was no stranger to extreme physical work.

Daniel rose from his seat. Placing an arm around the large African, he said, "I think everyone knows Mike Cousins, previously in charge of Special Projects attached to the Committee of Elders, but recently made head of security worldwide." Then, warmly greeting the other man with an embrace, he said, "And this is the angel Raphael, better known as Rafe. Rafe is a warring angel who reports directly to archangel Michael whom, as I'm sure you all know, is head of the warring angels and who reports directly to the Lord of Hosts, King Jesus. Gentlemen, I know that you're here to bring us the latest on the king's final planning, so please take the floor."

Mike was the first to step forward. "Our defense network worldwide has been divided into three sections. First we have the warring angels who, by their very nature, are able to operate both in the spiritual realm and in the physical. Michael, Rafe and the other warring angels report directly to the king and do his bidding as far as the war in the spiritual realm is concerned.

"The rest of us – let's say the 'non-angels' – are made up of both mortals and immortals, like me. Our job will be to counter the advances of the mortal returnees, that is, members of Kratos' Shadow Brigade. Bear in mind that any mortal could be killed in the action that is to follow, but mortals whose names are in the Book of Life will certainly be resurrected into New Jerusalem very shortly, following the White Throne Judgment. Unfortunately those not in the Book of Life, as I suspect will be the case for most of the unrepentant Shadow Brigade, will face the Lake of Fire. We immortals obviously cannot be killed, so we will be in the forefront of any confrontation, meaning that mortals will only get involved if absolutely necessary. Let me hand over to Rafe to explain further."

Rafe stepped forward. "As Mike said, we warring angels will deal with Kratos and his demons, and that battle will be mainly in the air, not on Earth."

A voice came from the floor, "But are there enough of you to ensure that Kratos won't overrun us? My understanding is that Kratos has millions of demons at his command. He also has thousands of missiles aimed at all the major cities of the world; how on earth will you stop them?"

Rafe smiled. "If I'm not mistaken that question came from the apostle Thomas. Thank you for voicing a concern that many may have. Yes, Kratos has millions of demons, but most of them are extremely weak and largely powerless. Many immortals, and even certain mortals, have in the past successfully dealt with these lesser demons. If anyone doubts this, speak to Xantho from the MMOD office." Rafe smiled and pointed towards Xantho who, looking embarrassed, raised a finger in recognition.

"As far as the missiles are concerned," continued Rafe, "all our large cities have been equipped with updated versions of the old Sky Shield anti-missile system used in the pre-Millennium wars. If the unexpected happens and any missiles get through the Sky Shield, we will have warring angels ready to deal with them. Some of you may remember that we dealt with the Antichrist's missiles in a similar way during the Tribulation. I still have my burned T-shirt to show where I got too close to a missile's backburner," he smiled.

"Bear in mind that Jerusalem is Kratos' obsession. We believe he will not use nuclear weapons against the city he hopes to make the capital of his new empire; instead he will rely on his overwhelming ground forces to take the city with minimal damage. If, however, he finds that he cannot achieve his goal, he may try more destructive tactics. He is on record as stating that if he can't have Jerusalem he will destroy it.

"What we need more than anything else is for every leader seated here today to ask the folk in their charge who will not be directly involved in defense activities, to stay at home and pray that God's will be done swiftly on Earth. The ultimate result has been prophesied, but the means to get there will be worked out depending on local circumstances. But don't be afraid, you are all on the winning team. Very soon we will be enjoying the splendor of New Jerusalem, so look forward and not back. I thank you all."

Daniel rose to close the meeting. "Our strategy is simple: the war in the heavenlies will be fought by the king himself and his warring angels. The immortals, who largely make up the security force in each city, will deal with the armed Shadow Brigade, while our mortal members will only become involved in direct conflict if it can't be avoided. Mortals will take their orders from their immortal zone leaders. Zone leaders must please pass all this information on to those in their areas worldwide, so everyone knows what's expected of them."

Then Daniel stretched his hands out over the gathering. "Go in peace and never lose faith, for we know how this final conflict will end. I look forward to seeing you all at the banquet that will be held soon in New Jerusalem. This is the final hurdle; until we meet again."

CHAPTER 58

DRACO ENTERPRISES LAUNCH SITE, SIX THIRTY P.M.

General Kurt Zurlich entered the security control room of Draco Enterprises and glanced around the semi-circle of video monitors and the security men manning the positions. On seeing him enter, Gustav Bruins, his second in command, hastened over to him.

"Evening General, everything's clear around the campus; the spacecraft have been loaded and everything seems ready for take-off. You looking forward to the trip, sir?"

"What I'm looking forward to is getting the hell out of this place before the so-called 'judgment day'. I know that Kratos is taking care of that, but just to be safe..."

"Wish I was going with," said Bruins with a rueful smile. "I've got plenty of reason to avoid any judgment; sure hoping Kratos comes through for us."

"I'm sure he will," replied Zurlich. "Look after the place while I'm gone, Bruins. I'm on my way to report to Draco, then it's up and away to what should be a very lucrative future." With that he turned and left the building, hurrying across an open lot towards the main reception hall where the farewell ceremony was still in progress. As he passed a clump of trees, a voice called out.

"One moment, General, could we have a word with you?"

Zurlich turned and saw two men approaching, one short and slight, the other tall and broad. He groaned inwardly as he recognized them to be two of his least favorite people – Greg Madison and Barend Barnes.

Zurlich glared at the two men. "Make it quick, I need to get to Draco right away. What's on your minds?"

"Tell us more about your mission to the planets of solar system 103, particularly about the mining project."

"You mean the drilling for water?" Zurlich asked after a barely perceptible pause.

"We know about the water; tell us more about the xerlite, especially the bit about making us all slaves to mine it. Isn't that why Draco hired someone with your ... talents?"

"I don't know what the hell you're on about – I know nothing about xer–"

Zurlich's words were cut off by a vicious chokehold from behind. Barnes had moved behind him while Madison was asking the questions. Zurlich felt himself being lifted off his feet by Barnes as the grip around his throat tightened.

"That was the wrong answer," said Madison softly. "Try again. Does Draco intend to make slaves of us with you and your goons guarding us?"

"Go to hell," blurted Zurlich. "I've got my orders and I'll carry them out whether you like it or not, and believe me you two will be marked men."

Madison reached into his coat pocket and pulled out a stiletto. There was a *swish* and a click as the blade jumped into place.

"Let's think about those answers again, *General*." The menace in Madison's voice was clear. "I've killed many times before, and if I cut you up now I'll be doing many people a favor. Tell us what you know about Draco's real intentions and how you fit into the picture." With that he plunged the stiletto about half an inch into Zurlich's belly. Zurlich lurched and began struggling, but Barnes tightened his grip around the guard's throat.

Knowing that Madison was not lying about his past killings, and already feeling the warm blood trickling down from the wound into his crotch, Zurlich, who delighted in applying bullying tactics to others, howled in fear. Barnes loosened his grip so the other man could speak. "Okay, I'll talk. I'll tell you all I know," Zurlich gasped. "You're right, Draco does intend to use the people as slaves in the mines."

"And what's your role in his little plan?" Madison started to twist the blade.

Zurlich cried out in pain and struggled in vain to free himself. Realizing that escape was impossible, he blurted out, "There will be a team of experienced mining engineers at each site to advise on the actual mining operations. The hard work will be done by the men. The women will be used to clean and pack the xerlite for shipment to markets throughout the universe."

"What's your role in the whole sordid plan?" repeated Madison, giving the blade a further twist.

Zurlich grimaced and squirmed as he felt the blade dig deeper. "My role is to maintain discipline and to make sure that the workers don't slack off. I must organize both the miners and the guards into shifts so that the mining operations will carry on without any breaks. All boys over the age of twelve will be forced into the mines. Draco will set targets for production and I am to drive the workers to achieve these targets."

"Thanks *General*, that's all I needed to know." With that Madison plunged his stiletto further into Zurlich's abdomen and nodded to Barnes to release his grip on the man's neck, allowing him to drop to the floor.

"That takes care of him," said Madison wiping the blade on Zurlich's tunic, "and good riddance. I never liked him anyway. Now let's find out what Draco has to say for himself."

CHAPTER 59

MAIN AUDITORIUM, DRACO ENTERPRISES LAUNCHING SITE, WASHINGTON DC

The departure celebration was still in full swing when Madison and Barnes entered the hall via a side door. Draco was ending off a lengthy speech to rounds of applause as he assured the travelers of a rosy future free of any form of judgment. He promised that their children would grow up free of any threats or bondage and that they would live off the abundance of the land and be eternally free.

Draco pointed to Seth Baron sitting in the front row and explained to the travelers the role Seth had played in ensuring that the spaceships were constructed timeously with the very best materials available. He asked Seth to rise and the supplier was greeted with enthusiastic applause. Just then Draco caught sight of Madison and Barnes who were on the side of the auditorium, moving towards the podium. "Ah, I've just spotted my two group leaders; Greg, Barend, please come forward, I would like to introduce you to everyone."

As the two men climbed the stairs onto the stage and approached the podium, Draco moved to one side. "Greg, please introduce yourself to those who may not have met you, and give them a brief view of how you envision your new life."

Madison moved to the right of Draco and placed an arm on the man's shoulder. Barnes, guessing how the next few minutes might play out, took up position on the other side of Draco where he stood, hands behind his back, towering above the other two.

"Fellow travelers," Madison began, "I think you all know what a special person our friend Draco is and how much he is doing for us." With that Draco beamed widely and gave a little bow. Madison continued, "He is a man who has always placed his fellow man, in this case all of us present today, ahead of his own needs and ambitions. In fact, when I explain to you to what lengths Draco will really go to in order to ensure that we have a prosperous future, every one of you will want to come forward and thank him in an appropriate manner."

At this Draco gave a puzzled glance to Madison, but continued smiling broadly. Madison tightened his grip on Draco's shoulder and, taking his cue, Barnes shuffled up against his left shoulder. "Not only has our good friend here taken care of our future, but he has also made sure that we will not be bored while living in luxury on 103's planets. He has gone to a lot of trouble to provide us with endless fun, recreation and gainful employment. There is one particular surprise that he was keeping from you until we arrived at 103 – you will be allowed to be special guests in his mines where you will dig out a newly discovered mineral called xerlite, the sale of which will make Draco here an even wealthier man than he is already. And because it's an honor to be working for a great man like Gorgonius Draco, you wouldn't be compensated in any way for your labors; you would be slaves under the watchful eye of the late General Kurt Zurlich."

Draco squirmed and tried to move out from between Madison and Barnes, but Barnes placed a huge hand on his collar and held him firmly. "It's lies, lies I tell you! I don't know where he gets it from, but none of it is true," Draco protested loudly.

Madison removed a gizmo from his pocket and connected the device to the auditorium's sound system. He spoke a command into the gizmo and the recorded voice of Zurlich could be heard confirming Draco's intentions regarding the travelers.

"That means nothing! Anyone can hear that Zurlich said those things under duress. You forced him to lie about me! Friends, don't believe a word this man is saying."

"Oh, but I believe him," called a voice from the back of the auditorium, and Professor Joel Lipton made his way down the main aisle towards the stage. Receiving a signal from Greg Madison to speak, he turned to the audience. "Yesterday I received a tip-off from a very reliable source informing me of our friend Draco's intentions. In a nutshell, I learned that Draco had discovered xerlite on the 103 planets, and that he made up this whole story about the promise of a new life far away from Earth and the king's judgment – not that I really believe one could ever escape final judgment.

"Since then I did a bit of checking up of my own and found out that the mining equipment Draco was taking up to the planets is far in excess of what is required to drill for water. In addition, I overheard one of Zurlich's security guards telling his friend that he had been assigned to lead a team that would oversee the slave workers on the mines. He seemed confident that all the guards would be given a good share of the profits from the sale of xerlite. I don't think we need to dig too deep to uncover Draco's whole evil scheme," Joel concluded.

By now the news was sinking in and the audience had grown restless to the point of rebellion. Shouts of "Lynch him! Let's string them all up!" resounded through the auditorium. Seth stood up from his front row seat and moved quickly onto the stage.

"Ladies and gentlemen, please give me a moment to address you before we make any rash decisions. Let me explain how I believe we can still get a good result from this very unfortunate turn of events."

Madison raised his arm. "Friends, I still believe we should lynch this scheming bastard, but I know Seth Baron to be a straight talker, so let's give him a chance."

Amid much murmuring, the crowd took their seats again. Seth turned and addressed the audience.

"For those who don't know me, I'm the owner of a company that supplies a variety of metal-based products. Although Gorgonius Draco was one of my customers, and my company supplied the sheet metal and other products used to build the spacecraft fleet, I also had no idea of his evil intentions. I did not agree with his idea of escaping judgment in a distant galaxy, as I don't believe escape anywhere will be possible, but I saw no reason not to supply him with the products he needed. So where do we go from here?

"As you know, Kratos and his mob are planning to stage a revolt against the king's government, which we believe is imminent. Had your flight plans gone ahead as scheduled, you would have left Earth sometime tonight and would have been well away before Kratos struck. As things stand now, there will be no flights leaving Earth in the near future – at least not until we get Draco sorted out, one way or another."

Shouts of "Kill him! Lynch him!" arose once again. Seth held up his hand and the crowd grew silent.

"I think you all realize that Kratos will not readily accept any of you into his fold. In the past he's made it clear that although he doesn't entirely agree with Draco's plans to flee Earth, he would not try to stop him in any way. It is my opinion that Draco and Kratos entered into some sort of alliance; a truly unholy alliance if ever there was one. However, Kratos made no bones about the fact that he viewed you all as part of a 'chicken-run', as he put it. Instead of joining him in his quest to overthrow the king and his government, you all chose to follow Draco and run away from the problem. Don't imagine that there will be a place for you in what Kratos hopes will be his new kingdom."

The crowd was silent for a moment, until someone at the back of the hall shouted, "So what do you propose? Do we let Draco get away with this, do we try to join Kratos, or do we join the king and hope he forgives us and takes us back?"

"That's up to you," said Seth, "but let me give you a bit of advice. Kratos will show no mercy to anyone who is not one of his disciples. As far as I know very few of you joined the Shadow

Brigade because you didn't plan on sticking around here. Kratos will deal with you the same as he will deal with the king's followers, and he has already stated that not one of them will live long once he gets into power."

"So should we try and join the White Robes?" a lady near the front asked. "They are the king's followers; he will surely not throw his followers into the Lake of Fire?"

Seth smiled at her. "No madam, the king will accept anyone who truly wants to be on his side. The Lake of Fire is only for those who harden their hearts against him and refuse to change their ways. I can't tell any one of you what to do, I can only advise you. I am one of those who came through the Tribulation more than a thousand years ago, so I've seen it all. If you are serious about wanting the best lives for you and your families, you only have one choice."

"So what do we do about Draco and his ilk?" asked another man in the crowd.

"Leave him for the king to judge; don't get yourselves into the muddy waters of lynching or murdering him. The judgment day is very close and you can be sure Draco will pay the price for his deception."

CHAPTER 60

MOUNT TABOR, NEAR THE SEA OF GALILEE

From his command post on top of Mount Tabor, eleven miles west of the sea of Galilee on the eastern fringe of the Jezreel Valley, Kratos surveyed his ragtag army spread in all directions as far as the eye could see. The hundred miles between Mount Tabor and Jerusalem to the south used to be largely desert, but during the fruitful years of the Millennium the adequate and predictable supply of gentle rain ensured the whole area was transformed into a lush expanse of rich farmland.

Kratos knew that most of this rabble in front of him could hardly pass as soldiers as they had virtually no training. His pride and joy was the elite, highly-trained detachment of 3,000 warriors drawn both from resurrected people of past ages as well as from malcontents born during the Millennium years. Divided into groups of 500 men, each trained and led by skilled commanders, the elite forces would form the spearhead of his attack against Jerusalem.

As far as the rest of the hordes gathered around Mount Tabor were concerned, Kratos had no real use for them. Most of them were driven solely by their fervor to overthrow the king and his government in the hope of avoiding their own final judgment. Whether or not they finally ended up in the Lake of Fire he did not care. Kratos' plan was to use them as cannon fodder in the towns beyond the Jerusalem area which he knew would be pro-tected by locals led by immortals.

Michael and his warring angels were Kratos' main concern. Although his elite troops were well trained and adequately armed with recently-developed weaponry, he knew he could not pit them against Michael and the warring angels with any certainty of success. His main strategy was to use his top commander, a powerful demon named Zolas, to lead the select group of warring demons against Michael, while his less skilled soldiers would take on the locals led by the small security force elements defending Jerusalem. His instruction to his commanders was to cause as little damage as possible to the infrastructure of Jerusalem. For this reason he would keep any aerial attack, such as the use of missiles, in reserve in case of emergency. Kratos had always dreamed of ruling the world and beyond from his cherished city, Jerusalem. He rubbed his hands together in an-ticipation – the time was almost here.

With a final look over the valley below, Kratos headed for the large camouflaged tent that formed the command post. He paused for a moment at the door and pulled his black hood firmly around his white faceless mask. Even at this late stage he preferred to keep his true identity a secret. As he entered, his six top commanders stood to attention, eager to receive their final battle instructions.

"Sit," he barked as he took up position at the head of the semi-circle. He silently studied each commander before him, finalizing in his own mind his strategy for the coming conflict.

To his left sat Zolas, leader of 500 warring demons who would lead the attack against the king's warring angels. Each demon in the group possessed both natural and supernatural powers, and they were finely honed in the art of physical and spiritual con-flict. Second only to Kratos himself, Zolas was the most powerful demon under his command.

Next to Zolas sat La Porte, resurrected French general of the Napoleonic era, and mastermind behind many of Napoleon Bonaparte's battles, including the Battle of Austerlitz, one of

Napoleon's most notable victories. La Porte's orders were to capture and secure the old city of Jerusalem, including the heavily guarded Temple Mount.

Next in line was Estevan, a cruel resurrected general of the Spanish Inquisition period who was responsible for the torture and murder of hundreds of Jews, Muslims and Protestants. During the fifteenth century Estevan became the chief inquisitor under Tomas De Torquemada, the Catholic priest appointed as Inquisitor General by King Ferdinand and Queen Isabella of Spain in 1483. His task in the coming conflict was to ensure the capture of the members of the Committee of Elders and as many local leaders as he could find. For this purpose Kratos had given Estevan and his selected leaders enough demonic power to kill mortals and to spiritually bind, and so immobilize, immortals.

Although Kratos wanted to preserve the buildings and infrastructure of Jerusalem, he had no need or desire to allow any of the civilian inhabitants to live. For this reason Klokvas, demon general of 500 resurrected former criminals and other low lifes, had been tasked with eliminating every last man, woman and child living in the city and its surrounds. Klokvas smiled and nodded as Kratos caught his eye. Kratos could feel the eager anticipation of his general to get on with his task. Killing was what stimulated him beyond all else, and the more pain he could inflict in the process, the better. But Kratos had an even greater task for Klokvas; he drew near to the demon, almost face to face.

"I want you to bring me Luke Baron – alive. I know how much you like to use your *other* skills on humans, but I want Baron in front of me alive and unharmed. Don't give this job to anyone else; I hold you personally responsible for carrying out this task – don't fail me. Is that understood?"

The smile left Klokvas' face as he felt the urgency in his leader's voice. He knew what had happened to others who had failed to carry out Kratos' orders to the letter. "Yes Mighty One, I will seek him out and bring him to you. I won't fail you."

At the end of the semi-circle sat his two female commanders – Tazmin and Anastasia. Tazmin was a resurrected high-tech systems developer who had been responsible for designing and implementing the advanced communications and weapon technology used by the Antichrist during the Tribulation period. Now she headed up the teams of technical experts responsible for coordinating Kratos' attacks on all the major cities. She would stay close to Kratos during the coming conflict in order to relay his commands instantly to the returnee generals leading the troops. There would be no need for such communications devices between the demons themselves because they had the ability to communicate telepathically.

Last in line, and significantly positioned close to Kratos' right hand, was his favorite commander, Anastasia. In possession of great physical and spiritual powers, she was both feared and respected by the other demons. Of all the demons in his hierarchy, Anastasia was the only one that Kratos really trusted. Fiercely loyal, she had on occasion destroyed lesser demons plotting against Kratos. In addition, the 500 female warriors under her command had been hand-picked and trained by Anastasia herself. Kratos had assigned Anastasia and her group to locate the Book of Life and the Books of Deeds – the books that would be used at the final judgment. Prior to the advent of the Millennium when Christ returned to set up his earthly government, these books had been located with him in the heavenlies, but they had been moved to earthly locations at the start of the Millennium.

The concept of the data being stored in book form originated at a time when the written word was recorded on papyrus scrolls. For this reason the Bible referred to 'books'. In actual fact the 'books' were minute data storage units that were constantly being updated telepathically by the angels assigned to every mortal and returnee. On judgment day the records would be telepathically accessed by the King of Kings. In this fashion the books would be "opened" and judgment would be passed.

For security reasons these records were now stored in seven earthly locations worldwide, to correspond with the seven continents. The storage location for Europe was Jerusalem itself, in a concrete bunker situated in the depths of the Mount of Olives.

Kratos knew that each location was heavily protected, but he surmised that once the action started the king would have to deploy his troops to actual battle zones, leaving the location of the books largely unprotected.

Kratos smiled as he imagined the frustration the king would feel at his judgment seat when he found out that his precious records had been destroyed, resulting in there being insufficient evidence to condemn anyone. Once the king had anguished over the loss of his Books of Judgment, Kratos planned to cast him and his followers into the Lake of Fire.

After going over the plans again with each commander he arose and stood before the group. "Any questions?" he asked. Upon receiving no response he added, "Ladies and gentlemen, tomorrow we end the king's reign and all this nonsense about judgments. We will meet again after the battle and you will receive your rewards. Till then."

As the group was leaving the tent the tall figure of Jan Vogel, clad in a khaki camouflage outfit, appeared at the entrance. "You sent for me, Commander?"

"Yes, come in Jan. Is that old-fashioned rifle of yours still shooting straight?"

"Straighter and further than ever before. Do you need a job done, sir?"

"Yes, Jan, this is a very special job, probably the most important hit you've ever made." Kratos reached into his robe and brought out a small black box which he handed to Vogel. "Open it," he said.

Vogel opened the box and saw that it contained a single bullet, bright silver in color, which he immediately recognized as being the correct caliber for his rifle.

"If all spiritual powers fail," explained Kratos, "you are to carry out my orders using your rifle and this silver bullet. I have given that bullet special power for the job I need you to do. Listen carefully."

CHAPTER 61

KAREN'S APARTMENT, JERUSALEM

Luke woke up as the sun streaming through the window hit his face. Karen was still sound asleep, her head resting heavily on his chest. He glanced at the time on his gizmo: eight thirty. His movement caused Karen to stir; she opened her eyes and looked up at him.

"You been awake long?" she asked, trying to stifle a yawn.

"Only a few minutes – I was enjoying watching you sleep and didn't want to wake you."

"You mean we actually slept together for the first time?" She gave a sly smile.

"Don't go telling people that, they might get the wrong idea. Let's see what's happening outside."

They stood up, both feeling stiff after sleeping in an awkward position, and together made their way out onto the balcony.

"Shouldn't we be doing something?" asked Karen, looking out over the city. "In a few hours from now Kratos will attack Jerusalem; it seems strange to just sit here and wait."

"I couldn't agree more," said Luke. "I have work to do at the MMOD office and I'm not going to let Kratos' threats stop me. In any case, no matter what happens today, in a very short time we will be entering New Jerusalem; there's no need to fear Kratos and his cronies."

"I agree fully," said Karen firmly. "I'm going with you. I'm not scared – much. I know how it will end; it's the bit in the middle that worries me a little."

Luke's gizmo buzzed. He glanced at the screen. "It's Maribeth. Hi Maribeth, what's up?"

Maribeth's excited voice came across clearly. "Xantho and I still can't believe that we are both safely out of Kratos' clutches, but we feel we can't just sit here and do nothing. We know we were told to stay indoors, but we both feel that we could be of some use somewhere. What are you two doing?"

"We feel the same way," said Luke. "Karen and I have work to finish at the MMOD and after that ... well, we'll see. What were you thinking of doing?"

"Xantho says that Dimitrov told him he will be heading up the defenses at the Temple Mount, so he wants to join him there. I'm going with."

"Dimitrov may enforce the instruction given to mortals to stay at home; he might order you to leave," warned Luke.

"Yes, he might, but when Xantho had a brief chat with Dimitrov at the meeting yesterday, Dimitrov was very interested to hear more of what Xantho could tell him about Kratos and the inner workings of his organization. The fact that Xantho was close to Kratos for some time enabled him to see and hear things that others were unaware of. Should we meet up somewhere?"

Luke thought for a moment, then said, "Let's see how things unfold today. We know it is written that God will send fire down to devour his enemies, but at exactly what point this will happen we don't know. We trust Him, but we feel we must play our part too."

"That's exactly how we feel," said Maribeth. "Till later then."

"Till later," answered Luke, "and may God be with us all."

CHAPTER 62

MOUNT TABOR, ISRAEL

Kratos looked out over the plains surrounding Mount Tabor and grunted with disdain. He turned to his elite commanders standing with him, eagerly awaiting his instruction calling them into action. "We'll load that lot down there into the troop ships first and dispatch them to their designated areas. I don't expect much out of them, that's why they'll confine their action to the towns and villages around Jerusalem. It's you six who will lead your elite warriors in today's action and win the day for us. Let's get the rabble loaded up and on their way."

Immediately Zolas sent a telepathic message to the demon captains of the airborne troop carriers to draw near. A moment later the sky was darkened as the troop carriers arrived from their nearby airbase and hovered over the crowds below. Then they slowly landed, each in their designated area, and the troops began to embark. The pilots of each carrier had been given their disembarkation destinations, and as soon as the troops were on board the carriers moved off.

Next to board the troop carriers were the elite troops made up of the specially-trained returnees. Zolas' group of warring demons had the ability to teleport themselves any place they wanted, so they had no need of troop carriers. Their task would be to confront and neutralize Michael and his warring angels when the time came.

Tazmin, Kratos' communications coordinator, stood close to her leader, her high-powered miniature communications device secured behind her left ear. Her task was to await his commands and convey them to the resurrected Shadow Brigade leaders who would initiate strikes against key installations worldwide.

"Are you ready for my worldwide announcement at noon today; that's thirty minutes from now?" Kratos asked.

"Yes sir," Tazmin replied. "I've also checked in with all the other leaders. All the missile launchers are loaded and primed for their targets; everyone's ready and waiting."

Kratos smiled. "Good. Soon we'll see whether the king is willing to meet my demands. If not, I'll release all hell on this little planet of his."

CHAPTER 63

TEMPLE MOUNT, JERUSALEM

The Temple Mount on Mt. Moriah in Jerusalem has long been a focal point in the life of the Jewish nation. It was on Mt. Moriah that Abraham offered his son Isaac as a sacrifice in obedience to God's command, and where King Solomon established the First Temple in 950 BC. History showed that the First Temple was robbed and plundered by various groups until it was finally destroyed by Nebuchadnezzar in 586 BC along with most of the city of Jerusalem.

At that time many of the inhabitants of Jerusalem were carried off in captivity to Babylon. Among the captives was the prophet Ezekiel, who was given a detailed vision by God of a new temple that was to be built. After the return of the exiles from Babylon, the Second Temple was completed in 515 BC under the supervision of Zerubbabel. The Second Temple was, however, not built to the specifications given to Ezekiel. Shortly before the birth of Christ, Herod the Great extended the Temple Mount and carried out extensive reconstruction of the existing Second Temple. In 70 AD the temple was destroyed by the Roman General Titus who ransacked the city, killed most of the inhabitants and burned down the Second Temple.

Following the Great Tribulation and the triumphant return of Christ, the Third Temple was constructed on the Temple Mount, using the same plans that God had given to Ezekiel all those years before. This temple served as a place of worship and joyful celebration during the Millennium.

It was on the section of the Temple Mount that had been extended by Herod that Xantho and Maribeth found Dimitrov. He was briefing his security group in preparation for any possible onslaught on the temple.

"Hope you don't mind us being here," said Maribeth. "We decided we couldn't sit in our apartment and do nothing."

"My instructions were to keep all civilians off the Temple Mount, but considering what you two have been through, you can hardly be viewed as run-of-the-mill civilians." Dimitrov gave Maribeth a gentle handshake, then turning to Xantho he said, "I heard you whacked the pants off a couple of demons recently; glad to have you with us."

"So far there's only been one demon I crossed swords with, but he had it coming. I can't wait to meet his two buddies again – the ones who worked me over while I was drugged and bound hand and foot."

"Perhaps your chance will come pretty soon," said Dimitrov. "It's nearly midday which is the appointed hour Kratos promised to start his nonsense."

Dimitrov's second in command hastened across the plateau towards them. "We just got word that Kratos' troop carriers have taken to the air from Galilee, Captain, they should be here at any moment."

"Good, it's about time," said Dimitrov. Turning to his lieutenant he said, "Please take my two friends to the mobile armaments vehicle and issue them with a spectrum rifle and a sonic sidearm each, and show them how to use them. We'll need all the help we can get today."

CHAPTER 64

General La Porte rubbed his hands together gleefully as he watched his troops buckle on their anti-gravity belts in preparation for the short descent from the troopship to the ground below. He felt exhilarated in a way he had not experienced since leading Napoleon Bonaparte's crack 21st Regiment d'Infanterie de Ligne. He barked an order and the first group of 100 men took up their positions at the exit hatch.

"Remember men, your task is to secure the old city of Jerusalem, including the Temple Mount. You may kill any inhabitants who try to oppose you, but Kratos wants no damage done to any buildings or other infrastructure. Two hundred men will take up position around the Temple Mount. I estimate the temple guards will number about 130, so you should have no trouble securing the area. I will lead this group personally."

Soon each group had descended and proceeded to move through the streets. As they expected, they met with no opposition from the unarmed inhabitants; anyone who may have been on the streets hastily retreated into their dwellings when they saw the troops moving towards them. Each group moved purposefully towards the Temple Mount, leaving behind a number of men in strategic positions to ensure no unexpected rearguard action would take place.

In the meantime Dimitrov, realizing the temple itself would be the prime target, had placed his men in and around the site of the building. The men were equipped with newly-developed high power impulse rifles that could be set to a variety of options. The most deadly of these allowed a concentrated pulse which would vaporize the target. In less deadly mode the output from the rifle could spread out like shot from a shotgun, either killing its targets at close range or paralyzing them at greater distances. Knowing that his force would be greatly outnumbered, Dimitrov had opted to place most of his troops on shotgun mode, with a few of his crack marksmen acting as snipers.

Turning to Xantho and Maribeth, Dimitrov asked, "You two comfortable with the weapons you were given?"

"They seem pretty simple to use," said Xantho. "We fired off a few test shots at a target and Maribeth was much better than me. I prefer fighting with my hands – I'm not used to using a device to overcome my enemy."

Glancing up at the sky Dimitrov said, "You may need both soon – here they come."

CHAPTER 65

UNDERGROUND BUNKER BENEATH THE MOUNT OF OLIVES, JERUSALEM

For centuries the Mount of Olives, situated to the east of the Old City in Jerusalem, had been used as a Jewish cemetery and was the site of thousands of graves. Whether it was for this reason that the mount was chosen to house the European volumes of the Book of Life and the Books of Deeds, only the king himself knew.

Anastasia had done her homework well. All seven locations of the books had been sought and identified by the she-demon and her team, working quietly yet methodically to win the confidence of those in charge of the various locations.

Anastasia had placed Stella, her second in command, in charge of proceedings at the Jerusalem site. Stella had used her considerable charms on Lucas, the angel in charge of the Jerusalem archive, and due to her skill with graphics and her apparent dedication to the work on the books, Stella had quickly risen to shift leader at the archive.

Anastasia made telepathic contact with Stella, who confirmed that her shift was on duty, and consisted of two angels and thirty mortals who were responsible for ensuring that the recording process was working smoothly. At a prearranged moment Stella made an announcement to her workers.

"Attention everyone, please report immediately to the conference room for an important announcement." The two angels
working under Stella quickly ensured that their teams dropped
everything and moved through to the conference room. Knowing
that this was the day that Kratos had promised to start hostili-
ties, everyone waited with bated breath for the announcement.
Stella stood in front of them, but instead of addressing them she
turned and called out, "Anastasia, we're ready."

The next instant Anastasia swept into the room followed
closely by thirty female demons. "Nobody is to move from this
room," she ordered. The two angels in charge were seized by
demon warriors and held firmly. "If any mortal tries any heroics
they will be instantly terminated," she said. Anastasia and twenty
of the demons then left the room and headed for the storage
units, leaving the rest of her contingent in the conference room
to guard the workers.

The she-demon quickly contacted her team leaders at the
other storage locations worldwide. On receiving confirmation
that all seven locations had been secured, she felt a rush of
exhilaration filling her; now she and her warriors would prove
their worth to Kratos. "Right teams, we all know what to do. We
remove all the memory units and place them in our containers,
then we head back to Mount Tabor and await further instructions from Kratos."

With howls of glee the demon warriors began ripping off the
covers of the storage banks, exposing the memory units within.
Stella turned to Anastasia, "It will be good to see this little lot
end up in the Lake of Fire instead of us, and once Kratos has
defeated the king we will all be free forever!" The rest of the
crew shouted their approval.

CHAPTER 66

MMOD OFFICES, JERUSALEM

Luke and Karen had arrived at the MMOD offices at ten thirty that morning. "It seems strange to think this may be the last time we'll be in these offices," said Karen.

"Why should it be the last time?" asked Luke. "Don't you believe the victory will be won and Kratos defeated today?"

"Yes, I do, but as we mentioned earlier today, we don't know at what stage the king will take action. Will he let Kratos enjoy a few victories over us before throwing him in the Lake of Fire or will he do that before Kratos starts trouble?"

"Does it matter?" asked Luke, slightly irritated that Karen was entertaining any negative thoughts. "We know how it will end, that's the main thing."

For the next hour they carried on working as they would on any other day, yet despite his reassuring comments to Karen earlier on, Luke's mind was not fully on his work. He was about to suggest that they take a break when the door to their office suite was flung open and three men burst in. The first man was tall and thin with a hooked nose and ears that seemed two sizes too big for him. Karen drew a gasp when their eyes met. *Those are the cruelest eyes I've ever seen. This man is sent to kill us,* was her immediate thought.

The two other men with him were unkempt and unshaven and looked as if they would do anything for the right payment. One was short and barrel-chested with tattoos all the way up both arms and on his neck. The other looked and smelled as though his body had not seen water for a long time. He had a scraggy beard that barely covered a wicked scar below his left eye. Luke's impression of them was: *These two guys look like mortals, but the real "bad news" type.*

Hooknose eyed Luke up and down and said, "Luke Baron, I assume. You're coming with us – and the lady too."

"Who are you and who sent you?" Luke assumed a defensive position in front of Karen. "We're going nowhere, my friend; now you and you buddies can get out of here."

"Before we get ahead of ourselves, Mr. Baron, let me introduce myself. I go by the name Klokvas and I'm a general in Kratos' elite squad. I have orders to take you back with me."

With that the two henchmen came forward and made a grab for Karen. "You're coming with us, pretty lady; we'll treat you real nice."

At that moment the hours of self-defense training that Luke and his great aunt Britt had taken together on their Wyoming ranch flashed before him. Without thinking he pivoted to his left and caught Tattoo-Man with a vicious elbow strike to the side of the head. The blow was effective; the man dropped like a sack of potatoes.

Before Luke could confront Scarface the latter made a grab for Karen. He put both hands around her neck and yanked her off her feet. Acting partly out of impulse and partly from her memory of moves that Luke had shown her during their friendly sparring sessions, she brought her knee up as hard as she could between the man's legs. He let out a grunt and dropped to his knees, releasing his grip on Karen's neck. Luke saw his chance and struck a hard blow to the man's temple. Scarface fell sideways and lay still. Luke turned to face Klokvas who had stood watching the action with a smile on his face.

Klokvas clapped his hands together in a brief round of applause.

"Very good, you two; not bad at all for people who have lived in peace all these years. But I know all about your ancestry, Luke, being descended from Mark and Britt Baron, the two who played such a big role in defeating the Antichrist at the end of the Tribulation. If you ever see them again – which I doubt – tell them their offspring did well. But the games are over; the two goons on the floor are resurrected rubbish, they deserve the Lake of Fire. Now you're coming with me, and there'll be no further arguments."

"I told you to get out," said Luke advancing on Klokvas. "Go tell your boss to make himself scarce before the Lord's army gets hold of him." With that Luke grabbed Klokvas' arm and tried to turn him around. To his surprise Klokvas didn't budge; in fact it felt like the man was made of steel and weighed a ton. Klokvas grabbed Luke by his trousers and shirtfront, then lifted him above his head and hurled him against the wall. Luke hit the wall with his back, banging his head on the floor as he landed; his opponent towered over him.

"Did I forget to tell you I'm not one of the resurrected rubbish? I'm a high-ranking demon. You've had a small taste of what I can do; don't make me really mad. Kratos told me to bring you to him without too much damage, but I'm quite prepared to push the envelope a little. Anyway, I'm sure you don't want to see the lady hurt." Reaching down Klokvas grabbed Luke by his shirtfront and yanked him to his feet. He pushed Karen ahead of him. "Walk!" he ordered.

Realizing that resistance was useless, Luke shook his head to clear the cobwebs and followed Karen to the door. Before leaving the room Klokvas turned to his two henchmen who were pulling themselves off the floor. He extended his arm and pointed his forefinger in their direction. Luke could see nothing except his hand, but the two men were immediately catapulted backwards where they lay completely still.

"Are they...are they..." stammered Karen.

"Dead," Klokvas finished the sentence. "You can't get good help nowadays."

CHAPTER 67

GOVERNMENT BUILDING, JERUSALEM

The Committee of Elders filed silently into the main boardroom of the government building in Jerusalem. The usual cheerful banter among the members was significantly absent as they took their seats, awaiting Daniel, the chairman, to appear. A few minutes later Daniel entered and took his place at the head of the conference table.

Daniel looked at the worried faces around the table. "Ladies and gentlemen, I have met with the king and Michael. They have been monitoring events around the globe and, in a nutshell, the position is as follows. Kratos' forces have surrounded all major cities around the world and are awaiting his command to occupy these cities. In addition, they have arrived at the Temple Mount, which they plan to take control of by sheer force of numbers and superior weaponry."

"Did the king give any indication when and how the victory predicted in the Bible will be carried out?" The question came from Joshua who remembered the times when superior strategy defeated numerical superiority.

"Like the true savior that he is, the king's main aim is to give everyone sufficient time and opportunity to turn to him. Even at the very end, which is where we are now, he will not give up on anyone. But what he made clear was that when the time came, he himself would be leading the heavenly host against Kratos – the devil. There has been no change to events as they are written. We are to be patient and trust him to lead us into glory."

"What do we do in the meantime?" asked David, himself itching to be part of the action. "Do we really have to just sit here and wait?"

"That is what we have been commanded to do," replied Daniel, realizing that this answer was not what many of the elders wanted to hear. "Once this is all over we are going to be pretty busy with ..."

A loud explosion outside the conference room caused him to stop in mid-sentence. The door to the conference room was thrust open as Estevan, resurrected general of the Spanish Inquisition period, and fifty of his troops piled into the room. Estevan moved quickly to the podium while his men formed a circle around the perimeter of the room, surrounding the seated elders.

"Sorry to disturb your meeting, but we have *other* plans for you," he announced with obvious disdain in his voice.

Immediately Joshua, David and Gideon rose from their seats and advanced on him. "I don't know who you are," shouted Gideon, "but we have dealt with far worse than you. Get out of here right now, and take your motley crew with you."

Estevan smiled and pointed to one of his men. "A little demonstration might help you to see things more clearly." The man to whom he pointed stepped forward and raised his arm. Immediately Joshua, David and Gideon froze where they stood. They were fully aware of what was going on around them, but they found they couldn't move.

"You might think that we're nothing but resurrected scum," said Estevan, addressing the entire committee, but many of us have been given special powers by Kratos himself. You bunch of heroes sitting here have caused enough trouble throughout history – you and your soon-to-be-dethroned king. Even though you are all immortals with glorified bodies, you will not be able to match our powers."

Daniel remained calmly in his seat. "We were informed that Kratos has given some of his forces special powers that may give you temporary success over immortals, but as you know you can't kill an immortal. On the other hand, you are not immortal and therefore you are now faced with a perplexing problem: you either do some serious repenting and turn to God, or you will very soon be cast into the Lake of Fire. Sobering thought, not so?"

"That's where you make your mistake," said Estevan, his voice sounding a little less confident than before. "Once Kratos and his army have defeated Michael and his angels, the king will realize that he grossly underestimated us. When threatened with the imminent destruction of Jerusalem and all his main cities of the world, he will quickly reconsider his refusal to rewrite the sections of the Bible that refer to Kratos and the rest of us being thrown into a lake of fire. I don't know what Kratos has planned for you after that, but I reckon all of you who so smugly condemn us to the Lake of Fire will find yourselves singeing your own tail feathers."

With that he gave a command to his men to release Gideon, Joshua and David from their immobilized state. Then, pointing to the door of the conference room, he beckoned the group to follow him. "You illustrious ladies and gentlemen will now accompany me to meet the person you have been trying to find all this time. One thing's for sure though, you're not going to enjoy this little party."

CHAPTER 68

TEMPLE MOUNT, JERUSALEM

Meanwhile General La Porte and his men had surrounded the Temple Mount. At a quarter to midday La Porte gave the order to breach the northern, eastern and southern gates simultaneously, and his troops poured through. From their position on the balcony of the temple Dimitrov, Xantho and Maribeth watched as La Porte entered. Dimitrov raised his right hand and signaled to his men to hold their fire until his command.

"Looks like they are about 500 to our 150 men," whispered Dimitrov to Xantho who was lying next to him, their spectrum rifles leveled on the troops that had now taken up position in a semi-circle about 100 yards from the temple building. "Daniel's instruction was that we only retaliate if directly threatened, because the battle will be won by the king himself."

"Well, it sure looks like we are about to be given some kind of ultimatum," said Xantho, watching as the troops in front of the temple parted and three men strode forth.

"That's La Porte himself," whispered Maribeth. "I met him at Dartmoor once when he visited Kratos. He actually tried to come on to me."

"Vive la France," said Xantho grimly.

"I recognize the other two from images I've seen elsewhere," continued Maribeth. "The one on La Porte's left is Le Doux, another of Napoleon's generals and the other is Alaine Roux, one of the chief architects of the French revolution."

"Do they think this is the storming of the Bastille all over again?" muttered Dimitrov. "Wait; La Porte is holding up his right arm."

La Porte's voice boomed out over the Temple Mount, obviously making use of an integrated speaker system.

"I have no desire to cause any damage to the temple or any of the surrounding infrastructure. Send out a team of three to meet me and my two generals, and we can discuss the terms of your surrender. I will give you five minutes."

"Think he's serious about this?" asked Xantho.

"There's no way we'll surrender, but I'll go out and see what he has to say," replied Dimitrov.

"Not by yourself, you won't," said Xantho.

"I'm coming too," declared Maribeth.

"Think you'll charm him into surrendering? You did say he fancied you—" teased Xantho who received a punch in the arm from Maribeth for his trouble.

They descended the stairs and strode out towards the three waiting generals, stopping about three yards from them. Dimitrov and Xantho looked like two giants next to La Porte and his two henchmen.

La Porte smiled and turned to Maribeth. "Ah, the beautiful Mademoiselle Markham, fancy meeting you here," he said, his eyes giving Maribeth a lingering once-over. "Last time we met you were on the winning side, and so was my friend Xantho here; what happened to make you lose faith?"

"Let's cut the crap," said Dimitrov abruptly. "You know you're on the losing side – you can read, you know how this will end."

La Porte smiled, then answered. "The 'crap', as you so crudely put it, is about to become a fact. Within hours from now all of you, including your king, will be feeling the heat of the Lake of Fire. In the meantime I want you and your ludicrous little army to come down from the ramparts and surrender your weapons."

"It's not going to be as easy as that, I'm afraid." It was Xantho who answered. "What makes you think we'll surrender without a fight?"

"What if I prove to you that your weapons – the spectrum rifles and sonic side arms – can't hurt us? On the other hand if we open fire on you and your men, we will destroy not only the people but also the infrastructure your men are standing on. I'm sure I won't have to annihilate too many of your men before you see the light."

"I don't believe a word you're saying," said Dimitrov. "If that's your offer, the fight's on." He turned to leave.

"Not so fast," said La Porte. "A small demonstration may change your mind." He turned and shouted an instruction to his men, whereupon a soldier came forth from the ranks carrying a spectrum rifle.

"You will recognize this as being identical to the standard spectrum rifle you are using – a weapon that can cause an enormous amount of damage." He ordered the soldier to take aim and fire at one section of the wall surrounding the temple. The soldier did so and, as expected, that section of the wall collapsed in a pile of rubble, dust and smoke.

Dimitrov turned to leave again. "We know the spectrum rifle can do that," he said, "and we're quite prepared to use our weapons on you if you don't leave immediately."

"Ah, not so fast, my friend; stand well back and you will see the next part of the demonstration."

Not knowing what La Porte had up his sleeve, the three took a few paces backwards.

La Porte issued an order to his rifleman, "Do it now!"

The soldier turned his rifle on his three generals and fired a ten-second burst. The rifle seemed to have no effect on the three men.

"Another ten-second round," ordered La Porte.

Again the rifleman aimed and fired. Again no effect.

"Your rifle's jammed or something," said Dimitrov, obviously taken aback by what he had seen.

"Give your rifle to Captain Dimitrov," ordered La Porte, whereupon the soldier handed his weapon over to Dimitrov.

"Fire at the wall again," said La Porte, as Dimitrov carefully inspected the weapon. Dimitrov took aim to the left of the section of the wall that had been damaged previously and pulled the trigger for five seconds. In an instant that part of the wall disintegrated.

"Looks like the rifle is working just fine," said La Porte with a superior smile. "And so is the protective shield that our scientists have developed. Now go back to your troops. I'll give you ten minutes to bring your men down here – without their weapons. I will then decide what to do with you."

"What do we do now?" asked Xantho as the three made their way back. "Obviously we can't fight them; we can't even put a scratch on them."

"Let's do the only thing left for us," said Maribeth. "Let's pray."

CHAPTER 69

Dimitrov, realizing the futility of placing his men in the path of certain death, instructed them to leave their positions on the temple walls, discard their weapons and form up on the flat area of the Temple Mount. In was not in Dimitrov's make-up to surrender without a fight, but in view of the fact that La Porte's earlier demonstration had proved that he and his men had some sort of shield around them rendering them impervious to even an impulse gun fired at close range, he decided to play for time. After a brief consultation with Xantho and his second in command, he decided to bring everyone down from the temple walls and other high places, but to leave Sergeant Butler, a specialist sniper equipped with a high velocity custom made rifle, on the roof of the western lower chamber, from where he would have clear sight of the proceedings in the courtyard below. "Only as a safety back-up," he told Xantho.

"Surrender was a wise decision, Captain Dimitrov," said La Porte with satisfaction when the small security force stood before him. "If you had chosen to fight us you and your men would have been vaporized by now."

"Okay, you have us here where you want us," said Dimitrov, not willing to enter into pointless dialogue with the Frenchman. "What now?"

"My original plan was to turn you and your team into an unpleasant vapor, but unfortunately for you, you won't be offered this easy way out. I have just received word that some of your friends will be arriving within the next few minutes, and so will our supreme leader. He has ordered us to wait until he arrives as he wants to have a final chat with you all before he ... makes any further decisions."

The words were barely out of his mouth when a troop-carrying cruiser swept into view, hovered over the Temple Mount, and then landed gently. Almost immediately the door sprang open and out stepped Klokvas followed by Karen and Luke. Klokvas headed over to La Porte and, after a brief conversation, La Porte ordered Luke and Karen to join the others. Karen and Maribeth embraced.

"Are you and Xantho okay?" asked Karen, her eyes filled with tears. "I was so worried about you."

"I too was worried, especially about Xantho," said Maribeth, her arms tightly around Karen. "But we must be strong; it's only a matter of–" Her sentence was abruptly cut short by La Porte.

"Cut out the dramatics, ladies, and stand together quietly – your leaders are arriving."

The spacecraft carrying Estevan and the Committee of Elders hovered above the Temple Mount before slowly descending. Estevan came out first accompanied by six armed guards; he was followed soon afterwards by Daniel and the rest of the committee. The guards herded the elders to where Dimitrov and the others were standing.

Daniel caught Luke's eye and whispered, "Play along with them for the time being; soon it will all be over." Luke acknowledged his instructions with a nod of his head.

"Cut out the chatter," shouted La Porte. "Kratos is on his way and then you can start pleading for your miserable lives; not that it will help, of course."

Thirty seconds later there was a flash in the sky above the Temple Mount and in an instant Kratos and twenty warring demons were standing in front of the gathering. This time he was not wearing his usual featureless mask, and his face no longer took the handsome form of Martin Petrovic so familiar to Luke, Karen and the others connected to the MMOD. In fact, he bore no resemblance to the colleague they had known and trusted. Instead his features reflected what could only be described as pure evil. He was visibly about a foot taller, and his eyes, normally a piercing blue, were red and glowing. He wore a short beard with a moustache that curled upwards at the ends, giving his face an almost theatrical appearance.

Kratos headed over to the group of elders and called Daniel out.

"Why is your leader not here?" he demanded. "Is he so scared of me that he can't show his face?"

Daniel merely smiled. "He will arrive when the time is right."

"I hope for your sake he's rewritten the ending of his little book. If he has rewritten it to my satisfaction I might be a little more lenient towards you all."

"You can count on the fact that he hasn't changed a single word of scripture," said Daniel. "Before this day is over you and your followers will be where you deserve to be, and I can assure you, you will feel the heat."

Kratos' voice became low and threatening. "Before this day is over your king will be defeated and he and all his followers will be in the Lake of Fire where you're hoping to put me. But seeing that your king doesn't seem keen to meet me here, let's have a bit of fun while we wait. My forces can't wait to try out their new toys because my scientists have improved the old weapons and they are confident that even one little missile could destroy any major city. Let's start with New York."

Kratos abruptly turned to one of his warring demons, a huge creature about eight feet tall with craggy features resembling a gargoyle. "Zoltan, go to sector six in the United States and instruct the commander to launch a small one megaton strike on New York. I could communicate telepathically with my demon commanders, but I think your presence will ... encourage ... them to make no mistakes. Report back once the result is known. Then, if the king has not appeared with my demands carried out, we will obliterate a few more of his cities."

In an instant the demon was gone, having teleported to do his master's bidding.

"You still haven't read the last chapter of God's book, have you?" asked Daniel. "If you had you would know that your efforts are futile."

"I probably know that book better than most others," retorted Kratos, "but if your king has any compassion for his own people he would have rewritten many parts of his book of rules, as I advised him to. You had better hope that the changes have been made, or many of your beloved people are shortly going to disappear in a ball of fire."

CHAPTER 70

AIR DEFENSE CENTER, WASHINGTON DC - FOUR HOURS AGO

The bulky frame of Mike Cousins squeezed through a door leading to an underground air defense control room situated deep below the Capitol building in Washington DC. He entered a narrow passageway that lead to another door – this time a formidable steel door. The door had no visible handles to allow access; instead a bright orange light flashed in the center of the door. Mike looked straight into the flashing light and, in his mind, recalled the password phrase for that day: "From darkness into light." Instantly the door opened and he entered the control room. Glancing quickly over the myriad of virtual screens, Mike quickly spotted the man he was looking for – Captain James Kahn.

Captain Kahn was a resurrected US Marine who lived during the final days of the Great Tribulation. Having grown up in a home with an atheist father and a mother who was more often drunk than sober, the young James never set foot in a church of any nature.

After serving as a fighter pilot aboard a US aircraft carrier, he was eventually forced out of the air force due to his persistent drinking problem. In an attempt to pull himself together he completed his studies in aeronautical engineering and was accepted into the Sky Shield program, America's air defense system. Despite his best efforts, alcohol eventually got the better of him and he choked to death in his own vomit in a dingy alley behind a bar.

At his resurrection into the Millennium Kingdom Khan found himself with a group of men deeply involved in the White Robe organization. Realizing that this was his final chance for redemption, he too joined the White Robes and when the troubles started he was asked to join the fledgling defense system in the king's government. Here he was quickly placed on the revived Sky Shield program, hastily established to counter the rising threat of Kratos' ambitions at world dominance.

"What's our state of readiness, James," asked Mike, extending a huge hand in greeting. "Are we ready for Kratos' missiles which could be imminent?"

"Not sure on that one, Mike," said Kahn shaking his head. "We've installed a new guidance system that the lab boys have come up with. On paper it's streets ahead of the old systems, but it's untested. We haven't had time to test it properly. Have you heard any news of what Kratos is planning?"

"Bad news, I'm afraid," said Mike. "I've just heard from Daniel at the Temple Mount that Kratos plans to 'teach us a lesson'. He could be launching against New York at any moment now."

"I was hoping to test the system to iron out any unexpected problems, but I guess we must trust that the theory will work in practice. The lab guys seemed pretty sure of their work."

"And they're the best," said Mike, "but there could be an alternative. You worked on the pre-trib missile systems, on which Kratos' missiles are based."

"Yeah, what of it?"

"If you had access to their control systems, would you be able to do something that would prevent missiles from launching?"

"I often used to think about installing a 'total abort' mechanism into our systems, in case the top brass decided on a last-minute recall of a strike. I even wrote the program for a total abort, but what's that going to help now? We don't have access to their systems – and their software is heavily protected."

"But what if we could get access; could you still do it?" Mike looked serious now, serious enough for Kahn to realize that the big man was not bluffing.

"If they haven't made too many changes to our old software it might be possible, but how do we gain access? Even if we could hack the systems, we could never test it."

"Leave that to me," said Mike. "I'm going to contact my friend Rafe, a warring angel, and put my idea to him. In the meantime brush up on your 'bug'. We must act quickly - I'll contact you shortly."

This time Mike did not use the doors – teleporting was much quicker.

CHAPTER 71

THE TEMPLE MOUNT, JERUSALEM

A cold January wind was blowing over the Temple Mount, and heavy clouds threatened an imminent deluge. In spite of the dark and heavy weather the mood among the elders was cheerful, a fact that annoyed Kratos.

"You people should be worried about what's going to happen in a few minutes' time. Your king should be appearing with evidence that he has rewritten the book as I instructed him, and if not then I will set about destroying cities according to the feedback I get from my teams. I also have some very special plans for your little group. But wait, Zoltan is returning."

There was a flash in the sky and Zoltan appeared before Kratos.

"Is it done?" demanded Kratos.

"No, not yet," stammered Zoltan. "They couldn't get any of the missiles to launch. There seems to be a problem with the controls, but they're working on it. Should we try another city?"

"Nobody fails me!" screamed Kratos. "When I find the person responsible for this, they'll die slowly and painfully."

"I'll go back and tell them, chief." Zoltan was clearly shaken, knowing that his leader could easily take his frustration out on anyone he thought to be involved with this failure.

"No, I'll handle this myself," said Kratos, his voice once again quiet and composed. His close followers knew that was when their leader was at his most dangerous. Kratos turned again to his assembled warring demons and selected five of them.

"Now I mean business. Go to my commanders in London, Paris, Moscow, Rome and Washington. I want a five megaton warhead on each of those cities. If there are any failures, I order you to give the commander that fails a fitting sendoff. Make his demise slow and painful – my people must learn that there is no excuse for failing me! Report back to me in five minutes. Go now!"

In a flash Zoltan and the other demons were gone to do their master's bidding. Five minutes later Zoltan communicated telepathically with Kratos.

"Something is drastically wrong, Chief, not one missile can fire. Dr. Cleveland, head of the guidance system software, is convinced the systems have been tampered with – someone has inserted a bug that prevents the systems from going active. They're working furiously on a solution. What do you want me to do? Must I terminate all of them, or should I let them carry on to find the problem?"

Kratos could hardly contain his anger. "I don't want to hear any more excuses for their stupidity. Terminate all of them then get back here! No more fooling around with outdated weapons; now they will feel the power of darkness like never before!"

CHAPTER 72

The group of elders stood together in a huddle. Having communicated telepathically with their leaders in New York, DC
and other key areas, they had been informed that the planned
missile strikes had not gone according to plan. They realized too
that Kratos would now be both furious and desperate enough
to wreak havoc and destruction, perhaps even to the extent of
destroying Jerusalem.

Kratos stormed up to the group. "I know you are somehow
behind this; I can see by the looks on your faces that you know
what's happened. I wonder if you realize the position you are
in right now? You might all be chosen immortals, but what
you don't know is that I have spent my thousand years locked
in the abyss very profitably. I have developed my powers to a
point where I can destroy anything I choose, even an immortal.
I have also bestowed these powers on my top warring demons.
Although they don't have exactly the same amount of power as I
do, they can cause a lot of damage."

Moses, known to be a man who could become swiftly irritated
by braggart behavior, spoke up from the group of elders. "Can
one of your demons pass over a huge army and kill every last one
of them by merely breathing on them? God's angel did that to
the Assyrians. Or can you destroy an army by sending a flood out
of a cloudless sky; or cause a twenty foot thick wall to crumble
into dust by merely walking around it? I think you may still have
a long way to go!"

Kratos answered by pointing at the eastern structure of the temple. There was a brilliant flash of light and that section of the temple collapsed with a sickening roar, as stones, bricks, wood and golden ornaments were reduced to a smoldering pile of rubble.

"Now it's your turn," he said, turning to the group watching in horror as the focus point of their Millennium worship crumbled before their eyes. "I'm going to start with my ex MMOD colleagues. I want Luke, Karen and Maribeth to step forward and stand before me."

Karen was about to move forward when Luke pulled her back. Instead he stormed forward and stood before Kratos. "You leave Karen and Maribeth out of this. I'm the head of the MMOD and I'm the one you totally deceived. I don't know whether you think we should all shiver in our boots when you speak, but I for one know you for what you are. You're nothing but a worthless liar, a deceiver and, worst of all, an arrogant bastard."

Kratos raised his right arm as if to strike Luke, but Xantho, who had followed closely behind Luke, moved in next to Luke. "I agree with what Luke said; I am utterly ashamed that I ever thought you and your Shadow Brigade had all the answers. You can try to burn me to a frazzle, but I might still get one good punch in, and that will be enough."

Immediately Zoltan moved his eight foot frame forward and stood beside his master, his gargoyle-like face a mask of furious menace.

"Enough of this!" roared Kratos, his voice echoing over the Temple Mount. "I want Daniel and the rest of you elders to move forward and join your MMOD friends in front."

Daniel indicated to the elders that they should follow him as he moved forward.

Kratos eyed the group in front of him, then smiled. "So, here we have all the great men of the ages. I see Moses, Joshua, Gideon and all the rest of you. I actually want your king, but let's start with you. I want you to start by acknowledging me as the supreme leader of the universe. You need to pay me the respect I'm due. Get down on your knees before me – do it now!"

Nobody moved.

"Do you think you're safe because you're immortals? Let me prove you wrong." He turned and aimed his finger at one of his own warring demons. "My warriors are also immortal, but watch this." There was a flash and only a heap of ash remained where the demon had stood.

"If I do that to one of my own, imagine how much pity I will have on you. Now get down on your knees and worship me!"

Again nobody moved.

"Very well," he said more quietly, "I'll begin with Daniel. Daniel, step out and stand before me."

Daniel obeyed. Kratos pointed his finger at Daniel's chest. At that moment there was a flash of light and a faint crack from the roof of the western section of the Temple as Sergeant Butler, who had been left there by Dimitrov as a possible back-up, opened fire with his custom-made sniper's rifle.

The high-velocity ordnance hit Kratos in the face. "That stung my cheek," he commented, annoyed. He called Tazmin nearer. "Call Jan Vogel and tell him to take out that other sniper." Tazmin, knowing that Vogel did not have telepathic powers, made the call.

"Last warning!" bellowed Kratos. "Everyone down on your faces, now!"

CHAPTER 73

Jan Vogel peered down the lens of his high-powered telescopic sight. Even before Tazmin had made contact Vogel had heard the crack of Butler's weapon and was searching methodically to find the location of the unknown sniper. He had instantly recognized that the sound came from a weapon other than the rather inaccurate spectrum rifle, and the presence of an unknown marksman worried him. Years of experience in his previous life had taught him that two snipers could not co-exist in the same arena. One had to go.

As he swept his sights over the roof of the western lower chamber that still remained intact, he caught a glimpse of the sun flashing off the glass lens of a telescope. He focused his own sights and saw Butler preparing to take another shot at the group below.

Got you, you swine; you've taken your last shot. Vogel focused in on Butler's head and took up the pressure on his trigger. The shot found its mark.

***

Back on the surface of the Temple Mount Kratos yelled his order again. "This is the very last warning; I'll destroy the lot of you if you don't immediately get down flat on your faces before me. Before I kill you I want to hear your praises rising up to the heavens. Do it *now!*"

As before, nobody moved.

"Very well, don't say I didn't give you every chance." Kratos raised both his arms above his head and screamed something totally unintelligible. There was a sound like the rushing of wind and about 500 warring demons appeared out of nowhere and hovered about fifty feet above the ground, forming a ring around the inside perimeter of the Temple Mount.

Kratos, hands still raised above his head, shouted: "My hour has come! We have the whole of Jerusalem surrounded, and I have the king's little group of leaders in front of me! Seeing that your king has deserted you, I will begin by destroying all of you, followed by every last person in Jerusalem. After that I will call my followers out of all the world and destroy the rest."

Then, Kratos, his face a mask of fury and hate, pointed for the last time at the group in front of him and shouted: "'Chosen ones', I have chosen you to roast in the Lake of Fire instead of me. Now go!"

A blinding flash of light illuminated the sky and instantly Daniel and the group of elders fell to their knees. "The king has arrived!" shouted Daniel. Luke, Karen, Maribeth and Xantho looked skywards, then they too fell to their knees. Luke opened his eyes for a moment and stared upwards, a look of unbelief on his face.

A smile creased Xantho's craggy face. "Praise God," he said for the first time in his life, "it's the warring angels – they have the demons surrounded."

The huge demons that had formed a ring around the Temple Mount were now themselves surrounded by legion upon legion of angels dressed in shimmering armor. Each one had on a bright silver helmet and a breastplate that seemed to shine with its own light.

Kratos momentarily shielded his eyes with his arm, then hastily withdrew it and screamed at his demons, "Don't just stand there, attack them; banish them all to the Lake of Fire!"

The ranks of angels suddenly parted and the sound of trumpets filled the air. Then a figure appeared from between the parted ranks, dressed in purple robes over his shiny breastplate. He was seated on a huge white stallion. Horse and rider slowly descended to the surface of the Temple Mount and stopped about twenty yards from the east gate.

Kratos turned and stared at the rider for a moment, then he shouted a command: "Zoltan and Zolas, join me here!" Immediately his two most powerful warring demons took up position beside their leader.

"We'll hit him with our combined force so that he'll wish he had never come here!" Kratos cried, raising both arms and pointing at the approaching rider. Zoltan and Zolas assumed the same deadly attacking position and, at Kratos' command, a blinding flash emanated from the three demons, striking the rider squarely in the chest. After twenty seconds the three dropped their arms and stared in disbelief. The rider was still approaching.

By now Kratos was mumbling almost incoherently to himself. "I still have one more arrow in my sling, one that he will never expect. A weapon so old and yet so effective." With that he called Tazmin and told her to contact Jan Vogel once again. As soon as Vogel answered, Kratos grabbed the device from Tazmin.

"Jan, you are my last hope. Do you have a clear sight of the king on his white horse?"

"Yes sir, I see him clearly."

"He is immune to my dark powers, but he can be injured and he can bleed. When he was crucified he was a mess. Even now I believe you can kill him."

"I believe so too, sir. Do you want me to use the silver bullet you gave me?"

"Yes Jan, but listen carefully. Don't go for his breastplate or any other part of his body. Hit him between the eyes – that is our only chance."

"I understand, sir. *Ek sal so maak.* (I'll do it.)"

CHAPTER 74

The rider on the white stallion started moving forward again, slowly approaching the group of warring demons surrounding their master. Vogel brought his high-powered rifle to bear on the rider, and peered down the sight. The rider was looking straight ahead, obviously focused on Kratos and his group. Vogel took aim between the eyes then gently began to apply pressure to the trigger.

At that moment the rider halted his steed and moved his head, causing Vogel to momentarily release the pressure on the trigger. He had one shot available, and he knew he had to strike between the eyes as Kratos had said. For an instant he looked up from the rifle sight to take in the total picture, then he once again placed the rider's head in the cross-hairs. Suddenly he froze.

He's looking straight at me.

Vogel adjusted the sight to full magnification and looked again. Now he had an even clearer view of what had startled him. He was looking into eyes such as he had never seen before. The horseman was not only looking his way, but those eyes were burning into his very soul. The eyes bore no fear, nor hate, nor condemnation, instead Vogel felt the strangest sensation of peace fill his whole body. Nevertheless, he was a soldier who had never in his life disobeyed or questioned an order, and his leader had given the order to kill this man. Forcing himself to carry out his task, he lined up on the target and took up pressure on the trigger.

Jan, sit neer jou wapen. (Jan, put down your weapon.)

The words, in his beloved Afrikaans language, seemed to come out of nowhere. Vogel felt them rather than heard them. Once again he released the trigger and looked around him, half expecting to see Piet Snyman, his fellow sniper, behind him. Nobody else spoke Afrikaans in these parts, but he was still alone.

You are a soldier, Jan. Although you have killed many, you were never a murderer. I want you in my army – from now on you will fight for me. Come down here immediately.

Once again Vogel heard these words in his spirit rather than with his ears. Without knowing fully why he was doing it, he put his rifle down and started running for the steps leading down from the rampart.

Meanwhile Luke and Karen, who had thrown themselves down on the ground before their approaching king, looked up when they heard running footsteps. On seeing the figure in camouflage fatigues exiting the rampart and running full tilt towards the mounted king, Luke cried out to Daniel.

"Daniel, one of their soldiers is charging at the king; maybe he plans to kill him!"

Daniel smiled, "Kill the king? That could never happen. Look, the king is dismounting; he's embracing the guy."

As they looked on in amazement, the king released the soldier. Now instead of being dressed in battle fatigues the man was wearing a robe of shimmering white. The king once again mounted his steed, but this time extended his arm and gripped Vogel's arm, hoisting him onto the steed behind him.

Vogel, blinded by his own tears, immediately felt at home on the horse. He had grown up on a South African farm and had been riding horses from early childhood. He looked down at his flowing new robes and remembered something his mother had told him when he was forever soiling his clothes in the red sand of their farmyard. "Jan, look how dirty you've made your clothes. *Weet jy, my seun, een dag sal die regverdiges wit mantels dra; wat gaan jy dan maak?* (Do you know, my son, one day the righteous will wear white robes; what are you going to do then?)"

Jan Vogel sat behind the king and wept for joy.

CHAPTER 75

Kratos realized that things were not going his way. He had summoned all his dark power against the king and failed. And now even the slim hope that the silver bullet Vogel had loaded into his rifle, the bullet he had cursed for the task of killing the only one who could destroy him, had come to nothing. Kratos felt the rage coming up inside him. He had planned this day during the thousand years of incarceration in the abyss. He had planned everything to the smallest detail. And now....

As his rage reached fever pitch, he lifted his hands into the air and gave a telepathic command to his forces surrounding Jerusalem.

"Bring down fire on the city and all its inhabitants! Burn it to the ground! If I can't have Jerusalem, neither will anyone else. Do it now!"

At the same time the king sent a message to Michael, leader of the warring angels: *The time has come to fulfill all prophecies. The forces of darkness must be consumed by fire. I will deal with Satan the devil as prophesied in scripture.*

Suddenly the sky was lit up as if by millions of simultaneous lightning bolts. In an instant the legions of warring demons were gone, as was every demon spirit that had ever plagued mankind. Kratos was left standing alone on the Temple Mount, with only the now terrified mortals of the Shadow Brigade around him.

Xantho, new to the faith, turned to Luke and asked, "What now? Don't tell me Kratos is going to get away with all of this?"

"Definitely not; I'm sure this is where it all ends."

The king raised his arm, now holding a shimmering sword, and addressed Kratos in a voice that boomed out over the entire Temple Mount. "Prepare to join your other disciples, the Beast and the False Prophet, in the Lake of Fire. You have been given every opportunity to repent, but have chosen the path of destruction. Go therefore to the place prepared for you. Never again will you be permitted to deceive my beloved people. Go *now*...."

In an instant Kratos was gone. That left only Kratos' non-demon followers, the remnant of the Shadow Brigade, behind.

Continuing in a voice that seemed not only to echo over the immediate surroundings, but also penetrate every heart and spirit on Earth, the king said, "The heaven and the Earth that you have known up to now is soon to vanish and in its place will be a new heaven and a new Earth which will be in the form of God's glorious city, New Jerusalem. I will shortly begin my final judgment to determine who will enter into New Jerusalem. Every person on Earth today will be judged according to the records in the Books of Deeds and the Book of Life. Kratos, the devil, made a vain attempt to capture and destroy the books, but nothing in creation can be hidden from me. I have said it before; *I am the Alpha and the Omega*, I am the Beginning and the End. The faithful need have no fear of judgment, and those who are still hard of heart must now decide whom to follow. Your old leader is no more, so make a wise decision."

Once again trumpets sounded and the ranks of angels ascended up into the heavens, led by the King of Kings on his white steed. Then all was quiet on the Temple Mount.

Daniel turned and faced the people remaining. "Today we have seen the fulfillment of prophecy. Soon the faithful will be entering eternity in New Jerusalem; go therefore and prepare. This message I am bringing you now is going out to all peoples on Earth. Anyone who has not committed his or her life to the king yet must not waste any time. As always, the choice is yours, you have free will. But you have seen today what has happened to the greatest deceiver that has ever lived – it would be unwise to try to follow him any further. You all have immortal leaders near you; consult with them if you have any questions.

"Now we will leave this place of the temple forever. There will be no temple in New Jerusalem as God will be with us all the time. Till we meet again on the new Earth – go in peace."

EPILOGUE

The city of New Jerusalem is in the form of a huge block, measuring 1,380 miles in length, breadth and height. It is a dazzling place, lit by God's glory radiating throughout the city.

Its twelve foundations, consisting of every kind of precious stone, bear the names of the twelve apostles. Each of the twelve gates to the city is made of a single pearl, and each gate bears the name of one of the twelve tribes of Israel.

Luke and Karen sat together on a lawn like no other lawn they had ever seen. Each blade of grass was perfectly formed, and the bright green color seemed to shine from inside each blade.

Next to them a stream bubbled as it made its way towards a distant destination. Luke bent, scooped some of the water into his cupped hand and drank it. It tasted sweet, not from any sugary substance being added, but its natural flavor was like no other drink he had ever tasted.

Next to him Karen lay back and stretched. "You know, I was never really sure whether we would actually be married to each other in New Jerusalem."

"I told you many times that God's intention was always that a man should have a wife. From the very beginning in the Garden of Eden – even before man's sin corrupted the world – God placed a man and a woman together as husband and wife. Why should he change that in the perfection of New Jerusalem?"

"I'm so grateful the way things have turned out," Karen replied. "It was wonderful to have Xantho and Maribeth share a double wedding with us, and having Daniel himself conduct the marriage service was such an honor."

Luke stood up and took Karen by the hand. "It sure was special. I could sit here forever, but remember we're meeting the others for a meal soon."

"I still can't get used to not having time measured in hours and minutes," Karen laughed, "not that we need to keep time here, but we also can't keep the others waiting. Let's move."

Luke communicated telepathically with Xantho, "Where are you guys meeting?"

Instantly the answer came back: "We're on the tenth level of the Juniper restaurant next to the waterfall. Mike is with us. He says he's hungry, so don't keep him waiting."

Luke communicated the message to Karen, who laughed, "That's just like Mike – one big hungry bear."

In an instant they teleported to the venue and were met with kisses from Maribeth and enormous bear hugs from Mike and Xantho.

"So it's really all over at last," said Maribeth, "and it's wonderful to be here."

"Sure is," said Karen. "But I still can't get over the fact that our colleague, whom we trusted, was Satan himself."

"Not 'was', but still is Satan," said Mike. "Remember, he is not dead; rather he was cast into the Lake of Fire where he will remain forever more."

Karen shuddered. "Serves him right, but it's still a terrible thought."

"Don't feel too sorry for him," said Xantho. "He would have thrown us into the Lake of Fire if he had half a chance."

"Let's not dwell on him," said Mike. "I'm starving; let's eat."

"Not without me," came a voice they knew well. The next moment Daniel was standing at their table. He greeted each one warmly, then took a place offered him at the head of the table.

"And how are the two pairs of newlyweds?" he asked. "Settling in okay?"

"I knew it would be wonderful in New Jerusalem, but I never imagined anything like this," said Karen. "When you see the king again, please tell him that we are happy beyond all measure."

"Well, you can tell him yourselves," said Daniel.

"What do you mean?" asked Luke.

"That's why I'm here," said Daniel. "The king wants to meet the four of you."

"You mean in person?" Xantho couldn't believe what he was hearing. "Do you know why?"

"Don't for one minute think that you have no duties here in the City of God," Daniel replied. "The king has given me a hint of what he wants you four to do, but it's up to him to tell you."

"I'm probably the least deserving to be in this wonderful place," said Xantho. "My previous life was a total mess. I've killed people. At least you guys always lived good clean lives. I'm..."

Daniel raised a hand. "No Xantho, it doesn't work like that. Once you've confessed your sin and repented, you're clean as a whistle. Never doubt your worthiness. If you didn't deserve to be here your name wouldn't have been in the Book of Life, but it was. You turned your life around and so you're here."

Blinking back a tear of joyful gratitude, Xantho nodded. "I do know that. I only served Satan until Maribeth planted a seed."

Mike stood up and placed his huge arms around Xantho's shoulders. For a moment the two big men embraced, then Mike said, "You're correct, my brother; Maribeth planted a seed, you allowed it to grow, and King Jesus harvested it. That's exactly how it was meant to be."

THE END